THE SURVIVORS BOOK EIGHT
THE GATEKEEPERS

NATHAN HYSTAD

Copyright © 2019 Nathan Hystad

All rights reserved.

No part of this publication may be reproduced, distributed, or transmitted in any form or by any means, including photocopying, recording, or other electronic or mechanical methods, without the prior written permission of the publisher, except in the case of brief quotations embodied in critical reviews and certain other non-commercial uses permitted by copyright law.

This is a work of fiction. All of the characters, names, incidents, organizations, and dialogue in this novel are either products of the author's imagination or are used fictitiously.

Cover art: Tom Edwards Design

Edited by: Scarlett R Algee

Proofed and Formatted by: BZ Hercules

ISBN-13: 9781079543377

Also By Nathan Hystad

The Survivors Series
The Event
New Threat
New World
The Ancients
The Theos
Old Enemy
New Alliance
The Gatekeepers
New Horizon

The Resistance
Rift
Return
Revenge

Red Creek
Return to Red Creek
Lights Over Cloud Lake

PROLOGUE

Their scent was overwhelming, luring him to the nest from miles away. He was starving, and the idea of food motivated him to speed up. His paws plodded along the rough ground; rocks littered the landscape as if they'd originated from the sky. Otherwise, the night was cold, close to freezing.

The hunter paused in the middle of the open space, raising his head to sniff. The land was sterile, fruitless, and he caught a whiff of impending precipitation. If he was correct, it would be falling as white flakes before the night was over. This only made him move faster, his thin limbs quickly carrying his emaciated body across the terrain.

His target was half a mile ahead; their smell filled his olfactory sensors now, filling him with blood lust. *Food*. Finally, after a week of eating nothing but grass, he'd found meat. His pupils widened as he remembered the feel of flesh between his lips, the blood of the kill dripping off his snout.

It was dark out; the dense clouds concealed the pricks of light he'd grown accustomed to over the years. As he neared the rocky outcropping his prey was using as a nest, he paused, seeing snow fall for the first time this season. A flake slowly dropped, landing on his nose before melting. He licked his lips and crouched low, trying to obtain a visual on his targets.

There were three of the six-legged creatures: a male, a female, and a baby. Life was tough out here, and that was why he was the last of his kind. Slowly but surely, they'd all died. His pack was gone. He was alone. The prey was half his size, but they needed less to survive. He envied their small stomachs and their hibernating ability.

He slunk around their nest, climbing above the rocks to peer over at the family. The male was sleeping, the baby nestled into his mother's embrace. She was awake, watching, listening as the protective matriarchs always did. For a moment, he felt guilty for what he was about to do, but life was like that. It was the only way to survive, and instinct took over.

He jumped down, landing on all four paws. He bit the female's head first, ending her with a snap of his powerful jaws. The male was next, raking his claws out, thrashing his tail without success. He died seconds later. The infant was flailing, six legs pulling it away from the bloody scene.

The attacker let it go. There was no survival for the child. This harsh world would eat it up before sunrise. Snow fell heavily now, and the hunter ate, consuming every part of the two victims. His eyes rolled back in euphoric triumph and he moved into the open, away from the nest when he was done.

He already felt the changes happening, and he allowed them to expedite. His snout shortened, and he felt every stitch of his face pull inward as his head twisted and deformed. His long, lean legs morphed, and two more stubby, leathery legs pushed out from his sides. His bushy tail shed its hair and lengthened until it was two feet long; a spike grew from the end.

A howl emerged from his throat, a primal sound, before his voice gurgled and changed to match that of the prey he'd recently consumed.

The hunter was now lower to the ground, and he took a few tentative steps, practicing walking with six appendages. He stumbled around, trying to recall how to walk smoothly. He'd Shifted into one of these creatures before, but that had been many seasons ago.

When he was confident in his ability, he started toward the mountains in the distance. His stomach extended, a bulbous sack containing the bones and blood of his recent victims. Already their cold blood made him acclimate to the weather more easily.

He felt stronger than he had in many cycles of the pink moon. His mind wavered, drifting into a catatonic state as he moved through the cold damp night. By the time he arrived at the base of the mountains, he was exhausted, ready for a brief hibernation to digest and consider his next move.

When he awoke again, the ground was blanketed in snow, and he wished his legs were a few inches longer so his belly wouldn't drag in the powder. It was going to be a long season. He needed to find a food source, and then he'd find a cave to rest in, waiting out the weather.

The hunter scuttled on six legs through rocky paths,

over small hills and ridges, climbing with a skill his previous animal body couldn't have managed. Miles later, he smelled the newcomers before he saw them. His kind always had an acute sense of smell, no matter what form they embraced at the time. It was a skill that should have allowed them to thrive, if only the land weren't so deadly.

He pushed the thoughts of his people away and waited for the two creatures to walk into the valley below. They were on two legs, and he found this disconcerting. Nothing here had that capability, at least that he'd seen – other than the winged creatures, but these were nothing like those. They were tall, shiny, and didn't seem to mind making noise.

He crept along the mountainside, following behind them for a mile before they stopped. He watched with interest as they erected a shelter: a portable cave with strange smells. He didn't understand the scents; they were too foreign to his senses.

That was when it hit the hunter. They weren't from here. Somehow, these creatures had arrived on his land. He needed to find out where they came from. Perhaps he could follow the path and leave as well. The thought consumed him, and he waited, spying on them as they sat together, communicating animatedly. He listened, hoping to gain comprehension. His kind could emulate their prey's speech patterns, if not fully understand them. Perhaps if he could learn a phrase, he could lure one away. One was all he needed.

"You really want to risk using the portal table again?" one of them asked. The hunter smelled him as a male.

The female replied, "What choice do we have? This place is terrible. It's nothing but rocks and snow. Sensors aren't picking up anything larger than a dog in the area. I don't know about you, but this isn't what I signed up for. What do you think went wrong?"

The hunter stayed and listened, unable to decipher a single sound. "Dean Parker and Sarlun have been warning us that this might eventually happen. The damned Theos are leaving the stones. It's like everything is disintegrating. The way I look at it, we have portals on hundreds of worlds, the entire system is interconnected. The Theos are somehow powering the crystals, but they're also fueling the whole complex grid of connections. There's enough juice to run each world's portal stone, but the grid is broken. Unless someone fixes it, we're bound for random planets each time we use it…"

The female cut him off. "And since they unlocked the previously blocked symbols, we don't know where we could end up. The Theos Collective had good reasons to hide those from the Gatekeepers of old. Dean needed them to stop the Iskios from destroying half of the universe," she said.

"Exactly. So if we go through again, we could end up on one of those dangerous worlds. Do you really want to risk arriving on a planet of lava, or one full of deadly human-eating snails?" the male asked.

"How do we know this world wasn't on the list?" she asked.

"We don't."

The hunter watched with intense curiosity. He was

beginning to learn their speech, tiny bits and pieces funneled into images through his advanced cerebral cortex. He understood their term *portal* on a basic level.

He sniffed the air, picking up this pair's scent behind him. If he acted soon, he'd be able to follow their tracks and trace the smell to this portal they spoke of.

"I wish we hadn't signed up for this job. I'd much rather be working on Shimmal. How about you?" he asked.

That was when the hunter noticed they weren't the same species. At first he'd thought their smells separated their sexes, but it went beyond that. He spotted the snout waving beyond an artificial dome over the man's head.

"I'd be happy to return to New Spero. My first mission, and I'm not even going to make the festival on Haven. Dean Parker was going to introduce me as a new Gatekeeper. Only a handful of humans is allowed entrance," she said.

"There will be other festivals. I'm sorry your first mission has turned sideways. I was looking forward to some time on Pumorel's beaches, even though we were going for diplomatic reasons," the male said.

"So was I. It's been a long few years of hard work on New Spero. Anyway, I think we should wait it out. Someone will come for us. The Gatekeepers are a resilient and ancient organization. As soon as they know we're missing, they'll find a way to rescue us." She stood, moving toward the constructed shelter. "You mind taking first watch? I'm beat."

The male's head shook. "Not a problem. I'm going to scope out the vicinity. See if there's a better place to move to in the morning."

"Don't veer off too far," she said before entering the shelter.

The hunter was happy. He was far smaller than the new prey, but he had the element of surprise on his side. He tested out his vocal cords, trying one of their words: "Gatekeeper." It was gravelly, and he tried a few more times before he was happy with the outcome.

The male was already walking around, a bright light shooting from its hand. The hunter didn't understand. It was as if he'd harnessed the sun's power somehow. He tracked the male, staying fifty yards away at all times. The two-legged creature continued below him in the valley, the hunter on a cliff twenty feet above. When they were far enough away from their nest, he made the move.

"Gatekeeper!" the hunter shouted. And again: "Gatekeeper!"

The male's head snapped up, trying to find the source. The light shone around the hunter's small, hidden form.

"Who's there?" the male asked.

The hunter heard the prey's footsteps on the rock as he climbed over the snow-covered ground and onto a platform in the outcropping. It was time. The hunter sprang from his hiding spot, jaws spread wide. He clung to the prey's clothing, biting into the male's neck. He was almost swung off as the victim protested, but he held firmly. After chewing through layers of fabricated skin, the smell of pumping blood was stronger. The hunter bit again, this time finding blood.

He gurgled and fell to the ground, and the hunter didn't

waste any time. He began to consume the body. It twitched as he kept going, the entire process taking far longer than any previous Shift. This creature was larger than any others, and by the time his belly was filled, the transformation had begun.

The hunter writhed in pain as he stretched out, the bones from inside his stomach sack melting and emerging through his skin. The transformation took longer than devouring the prey, and by the end of it, the hunter wished he was dead. He howled and screamed in an unknown voice, but eventually, he lay there unmoving, naked and cold.

The body was strange, and he fought to stand on two legs. His snout twitched from side to side, and he fell a few times before understanding how to balance. It was challenging after being so low to the ground with six legs. His feet carried him toward the nest, where the female was sleeping. He needed her suit; he could tell this instantly. His breathing was labored, and now he comprehended the dome around the prey's head.

The hunter stood naked at the camp and moved toward the tent, as he now knew it to be named. Once she was dead, he'd head for the portal they came through and leave this dreaded world for good.

ONE

The sun peeked through my drapes as I blinked my eyes open. It took a moment to remember where I was. For a brief second, I expected to be on the Kraski ship, flying around searching for *Fortune*, Magnus and Natalia's missing Keppe vessel. Only we'd found them, and they were now on their way home, safe and sound.

I sighed out stale air and smiled in the dim room. Mary's chest rose and fell as she slept peacefully, and as much as I wanted to crawl over her and kiss her awake, I knew she needed the rest. Today was going to be a big day. Again.

Maggie stood at the foot of our bed, her tail lifting straight up. She must have heard Jules moving around before I did, and had jumped off the bed stealthily. I tried to emulate her, and tucked and rolled from the blanket, my bare feet slapping lightly on the floor.

The dog and I trod down the hall and into Jules' room, where a device spun a carousel of lights around the space. Jules was standing in her big-girl bed, pointing at the dancing display. Her bright green eyes glowed, and I stifled the dread inside me of what it might mean. She was an ordinary girl. Dr. Nick assured us monthly that nothing abnormal was showing up in her test results. And yet... those eyes, as beautiful as they were on my little girl, were off-putting because of the Iskios. It was the same green as the Vortex Mary had been controlling while possessed by the ancient beings.

"Papa!" Jules stuck her arms out to me, and I crossed the room to snatch her up. Maggie was at the bed first and had jumped up, licking my daughter on the face. "Puppy silly," she said between attentions from the dog, and I couldn't deny it.

"Puppy is very silly. Let's take you to the potty, then you can come outside with me and Maggie. Okay, honey?" I asked, and Jules nodded. She was a quick study and had hated diapers for nearly six months now.

I picked her up, and she struggled as soon as we were out of the room. "Down, Papa," she ordered, and I rolled my eyes, setting her to the floor.

She ran towards the hall, and Maggie and I patiently waited while she did her business. Maggie peered up at me as if to say it was her turn, and I went to the kitchen, turning on the coffee pot. Mary always prepped it the day before, and I was grateful today. My head was sleepy, my mind addled after the long journey to Magnus and then home.

I wished I had more time here, more time to spend with my family on New Spero before heading out to the mess the failing portals had left for the Gatekeeper team. Sarlun was expecting us today, and as much as I didn't want to be there, I knew there were lives depending on us.

"Papa. I wash." Jules stood there in her tiny PJs, hands dripping with water. I laughed and grabbed the tea towel, drying them off.

"Good work, JuJu. Now if you could teach Maggie to let herself out, then we'd be golden," I said.

"Golden," Jules repeated.

Maggie was at the door, and I pressed it open to the back yard. She ran out, off the deck and toward the patch of garden. Various vegetables were thriving out there, and I held Jules' hand as we descended to the grass. She ran around, hands in front of her as if she was chasing an invisible fairy, and I soaked it all in. Maggie chased her, barking with joy, and this went on for five minutes before the door creaked open, and Mary stepped onto the wooden deck holding two steaming cups of coffee.

"When did you get up?" she asked.

"Not long ago. Sorry about the noise." I jabbed a thumb toward the happy kid and dog.

She shook her head. "I was up. And there are worse things to wake to. Like… anything but this." She sat on the deck, and I joined her, feet on the stairs. Magnus and I had built these steps with our own two hands, and I grinned at the memory.

"I'm sorry, Mary," I said.

"For what?" she asked.

"For not being around like I promised. I wish it wasn't like this," I said.

"I do too, but it's not in our cards yet. This time will be different, though."

"Why?" I sipped the coffee, instantly feeling the kick.

"Because we're going with you," Mary said without meeting my gaze. She smiled as she watched Jules chasing Maggie toward the garden. Maggie stopped to sniff something, and my daughter bumped into her, tumbling over. Jules stood right up and giggled.

I had hardly heard Mary's words, but they finally clicked. "Wait… you're coming with me?"

She nodded, glancing toward me. "We can't separate this family again, not so soon. If you're going to help the Gatekeepers, let me help too. I'm one of them."

"Maybe we can leave Jules with Nat. I'm sure she'd love to spend time with her goddaughter. They might not be home for a few days yet, though," I said.

"No, Dean. I'm not leaving her side," Mary said. It had taken months for me to convince my wife to let a sitter watch our daughter after she was born, and even then it was never for more than a handful of hours.

"We can't bring Jules on a Gatekeeper rescue mission," I said flatly, and took another drink.

"Then you aren't going," she retorted.

"I know I only made it home yesterday, but for some reason, the others look to me for answers. I don't understand it any more than you do," I told her, being totally truthful. I'd never asked for a leadership role, and at this moment, I wished I'd never accepted one.

"You have to be kidding me, Dean. After everything, you still don't understand. We stopped the invasion… you kept the Bhlat from destroying Earth, you stopped the Iskios from decimating everything, and then outsmarted

The Gatekeepers

Lom of Pleva. And don't forget about creating an Alliance of Worlds..." Mary was sticking out a finger for each point.

I had to defend myself, to deflect the praise. "I didn't do any of those things alone."

"I'm not saying it to make you cocky or proud. I'm only listing facts. You want to know why people are drawn to you? That's why. And you did it all with a smile and more care for the people around you than anyone else would have. You have a rare trait: empathy." She leaned over, resting her head on my shoulder. "I understand how they all love you, because I love you more than any of them."

I touched her chin and kissed her, tasting the coffee on her lips. "You're the best, you know that? So we bring Jules along. This is going to be fun. I suppose she needs an EVA, then..."

"Done. It's already in her closet. Call it mother's intuition." Mary smiled at me and clinked my cup with hers.

I couldn't help but laugh. "Of course she has one. Why wouldn't she? She is a Parker, after all."

"Come on, Jules. Time for breakfast. We have a big day ahead of us," Mary told our daughter, who was lying in the grass staring up at the sky.

The lander settled inside Terran Five. We were going to leave for Haven using the device from J-NAK the robot soon, but I had a stop to make first. The device allowed us to uncross the pathways in the portal stones so we could choose our targets, and I now wished I'd bartered for a couple more of the things. I needed to find out if Clare could duplicate it.

"You sure she's going to be there?" Mary asked.

"I'm not sure. I asked Leonard and Clare to meet us at Isabelle's house," I said. Maggie ran out from the lander, pulling her leash taut as I held the other end. Mary had Jules in her arms, and we left our gear inside the ship.

Someone honked from the parking lot outside the landing pad, and I recognized James' familiar face behind the windshield. "Looks like we have a ride." I grinned and laughed at the scenario. I couldn't imagine making this trip with our whole family. I only hoped Isabelle and James didn't mind watching Maggie for us while we were gone. They had a dog now, and the two of them got along, so I didn't expect any issues.

"James," Mary said, hugging my old best friend and now brother-in-law. "Great to see you. I only wish we were staying to visit."

"Likewise." James came in and hugged me, picking me up as he did so. Maggie barked at him playfully as he set me down. "Dean. Everything went well?"

"You bet. Magnus and Nat are home, and that's all that matters. Thanks for seeing us on such short notice, and I'm sorry about using your house as a meeting place. I hate to intrude."

"Dean, our home is your home. You sister is going to explode when she sees you," James said with a big smile. "Come on, let's go."

The Gatekeepers

It was morning, only three hours after we woke up, and traffic was light as James drove us toward his house in our new mass-produced version of a four-by-four vehicle. Maggie sat in my lap, and Jules faced backwards in her car seat. I wondered if Mary was going to make her use that in a space ship.

We pulled into their driveway, and I was once again impressed with how far our race had come after overcoming the departure from Earth. Isabelle was a veterinarian, and they were near the outskirts of town, where they could have quick access to the farming community. Their house was small but quaint, not unlike mine and Mary's.

Another vehicle was parked outside, and I recognized the government label on the window, telling me this was Leonard's ride. I hoped Clare was here too.

Before I knew it, we were at the doorway, and Jules ran inside, Maggie close after her.

"Dean, it's been far too long," my sister's voice said, and my eyes widened as she approached.

"You're pregnant!" I shouted, surprised by the bump of her belly. I pulled her close before holding her at arm's length to survey the new version of my sister. "Why didn't you tell me?"

Isabelle glanced over at Mary, who smiled at me. "I wanted to tell you in person, but it seems like you're a hard one to keep track of these days. Mary knew, of course," Isabelle said.

"Congratulations, you guys. I'm so excited for you," I said, and we closed the door behind us.

Clare and Leonard were inside the kitchen, sitting at

the table, and we took a few moments to greet one another. It was like a small family reunion. Leonard seemed so much older, and he was starting to grow a beard. I smoothed my own facial hair without thinking and patted him on the shoulder.

"How's it going there, Councilman Leonard?" I asked.

Leonard gave me a grin. "Great. Tell us what happened."

Isabelle poured us all coffees, and we sat there for a good hour, going over the events of the past few months. I told them about the Inlor joining the Alliance, and about Sergo breaking the Relocator. Leonard had used it with me so long ago, and his eyes went wide as I told the tale. Mary had heard it the night before, but she gagged a couple times as I described the slugs, and everyone was creeped out by the story of the Collector.

"I can't believe you found another Theos. Karo must be thrilled," Clare said.

"He is. Wait until you meet Ableen. The two of them together is quite a sight," I told them. I pulled the device from J-NAK out and set it on the table, sliding it toward Clare. "We need more of these, but I have to take this one with me today. Did you bring the scanner?"

Clare was our best engineering mind, and she was behind most of the amazing inventions on our newly occupied planets. She was actively trading technologies with other Alliance members, and we were now hundreds of years advanced in so many ways.

"I brought it." She took the portal Modifiers and motioned for me to follow her. We ended up in the living room, where a large steel briefcase sat on the coffee table. Jules was on the floor watching a cartoon, and she barely noticed we existed. The two dogs lay on the floor on either side of my daughter, chewing treat bones.

She opened the case and powered it up. "This will scan it as thoroughly as we can. It should allow me to comprehend the functions and duplicate them."

"How long will it take to replicate?" I asked.

She shook her head. "We'll have to test it a few times first." She stared firmly at me.

I understood what she meant. Someone would have to use the duplicate Modifier on a portal, hoping it took them to the right target symbol. "Is there any other way?"

"I'll see what I can do. There might be a way. Leave it with me." She put it back into its case. "Are you okay, Dean?"

"Sure. Why do you ask?"

Clare was never one to keep from sharing her thoughts. "You look a little run down. Can you take a week first? I might have another one of these ready by then."

"No. Sarlun's expecting our arrival, and the others are waiting for us on Haven too. I'll be fine. I can rest when every last Gatekeeper is home safely, and we've either shut the portals off or fixed them." I hated the idea of not having the portals, though we'd be able to utilize other technology, like the gateway sticks I'd obtained from Fontem's collection.

"Promise me something," she said, all hints of kidding aside.

"Go for it."

"When this adventure is over, take time for you and your family. I know you're being pulled in ten different directions at all times. You have homes on three planets, for the love of God. You need to ground yourself somewhere and watch that lovely daughter of yours grow up," Clare said.

My chin lowered to my chest. "I know, Clare. I want that too. Thanks for looking out for me."

"Anytime."

"How's Nick?" I asked, hoping they'd continued to be an item. Her expression answered the question.

"He's great. Better than great. We're living together, you know," Clare said, and sadly, I wasn't even sure if I did know that. I needed to spend more time with my friends after this mission.

"Good. You two make a wonderful couple," I told her.

"How's Slate? Is he holding up okay?" Clare asked, referring to the fact that his sole girlfriend since we knew him, Denise, had turned out to be a version of a Kraski-human hybrid that Lom of Pleva had used as a plant.

"You know Zeke. He hides his pain behind a wall of muscles and jokes. I think he's hanging in there, though." Slate was my best friend. I had a lot of real relationships around me, but there was a bond between him and me that went beyond what Magnus and I had. He was my brother by choice, and that made the connection even stronger.

"Tell him I said hi," Clare said. She closed the case up and latched it. "Leave this with me. I'll work as quickly as I can."

I clasped her shoulder and smiled. "Thanks, Clare. Can

you believe how long it's been since we were sent from New Mexico to chase after Terrance and Leslie?"

She laughed, small lines forming at the edges of her eyes. "It feels like a lifetime ago, doesn't it? In some ways, it is."

Isabelle poked her head into the room and asked if anyone wanted another coffee. I couldn't say no, and I checked to make sure Jules was occupied. She hummed along with some song on the movie, and I left her there, heading for the kitchen. The dogs were now beside each other, my smaller cocker curled up near the golden retriever.

Mary appeared ready to leave, the impending journey making her anxious. The last time she'd gone on a mission, it had ended with her being possessed by the Iskios, and after breaking free from them, we'd been stranded on Sterona for months. She hadn't said as much, but it was clear those thoughts were on her mind.

I took the hint. "Maybe I should pass on the coffee. We have to travel to Haven soon, and then on to Shimmal."

Isabelle and James looked sullen at the words.

"Dean, they're happy to look after Maggie while we're gone," Mary advised.

"Thank you, guys. Poor Maggie doesn't even know what house is hers these days," I told them.

Leonard crossed the room and whispered in my ear. "Can I have five minutes before you leave? I wanted to talk to you about something." He locked gazes with me. "Actually, how about I drive you to your lander?"

That didn't bode well. "Sure. No problem."

We said our goodbyes, and once everyone was done hugging and shaking hands, I carried Jules to Leonard's vehicle, strapping her into the car seat. Maggie barked from the entrance, but the smart dog knew what was happening. It didn't keep me from feeling like I was once again abandoning someone.

I sat up front with Leonard and waved to my family as we pulled out of the drive.

"What do you need to tell us, Leonard?" Mary asked from the back seat. Jules was chatting nonsense beside her, pointing out the rear window.

"It's… I have to show you more than tell you," Leonard said, and I didn't like the sound of his ominous words. We talked about mundane things as we rode, me asking him about his job and him telling us the glorious things the council had been up to. It really was improving at all times, and with all the new Terran sites coming up, the quality of life for everyone was constantly increasing. Earth also was being rebuilt, and many people had already begun to colonize again. Only now, with the portals failing, there were some families separated and anxious to be reunited. We did have large vessels that could traverse the distance, but it was a few months' travel, even in hyperdrive.

A rumbling diverted my attention, and I tilted my head up to see one of the hovertrains cruise through the air above us. "How many do we have now?" I asked Leonard.

"The trains? We have lines going to each of the original five Terran sites and are building the rest, using three main sites as our hubs. It's pretty impressive. We can move supplies and people like never before. And because of their hovering, we aren't disrupting the ground transportation, which is busier all the time.

"Did you ever picture this when you first arrived on New Spero?" Leonard asked.

The colony had been here for a few years before we'd arrived, and it was a bit of a ramshackle town when we saw it. Now, years later, it was impressive; as advanced as many cities from old Earth had been. In the hovertrains' case, even more impressive.

"You and the rest of the Council are doing an amazing job. When are you going to take over as mayor of one of the sites?" Mary asked from behind Leonard.

I noticed the young man flush a little at the comment. "Well... no one really knows this, but Mayor Patel has offered me Terran Seventeen."

"And you're going to take it?" I asked.

He nodded as he pulled toward the landing site where our lander was awaiting our return. "I am. We have something special here, Dean and Mary. You go bring home the Gatekeepers, figure this stuff out, and I'll stick around, making sure our people are tended to."

I was so proud of the man Leonard had become. "You had to show us something?"

Leonard tapped the nav screen, and a keyboard screen projected from it. Leonard typed on the holographic lights, and I glanced over at Mary. This technology was new to me, but I wasn't surprised I hadn't seen it before.

"About two and a half months ago, only days before you went off on your mission to find Magnus, we caught this on film outside Terran Five." Leonard hit play, and a video displayed on the nav screen. Mary was in the center now, leaning forward to see the small monitor.

A man emerged from the portal room, and we watched the video feed from each camera angle as he slowly walked on the pathways and to the exit. He was stumbling around, his footing looking awkward. He stopped, turned his head from side to side, and trudged forward, heading for the direction of the town.

"What did we just see?" Mary asked.

"We're not sure. At first glance, it doesn't seem too strange. But this was around the time the portals started acting up. Let me show you something, and then you can tell me what you think." Leonard scanned the footage, pausing it on a specific shot inside the caves. He zoomed in, and that was when I saw the snout.

"It's a Shimmali man," I whispered. "And that's a Gatekeepers logo."

Leonard nodded. "He is, and that is."

"Who is he?" I asked.

"We don't know. We haven't been able to transmit information to Sarlun fast enough without the portals. That's not it, though." He fast forwarded to the part where the man stopped outside and zoomed again.

We watched as he turned his head, his snout and mouth tilted up. "He's smelling the air," Mary said, and as soon as she said it, I saw it too.

"Through his EVA helmet?" I asked.

Leonard shrugged. "Appears that way."

I noticed something else in the shot. "Is that blood on

his uniform?" I asked, pointing to the right shoulder.

"That's what we're thinking," Leonard said.

"So what are we supposed to do with this? Where did he come from?" Mary asked.

"We don't know, and we don't know where he went either. No one seems to have noticed him." Leonard shut the video off.

"But? I sense there's more," I told him.

"There is. People have been going missing."

"People? How many?" I pressed.

"Ten or so. We've had a few missing persons over the years, but nothing like this. No sign of any of them. The local PD found blood outside town, on the far side near the foothills. They tested it, and it matched one of the missing women's DNA," Leonard said.

"You're telling us you think this man might be stalking Terran Five, killing people?" Mary's voice cracked, and Jules started humming, a soft unknown tune. It was a little unnerving.

"That's what I'm saying. We need to find out who this man is, and why he arrived through the portals in a Gatekeeper EVA. I've sent the video and still shots to your arm console," Leonard said, and I glanced at my bare forearm.

"I'll slip it on later," I told him. I only wore it when I was in the field, not around the house. "Then we'll show Sarlun. I have a feeling he'll be able to identify the man. I really wish there was a way to track the portals better. If only we could determine where the man arrived from."

"That's beyond you and me. The Theos are the only ones that might know, and Karo said he doesn't have the knowledge," Leonard said.

"Wait… what did you say?" I asked.

"It's beyond you and me…"

"That's it. Maybe Regnig can help with that. We've read all we could on the Theos from him, and gained some valuable insight into how the Theos stored themselves into the stones." I'd even witnessed the event through the eyes of a Theos when I'd first met Karo. "But Regnig might have details on how to track the source planets and destinations of the stones. If he can do that, we'll be able to find out where the missing Gatekeepers traveled to. It might also allow us to find out where our Shimmali friend here arrived from." I tapped the blank nav screen with a finger.

"I don't think he's a friend of ours, Dean. I think he's dangerous," Leonard said.

"When's the last reported missing person?" Mary leaned forward, her hand settling on my left forearm.

"Three days ago," he said softly.

"Jeeze. Sorry I can't be more help. Walk with us," I said, and soon we were heading for our lander among the dozen other commuter vessels parked inside Terran Five's boundary. When we arrived at the ship, I went inside, grabbing one of the two communicators Magnus and I had stayed in touch with until he was swallowed by Cloud. "Keep this one. We'll be able to remain connected. I'll let you know what we find out when I show this to Sarlun."

Leonard grinned and stuck the device into his pocket. "Thank you. Let's hope we can stop him before more people die."

I wanted to warn my sister about the roaming killer,

and asked Leonard to do it for me. He claimed they were keeping it quiet so the city didn't panic, and I wasn't sure if that was the best move. If everyone knew who they were looking for, then they'd be able to track him down sooner.

Minutes later, we were lifting off the ground, heading for the mountain ridge we'd become so accustomed to visiting.

Mary and I lugged our supplies on over our shoulders, and she held Jules' hand as we trudged through the caverns, heading for the portal room.

Once inside, I closed my eyes and took a deep breath. I'd only come through less than a day ago and didn't feel any more relaxed for the brief respite. So much was weighing on my mind, and even though I had the added stress of ensuring my wife and daughter stayed safe, I was relieved to have them at my side.

"Together," I said, clasping Mary's hand as we stepped up to the glowing portal table.

"Together." She selected the symbol for Haven, and I slid the Modifier device onto the lit surface, engaging the power. Jules glanced up at me, her bright green eyes dancing in the dim room. She smiled, a look so sweet I had to fight the urge to pick her up in a bear hug.

When I was confident we'd arrive at our selected destination, I pressed the button and everything went white.

TWO

"Sorry I'm not coming with you guys," Terrance said from outside the portal room. We stood with the rest of the gang that was joining our troop.

"You have a world to run, and judging by the quick conversation, you have your hands full with everything," Mary told him. "Say hi to Leslie for us."

"I will. Good luck with the portals. Be safe." And with a last look toward Karo and Ableen, the hybrid leader of Haven stalked off, leaving our small group alone.

"Good night at home, boss?" Slate asked, breaking the silence.

"The best. Everyone ready to head to Shimmal?" I glanced over at Suma, who seemed distracted. "Suma?"

Her snout twitched. "Sorry, Dean. I was thinking about what's going to happen after they stop functioning. We'll all be so far apart."

"Maybe that's a good thing. It'll give everyone a chance to regroup and focus on their own worlds," Slate offered.

"You don't mean that do you, Slate?" Suma asked.

He shrugged. "I don't know. Sure, I want us to be able

to hop planets and all, but without the portals, we'd all be able to relax for a while."

"But we wouldn't be together," Suma said sadly.

"What do you mean?" Slate asked.

Mary and I were staying out of this one, while Karo stood protectively beside Ableen. I could tell Mary wanted to talk to the Theos woman, to ask her how she was holding up in the new timeline she found herself in, but my wife was waiting for the right moment. This wasn't it.

"You'll be on New Spero, Mary and Dean will be… probably on Earth, and the hybrids will be on Haven. Where does that leave me? I don't want to stay on Shimmal and work in a lab. I want to be out there searching the expanse… with you guys," Suma said.

Slate came over and wrapped an arm around her small shoulders. "We'll figure it out. We're a crew, and nothing will keep us all apart. Right, boss?"

I smiled, nodding my head, but she was correct. If they failed, we'd be separated; or at least, some of us would be. "We'll do our best." My answer was very obviously non-committal, and that didn't go over Suma's head, but she didn't comment.

"Time to go. My father will be happy to see us, at least," Suma said, scrolling to the symbol for Shimmal.

Once the device showed the same symbol, she pressed the icon, and we arrived in the sterile white portal room on Suma's home world. Two guards assessed us, and squawked something to Suma. I'd become fluent in the language and didn't need the translator. "Your father is waiting for you," they'd said.

The seven of us strode down the halls. We were all wearing white Gatekeeper jumpsuits, with the exception of Ableen, who had on a tall pair of leggings and a long-sleeved sweatshirt. I wasn't sure where the oversized clothing came from, but silently thanked Leslie for accommodating the Theos female. Jules was wearing a small red romper, and she stuck out like a sore thumb as she stood beside Mary, holding her mom's hand.

The halls were familiar here, though it had been a while since I'd occupied them. The last time, I'd been in a rage at Mary's disappearance and had almost assaulted Sarlun. We'd made up since then, and I couldn't wait to hear the progress of the rescue missions.

The second the female guard led us into the boardroom, I knew something was wrong. Sarlun appeared older than ever, and Suma ran to him. We all busied ourselves, letting them have their brief moment of reunion, and I noticed Ableen staring toward them, eyes wide. Karo whispered something to her, and she nodded, giving the Theos man a grin.

"Dean, Mary, Slate, and Karo," Sarlun said a few minutes later. "I wish we were seeing one another under different circumstances." He grabbed something from the table and passed it to Jules, who accepted the outstretched sweet fruit with glee. She popped it in her mouth and peeked up at me.

"Sarlun, I'd like you to meet Ableen," Karo said, motioning to the woman beside him. She was striking, almost as tall as Karo, with long white hair, the same gray skin, and a slender form. She extended her hand out to Sarlun in our customary greeting, and Sarlun looked like he'd seen a ghost.

"Hello, Ableen." He spoke in English. "Pleased to meet you."

"It's a long story," I started. "You'll want to sit for this one."

And for the second time that day, I told our tale since we'd parted ways during the festival on Haven. So much had happened to us. The whole time we'd been gone, Sarlun would have been working on understanding where his Gatekeepers were sent through the random portals.

When I was done, Suma and Slate taking over at certain points, Sarlun leaned back in his seat beside Suma and frowned. "What I wouldn't give to find the Collector. Imagine what we could learn from all of those aboard that ship." His eyes drifted to the far wall. "I suppose you want my update now?"

We all nodded. Jules was in my lap, and all the excitement of the day was coming to a halt. She dozed while we spoke in hushed tones inside the boardroom, her body warm and cozy against mine.

"Five teams are missing." Sarlun stood, activating a large screen on the wall. Faces appeared, with their names and brief bios underneath. He tapped a device in his hand, and it zoomed on the first pair of Gatekeepers. "Bee and Da-Narp are a team from the Oryan system."

I'd seen them before but hadn't spoken directly with them. They were a lanky race that walked on two legs, but could use four when they had to travel at vast distance and speed. Their faces were accented by dog-like muzzles, but were mostly hairless. They were heading to a new system, one rumored to be rich in minerals, Sarlun said, and a symbol appeared, one of the portal destinations. "Only they didn't make it there. This was before we knew about the issue. All five teams departed before you returned from saving Origin."

Sarlun went over the next four teams, each having disappeared or, at least, not having returned since leaving. It was going to be next to impossible to learn where they went, not without more information. I was hoping Regnig would be able to assist us with that. I was looking forward to seeing the peculiar bird-man again.

"As you'll notice, Polvertan is missing, alongside the other newcomer, Dreb." Sarlun pointed at their pictures, and alarm seeped into me.

"You have to be kidding me. I thought they were pairing up newbies with someone experienced. How could we miss two of the new recruits, and from new Alliance of Worlds members?" Slate asked.

Sarlun glared at him for a second before his face softened. "They were asked to venture here to meet with their actual partners. They never made it to Shimmal."

"This mission became more imperative. They're all important, don't get me wrong, but the prince of Motrill? Our relationship with them is strong, but mostly through their Keppe cousins. We need to mitigate the fallout. Also… the Empress is going to be upset with me if we don't bring her pride and joy, Dreb, home safely. She hand-picked him to join our Gatekeepers when we asked." I let out a deep breath, knowing this all added to the ever-growing pressure

The Gatekeepers

building up surrounding the job.

"We'll bring them back, boss. We always do," Slate said with a grin. I almost believed him.

The last duo's image zoomed in, and my breath caught in my throat. "Is that one of yours?" I asked, recognizing the Shimmali man.

Sarlun nodded. "His name is Soloma. He was with the first other human Gatekeeper, Sally Prescott."

I knew her, we all did. She was sworn in a week before the festival because of her mission. I knew how badly she'd wanted to go to Haven for the festivities. My gut was telling me we wouldn't be seeing her ever again.

"I have something to show you." I grabbed my console, strapping it over my forearm. I found the file and pushed it to the screen on the wall. My image filled up half the screen, and it showed the video Leonard had sent me. Sarlun gasped as Soloma roamed through the corridors, and outside.

"How?"

"We don't know. I guess he arrived two months ago," I told him.

Sarlun was standing, and he crossed the distance, staring at the image on the screen. "Do you have him now?"

I shook my head, and told them everything Leonard had told us.

"This can't be," Suma said. "I know Soloma. He used to help me with my engineering homework."

"He can't be a killer," Sarlun said point blank. "I don't believe it."

"Then how is he there alone? Where's Sally?" Mary

asked.

"I don't know. I suspect they were trapped on the other side of a portal, and he elected to try his luck solo. Maybe they each went their own way, in hopes one would arrive at a safe world," Sarlun said.

"Look closely. That EVA doesn't fit him, and there's blood on it. He killed her, Sarlun. He stole her suit, and traveled through the portal." I hated having to say it, but the evidence was there.

"Then something possessed him to do so," Sarlun said, and I could tell he hated his choice of words. He glanced at Mary, shooting her an apologetic look.

"That could be. I wanted you to know. I'll be in touch with Leonard, and hopefully, we can find out what exactly happened. We need you to send us this information. Since we know that Soloma and Sally don't need to be rescued, we'll work on bringing the other six teams home," I said before telling them my plan to meet with Regnig, to see if there was anything in his galaxy-class library that might be useful.

"What of the portals? How do we fix them?" Sarlun asked Karo.

Karo drummed his fingers on the table. "My people are leaving them. Ableen can feel them inside, as if they're calling out to be freed. With the Iskios banished by Dean's Shifter, there's no place for them any longer," Karo said, and I hoped he didn't think that meant there was no place for him and Ableen now.

"So we'll be without?" Sarlun asked.

"Soon, I think. Soon," came Karo's answer.

The Gatekeepers

Sarlun sat again; the weight of the last two months showed in his posture and slack face. Suma grabbed his hand and looked up at me. "Dean, I can't come with you this time. I have to stay with my father. Maybe I can help in the research. We need to find another way to power the stones, one that doesn't require an ancient race's life force."

I nodded, sensing this coming. She was such a great team member, but she'd been through as much as any of us. I had half a mind to ask Slate to stay behind too. I'd have to talk to him before we left for the mission. On the other hand, I selfishly wanted his expertise and experience alongside us, especially if Mary and Jules were coming with us.

"A well-deserved rest." I gave Suma a smile, and she lowered her eyes, as if she felt a great conflict in remaining with her dad. "We'll figure this one out. We don't have any big looming enemies for this one, just faltering portals. I think we can handle it with a smaller team," I told her, and she perked up a little.

"I, for one, will be glad to have my daughter around," Sarlun said.

We talked for another hour, grabbing every detail we could about the missing Gatekeepers. It was getting late, and Sarlun asked us if we'd like to stay for dinner. Slate's expression said yes, but I was anxious to keep moving. The sooner we finished this task, the faster we'd be home again.

"I think we'd better leave for Bazarn. Maybe Regnig will have a spot for us to crash for the night, or Garo Alnod might take us in," I told Sarlun.

"Very well. Dean, may I have a moment?" Sarlun grabbed my arm, gently leading me apart from the others.

"What's up?"

"I don't think this is going to be simple," he said.

"What? The job?" I asked.

He nodded. "That and more. If the Theos are dying inside, how will Karo and his new friend Ableen handle that?"

"Sarlun, the Theos are already dead. They don't have bodies; it's only their energy inside. And they're not necessarily conscious," I said.

"You pulled a few into yourself on Sterona, correct?" he asked.

I could see where he was going with this. "Yes, and their energy powered me, like the Iskios did to Mary." The only reason I'd been able to beat them was because of their opposing force inside me. I'd harnessed the energy from the portal to flow through me, granting me temporary strength and powers. My spine tingled, thinking about the foreign voices inside my head.

"Just be careful. Do you remember how to pull them out?" he asked, eyes wide.

I nodded. It wasn't something I'd forget any time soon.

"How about putting them inside?" he asked, glancing at the two live Theos in the room.

"You're not suggesting we'd need to…" I set my sights on Karo, who gave me a grin from across the hall.

"No, hopefully nothing so drastic. You've been stranded enough times, though. Let's make sure it doesn't happen again." He sighed. "Perhaps I should accompany you. They are my responsibility, after all. I should have seen this coming."

"How could you know they would fail?" I asked.

"Regardless, I should be there to bring them home."

Suma was standing near us, trying unsuccessfully to appear interested in something on her arm console. "Your daughter is home. Savor this time with her. She's special, and it won't be long before some amazing project takes her away from home for extended periods. Enjoy these next few weeks."

Sarlun leaned against the wall. "You're right. You take care of your family, Recaster," he said with a twitch of his snout. He used the title Regnig had named me, and it was strange coming from his lips.

"I will. Even though I suspect I'll be the one that needs taking care of."

"Can I send someone else with you? We have a large contingency of Keepers on Shimmal, idly sitting around," Sarlun said. "I can guarantee many of them would love to join your mission."

I considered this, very seriously, before answering, "Nah. The fewer moving pieces, the better. We'll do everything we can to solve these portals and bring the teams home." I patted my pocket, where the Modifier jutted out. "Once I can read where they traveled to, I'll be able to bring them home."

Sarlun interrupted, "As long as the entire network doesn't fail first."

I clapped him on the shoulder. "And that kind of positive thinking is what keeps me going every day."

He stared, open-mouthed, before laughing. "Dean, I've missed this. We'll have to do that dinner when you return. I have a few things I'd like to pick your brain about."

Any other alien asking about picking my brain might have thrown me for a loop, but Sarlun had easily picked up our colorful sayings.

Suma and Sarlun stayed behind as our small contingency passed the sterile halls to the portal room. Jules was awake now, being carried by Slate. She was tugging on his blond beard and laughing.

And then we were six, and a very unlikely six.

"Bazarn Five, coming right up," Slate said, activating the portal table. The symbols lit up, casting an eerie glow across the Theos' faces. We set the Modifier up, ensuring we ended up at our proper destination, and as Slate tapped the icon for Garo Alnod's world, Ableen let out a terrifying scream.

THREE

"What is it?" Mary asked. We were on the other side, inside the portal room on Bazarn. The immense guards arrived, and the Theos woman continued shouting. Her body was against the wall, and she crouched low, covering her ears with her palms, long fingers wrapped behind her head.

Jules was crying now, startled by the light and the noise, and Slate passed her to Mary, who began to console the small wreck.

Karo knelt beside Ableen and tried to calm her. "It's okay. You're all right, my dear," he said, and she glanced up at him with red-rimmed eyes.

"Did you not hear them?" she asked, and Karo nodded.

"I did, but perhaps not as acutely as you. Our ancestors sacrificed themselves into these stones so long ago. They struggle to stay, I think. They understand their function and fight to help us," Karo said.

Ableen had stopped screaming, but she was rocking back and forth on the ground as Karo hugged her tightly. "They are in pain. We have to help them. We must release them, Karo."

Karo glanced up at me, locking gazes. I instantly knew that they were right. We couldn't keep the stones alive for our own convenience. I had to support her on this. "Ableen, help us bring our brothers and sisters home, and we'll do everything we can to close the stones, freeing your people."

Her eyes went big, and she blinked innocently. "Do you promise?"

I cringed. The Alliance of Worlds relied on trade, and a lot of it was done through the portal system. We'd have to find another way. I felt confident making the deal. "I promise."

Karo smiled wide and helped the woman to her feet. I wiped Jules' red cheeks and kissed her on her smooth forehead. "You okay, honey?"

"Okay, Papa," she said softly.

The huge familiar guards strode up to us, immense guns pointed in our direction. I raised my hands and stepped in front of our group. "Good evening, gentlemen," I said, not knowing what time of day it was on Bazarn.

"It's you again. Should I alert the planet that we might be under attack soon?" The guard's alien words translated into my ear through my earpiece.

I laughed at this. "Always nice to see you too. Can you…"

"Let Alnod know you're here and send a ship for you?" The other guard finished my sentence for me.

"Exactly. See, we're good friends at this point," I told

them, trying not to think about how easily they could tear me limb from limb. The room was eye-catching, with its high walls and pillars. Images of various planets were carved into the ceiling, and the gold color was etched into every nook and cranny the designer could find.

"What's that all about?" the first guard asked, pointing to Ableen, who was on her feet beside Karo behind me.

"Nothing. Her cat died," I said, and the two guards frowned at one another, confusion spread across their faces. "Good to go?"

The giant armored guards stepped apart, clearing a path to the exit. "By all means. Don't cause any trouble while you're here, Parker." So they knew my name. Mary glanced at me. It was her first time here, though I'd told her a lot about the stints I'd been to the world.

We moved through the space beyond the portal room and found the halls empty, as well as the stairs leading to the promenade. No hologram women greeted us to give directions this time, and we emerged onto the boardwalk. I was glad to see it a hustle and bustle of activity. So Bazarn was once more open for business.

"Everyone watch your pockets," I warned, recalling the time we'd been pickpocketed in the middle of the crowd. We carried our packs with full EVAs inside, and Jules clung to Mary as we strolled through the center of the promenade. It wasn't that busy, but it was warm in the bright sunlight. Smells of foreign foods wafted through the air, and I found I was suddenly hungry. I hoped Regnig would have something other than birdseed available.

Perhaps I could convince the pilot of the transport

vessel to make a pit stop. I found the same ship Garo sent last time, lowering from the distant sky to land at the edge of the square. Slate took the lead, and many visitors and locals alike cleared the way for the large incoming blond man in a white jumpsuit.

I noticed Ableen cowering from the throngs of people. She was skittish, and I didn't blame her. All of this was so alien to a woman who'd never left her home world. She was young and frozen in time for centuries aboard the Collector's ship. Karo whispered comforts to her, and she appeared to accept his word as gold as we arrived at the awaiting vessel.

One of Garo's blue Molariun pilots opened the doors and waved us aboard.

"Dean!" Rivo ran over, jumping up and wrapping her arms around me. She was so tiny, she hardly weighed a thing.

"How did you even make it home?" I asked.

"I left the night of the festival, before things went to hell. Dad was sick, and I needed to be with him," she said.

"Is he all right now?" Mary asked, settling Jules to a seat. She pulled out a bag of breakfast cereal and opened it for our daughter.

Rivo's four eyes cast aside, telling me he wasn't fine. "No. He's not doing well. Part of me is grateful the portals have been closed, because it's given me a chance to care for him."

Everyone was on board, and Rivo glared up at Ableen, who was over twice the small blue girl's height. "What do we have here?" she asked.

The Gatekeepers

"Rivo Alnod, this is Ableen of the Theos." Karo stood proudly when he said this, looking like he was posing for an ancient Greek statute.

"What… you found another Theos? This is great!" Rivo grabbed Ableen's hand and tapped the top of it with a finger, as if checking if the woman was real.

"Rivo, if you expect our story, I'm not telling you until we're with Regnig. I think I'm all storied out for today," I told her as the ship lifted up.

"Magnus and Nat are home safe?" Rivo asked.

"They weren't quite yet, but they were on the way," Slate told her.

"Rivo, do you mind stopping somewhere for food? We only have road provisions, and I'd rather salvage what we can," I said, and she nodded, speaking softly to the pilot. Our detour only took a few minutes, and soon we were up in the air, heading away from one of the rich floating islands above Bazarn, moving toward the desert. The food smelled great, and already Slate was trying to sneak a peek into the crate it arrived in. Rivo slapped his hand away.

"And I see the offspring is here." Rivo nodded to Jules, who had a donut-shaped cereal bit stuck to her cheek.

Mary rolled her eyes. "Yes, the *offspring* is here."

"She's very cute. For a human," Rivo said, and my wife laughed.

"I suppose you're right. Thank you," Mary said in return.

I glanced out the vessel's display screen and saw the ship's nose diving toward the sand. Here we went again. We traveled through the holograph and into the tunnel leading far below the surface, where the secret library and its telepathic caretaker resided.

It wasn't long before we were on the cliff platform outside the door leading to the library. Rivo asked the pilot to stay put, and we poured from the ship. Jules tried running for the ledge, as if to peer over it, and I grabbed her by the scruff of her romper. "I don't think so. With me, missy." She giggled as I carried her over to the entrance, which swung open before I had the chance to knock.

I knew it was only a matter of time, Regnig said telepathically. Everyone appeared to have *heard* his words, because Mary broke out in a smile.

"It's great to see you again," Mary said, and the tiny bird man lifted a stubby wing, inviting us inside.

Karo smiled and nodded at Regnig, whose large eyes widened at seeing Ableen with our group. *Who is this?*

"Ableen," Karo said, ushering her inside the door. We made our way to the hall and settled inside the edge of the library. Slate set the crate of food on a table, and Regnig stuck his narrow tongue from his beak.

A female Theos. I never thought I'd see the day where I met you, Karo, and now that we've met before, I never thought I'd meet another of your kind. This is preposterous and amazing, Regnig said. *What brings you to my little nest?* He motioned for us to have a seat, and when he realized he didn't have enough chairs, he directed Slate and me to an adjoining room, where we found a dusty old couch. We wiped it off and carried it to the center of the library, where Regnig and I had first had a long chat.

Jules wobbled over to Regnig, and I laughed at how

close in size they were. She thought he was something akin to our dog, and she tried petting him, receiving a scowl from the one-eyed telepathic bird.

Perhaps she'd be more comfortable in a cage? Regnig said jokingly.

I scooped her up and sat down, passing her a tablet from my pack. She threw on headphones and watched her favorite show while we talked. We tried to limit her screen time, but there was a time and place for distractions. I guessed there would be a lot of that on this adventure.

"You asked why we came." Everyone had settled in, and Slate was passing out food. It consisted of something brown and sticky on noodles, but it smelled wonderful, and my growling stomach was grateful for it. Jules slurped a noodle from her plate, sauce stuck to her nose. "We need to find a way to track where a portal stone sent someone. Or groups of someones." I proceeded to explain to him the dying Theos, and how many Gatekeepers were trapped on other worlds, potentially dangerous places.

"Without tracking them, they won't be able to go home," Mary said.

Regnig appeared to consider this. *And you think the stones will be gone soon?*

Karo took this one. "My people are leaving them. They fight to cling to our world, but their energy is spent. They will be sent to their final resting place as soon as we can facilitate the Gatekeepers home."

Ableen brightened at this, and she returned to eating her dinner, slowly poking the food before eating it with hesitation.

I understand. This will be difficult. I've been a hermit my whole life, and only since you've visited me, Dean Parker, have I had… what you'd call a social life. I even visited Earth and saw your childhood home. You are family to me now: you, the Alnods, and the one you call Suma. Regnig sat in a petite leather chair and watched us all with his unblinking stare. *Without the portals, we'll need another way to move about with ease.*

"There are over two hundred portal planets, and perhaps more we don't know about," I said, deciding to tell everyone about the devices I'd found while searching for Polvertan the Motrill. "I have some portal devices that can replace the stones, only Clare hasn't been able to duplicate the technology. Sarlun's team hasn't either. They came from Fontem's room. Do you have the one I gave you?"

Regnig knew about Fontem's room, because I'd left him access to it so he could catalog the items. *I do, and I have found some real gems inside there. Actually… there might be something about the portals.*

My heart raced. We'd searched his library high and low before, and Regnig was sure we'd exhausted all his materials while I was searching for Mary and the real Theos home world.

"Can we go now?" I asked. Everyone was nearly finished eating, and I forced a few more bites from my half-full plate.

I don't see why not. Regnig stood, flapping his compact wings; a feather fell off, floating toward my slumbering daughter.

"Dean, I'm going to stay put with Jules. It's getting late," Mary said. Rivo was already dozing off, and we left her sleeping soundly.

"Boss, how about you and Regnig make this a solo trip? I'll stay behind," Slate said, and I knew he wanted to protect my family. I nodded, giving him a smile.

"We'd also like to join you." Karo spoke for Ableen and himself.

Regnig's beak opened, then closed tightly. *We would love the company.*

"It's settled. Let's go." I stood up, my back cracking at the change of posture.

I followed Regnig, stopping at the short desk on our way. He tapped a drawer, and a blue light emanated, scanning his face before the drawer opened. I recognized the half of the portal device as soon as I saw the sleek metal.

"What's this?" Karo asked, flipping a leather-bound book closed.

I read the title. *Dean Parker: A Modern Recaster.*

That's... the book I told you I was going to write. Regnig's thoughts felt abashed, and I refrained from opening it to read anything.

"I thought you were kidding," I told him.

Why would I joke about something like that? Perhaps I can convince these two to tell me their story one day. Regnig pointed at Karo and Ableen, who didn't appear to hear his words. I knew Regnig could direct his telekinetic thoughts to one or all minds in a room.

"I'm sure they would be more than happy to," I told him.

Would you do the honors? Regnig asked, grabbing the device and passing it into my outstretched palm.

I led our group of four to one of the library's side cubbies. It was a place with soft lighting where one could bring a volume and sit in peace, reading or studying the contents. I activated the portal device, and its line of light shone out, covering the walls and ceiling in a flat plane; the evidence of the portal disappeared once it was locked into place.

"I'll go first," I said, wishing I had brought my pulse rifle along. I doubted anyone would ever find Fontem's collection from the other side, but we'd stumbled upon it rescuing the Motrill prince, who was now a Gatekeeper, and one of the missing Keepers at that. It was a diplomatic mess: swearing Polvertan in, then having him go missing the next day.

I stepped through, arriving in the once-familiar space. Only I wasn't alone.

FOUR

The hunter sniffed the air, sensing a storm arriving. He was miles from his nest and didn't like the idea of being stuck out in the open for the impending rain. The region had turned colder in the last few months since he'd arrived on this new, lush land.

It was so far removed from what he'd known his whole life, and being in this body was… odd. Animals from the plains of his land were an understood capacity. These two-legged creatures were different. He knew it was time to change from this shape. There were no others like him. His snout was longer than their breathing apparatus, his skin a different color, his legs thicker and shorter.

His legs carried him across the open expanse between the city's fence and the hills, where he made a home away from the prying eyes of the locals. If they knew what he was, they'd have killed him long ago, and he felt his luck starting to slip away.

The bones inside his belly were fully digested, and he felt weak because of it. It was time to feed again. He had used the last few bodies he'd fed on to fuel this vessel, rather than go through the pain and struggle of shifting into their forms. Now it was time. He was strikingly dissimilar, even though they were all bipedal: two legs, two arms, comparable enough physiology, but far enough apart to elicit strange looks.

The hunter ran now, finally used to walking as this being. Once the brain of the prey had been fully absorbed, he understood the man he'd shifted into. He was from another world, one called Shimmal. He could only assume the man had traveled to the hunter's land through the glowing crystal. He also felt the fear as he'd pressed the symbol etched on the flat surface those many moons ago, a warning sent off by the prey's brain sitting inside his belly at the time.

He called them portals, and they were unreliable. The hunter had thought about returning to the cave he'd arrived to on this world and traveling home, but there was nothing left for him there, even if he could comprehend how to operate the device.

So he kept walking, returning to his nest as the rain fell hard from above. His clothing sat on his body like tattered rags, and the water poured on him, drenching him within moments of the first flash of light in the afternoon sky. He was glad the immense red star wasn't bearing over him today. The sight of it sent shivers through his spine. It felt too big, too alien for his mind to process.

The hunter heard the mechanical noise before he saw the ship lowering to the ground. His version of a heart pumped blood quickly through his thick veins as he recognized it. He'd seen them around the village, rising into the air, moving quickly. From the ingested brains inside him, he knew this to be a transport vessel or a lander, depending on which prey's memories he accessed.

He wanted to run, to hide in the treeline that was only a few hundred yards away, but he stopped, knowing the ship would easily catch him. He had to wait for the right time.

The hunter wiped rain from his eyes, his snout twitching as a door hissed open on the vessel. Two *humans* emerged. He knew that was the name of their race. There were many colors of them, and they had males and females as well; a fairly universal trait.

One of each stood there now, holding weapons pointed at him from thirty yards away.

"What are you doing out here?" the man asked, holding his weapon firmly in place.

The hunter knew he didn't look like them. He was in the form of a Shimmali, and his clothing was dirty, torn, and had his prey's blood all over it. He licked his lips, tasting dried iron on his chin. "Friend," he squawked, unsure what language he said it in.

The two armed humans glanced at one another, and the woman lowered her gun. She smiled despite being out in the middle of nowhere in the rain. "Why don't you come with us then, friend? We'll find you some help," she said, and the hunter knew he had them.

The large male lowered his weapon as well, and the hunter timidly stepped toward them.

"What's your name?" the man asked when they were close enough to stop yelling above the storm.

Water dripped off the hunter, and he was glad it had

wiped some of the blood from his body. "Soloma." He used the man's real name.

"Soloma?" The woman's brow furrowed.

He couldn't wait any longer. He lunged at the woman first, assuming her the most cunning. Her guard was down, and his stubby teeth easily tore through her throat. Her gun clattered to the rocky ground, and the hunter picked it up, firing two rounds at the man before he'd even had a chance to react. They lay there lifeless, and the hunter smiled.

He moved for the ship, checking to see if there was a pilot waiting inside. There was no one else. Good.

He removed the clothing from the two guards, finding the meals a much better experience without the fabric slowing him down. He'd had a stomach ache for days after the first victim. He ate the man first, crunching the bones to dust before swallowing. The woman, he swallowed what he could whole, and spent the next two hours inside the shelter of the ship, converting from the Shimmali man into the visage of the female human.

He screamed in anguish as he made the transformation, feeling every bone move inside his sac of flesh. When it was done, he dozed, comatose inside the lander. Eventually, he awoke. It was dark outside, and the rain was all gone, dried up in the rocky expanse of the foothills.

His body ached, and he blinked his eyes open and closed, feeling the raw sensation. He stared at his reflection in the glass of the lander's door and saw the long brown hair, the slender face, the strong but agile body. He smiled widely at the image and slipped into the clothing he'd peeled off the bodies.

The Gatekeepers

The hunter closed the door to the ship. All that remained outside was the washed-away blood of the prey. No one would ever know he was there. He'd carefully digested the brain of the male and understood how to pilot the ship.

He lifted it off the ground and headed for a different place on this planet. Terran One. The village name was a whisper on his mind, but important nonetheless.

FIVE

I ducked as the thing pounced toward me. I wasn't able to avoid its grasp, and it clung to me, long arms wrapping around my neck.

Dean, don't struggle. I should have told you about Bool, Regnig said.

I dropped my arms, going slack.

Bool, stop it at once. Regnig's words were a blast to my mind, and the creature jumped off, away from me.

"What is it?" I asked, seeing a short torso, long hairy arms, and four thin legs. Its head was undersized, big eyes curiously watching me. It was only three feet tall, standing higher than Regnig.

Karo and Ableen entered through the portal device, and she gasped at the sight of the animal.

Bool is a Noolathrocite. A local tree dweller. It appears he found his way inside from the tropical planet where Fontem hid the access to his collection. Bool came to stand at the birdman's side, holding out his hand. Regnig pulled a piece of fruit from somewhere in his outfit and passed it to the animal. Bool smiled, showcasing a terrifyingly sharp set of teeth.

"And those are for eating leaves and grass?" I asked, hopeful.

Quite the opposite. They enjoy eating meat more than anything.

Karo stepped between the creature and Ableen protectively.

But don't worry. He's friendly. I let him come and go as he pleases. So far, he hasn't done anything, nor has he summoned any of his friends inside. Regnig petted the animal as he devoured the fruit in seconds.

"I'll take your word on it." I took in my surroundings, seeing much more rhyme and reason inside the collection. Everything was lined up in rows; new shelving, likely borrowed from Regnig's library, was set up, and he crossed the room to grab a tablet in his tiny hand, passing it to me.

Every item inside is listed on here. That cross-reference book I had came in very handy. I know what sixty percent of this stuff actually is, Regnig told us.

"You mean forty percent remains a mystery?" I asked.

He nodded, and Karo walked over to a shelf, picking up a globe-sized object with a glowing barrier around it, hefting it in his palms.

Don't drop that.

"Why's that?" Karo asked Regnig.

Because it's a world.

Karo appeared horrified. "What do you mean, it's a world?"

Apparently, about a million years ago, a disturbance formed far away from here. It shrank an entire solar system before dissipating. Only one of the planets survived. This is it. Regnig found the location on the tablet, handing it to me.

I read the brief description and paled. "He's telling the truth, Karo. You might want to set it down gently. The world is frozen inside that barrier." I scrolled through the data. "According to this, Fontem found this on a backwater world about fifty thousand light years from its original system. It was already encased in this barrier. Who placed it there is a mystery, but Fontem always wanted to find a way to reverse the shrinking, and to bring the planet to life once again."

Ableen stepped over to it, her hand hovering above the energy barrier. "That is so sad," she said.

"What if we find a way, Dean?" Karo asked.

I nodded. "I'm afraid of looking at anything else, because we could forever be trying to figure these ancient puzzles out." I studied the globe and saw the clouds and oceans frozen in time. I wondered what kind of life had been put on pause and, if we could find a way to reverse it, if they would survive.

"We must help them," Ableen said, and Karo smiled at the Theos woman. I could tell he was smitten with her, not only because she was the last female Theos, but because of her big heart and her sensitivity to the plight of others. She had also been frozen aboard the Collector's ship for a long time. She understood more than anyone.

"Then it's settled. Regnig, while we're gone, can you see what you can learn about this world?" I asked him.

The feathered being opened his beak and stuck his tongue out to the side, his one eye boring into me. *I have started already. I had to put your book on pause, though.*

I wanted to tell him that was a good thing, because no

one cared about reading a book about me, but I held back. "Great. Where do we start?" I asked, flipping through the program on the tablet menus.

I've made as many notes as I could. I must admit, this last year has been exhausting, but also the most exciting of my career.

I didn't ask him how long that was, because I knew it would only make Regnig feel old. "I can imagine. Who better than you to catalog a collection like this?"

I can think of numerous others, but I digress. I was the one lucky enough to be offered the opportunity. Let's use the keywords: portal, stones, crystal, Theos, map, reverse, pathway, and any others you can think of, Regnig suggested.

I keyed them all in, along with a few more, and seven files highlighted. We opened them one at time, searching for something that would assist us in deciphering the secrets of the portals within Fontem's horde of history.

"Let's begin," I said. Fontem had a collection of computer software files loaded onto countless different systems, some from long dead races from thousands of years ago, to books in hundreds if not thousands of languages.

Karo, take this and locate these books. Regnig passed him a screen from a nearby desk. *Hover this over the book and choose your language output. It will translate, and you can digitally record anything you want. So if you find details on the mapping and tracking of portal destinations, tap this icon here to imprint for later analysis.*

Karo nodded, and Ableen was already moving across the space, heading for the bookshelves where so many priceless volumes from around the universe sat. I was in awe of the sheer amount of information stored here. No wonder Regnig had such a great time. Here was a man who'd devoted his life to guarding and studying the universe's greatest library, and now he was gifted access to so many more secrets of time and space.

Dean, you and I will use the system to decode these three files. Regnig perched onto a feathery pillow, and Bool leapt over to his side, curiously watching Regnig's tiny hands fly across the keypad. I watched the almost monkey-like animal from the corner of my eye for a few moments before trusting it wasn't going to take a bite out of Regnig or me.

I cracked my knuckles, fully aware a research project like this could take some time.

It was hours later when Karo shouted from across the room, and I blinked my eyes open, not realizing I'd even been drifting off.

"We found something," Karo said firmly. Pride beamed from his smile. "Or Ableen did."

We stood, heading over to their seating area on the floor. Ableen passed the screen to me, and I saw the translated message, feeling my heart race at the words.

The Crystal Map is a tool few know about, but many wish they had. Each trip through the crystals leaves an imprint that fades with time.

It went on to discuss other things, and I scrolled through the prior pages as well as the next few, not seeing any more about the subject.

"What does it mean? Crystal Map. Let's search it!" I ran to the tablet and brought it over. Everyone waited with bated breath as I searched the keywords Crystal and Map. There were no results, not when typed together.

Perhaps we're doing this wrong. Dean, remove the translation to

English. We need to search it in the original form, Regnig suggested. I did as he bade, and found the word in some unfamiliar language. The lettering was strange, a distant series of symbols and sketches. I pasted the details into the search field on the tablet, and we watched it scroll through the millions of files, to return one result.

"We have a hit," I said, opening the file. I didn't understand what I was looking at.

This is good. Item number three hundred and eighty-two. Regnig was off, flapping his wings in excitement. Bool ran after him, squeaking as if they were playing a game. I assumed he really wanted another piece of fruit.

The shelf was too tall for Regnig. He made a series of unfamiliar commands to the creature, and Bool climbed the tall shelf, returning with a metal box, setting it into Regnig's talons. I was beginning to understand why our friend kept the monkey-thing around.

We gathered around Regnig as he opened the box. My heart sank as it sprang wide to reveal nothing inside.

Regnig stuck his tongue out and poked his beak inside the box. A secret compartment clicked open, and now we found what we were looking for. It was clear and sticky to touch, about the length of a pen, but flexible. I pulled my finger away, and the device stuck to it.

Place this on the stone, and the other end onto this tablet, and you will locate your destination symbol. It should be as easy as that, Regnig said.

"Can it be that simple?" Karo asked.

I shook my head. "Things rarely are. Thank you for your help, Regnig. Good catch, Ableen."

I was anxious to test it. Would it show us a full catalog of each portal, detailing each trip through that particular stone, and where the user traveled to? The brief message said that the imprints faded with time, but how much time? Centuries? Days? Hours? We didn't know.

We headed for the exit, and Bool accepted another piece of food from Regnig before we stopped at the portal device. Ableen glanced at the shrunken world, and I silently promised the inhabitants that we'd return for them one day.

Seconds later, we were inside the library, closing the portal behind us.

"Does Bool come and go as he pleases?" I asked.

As far as I'm aware, yes. Regnig led us to the center of the room, where Slate had erected a makeshift camp for us all. Mary and Jules were tucked away inside a tent; Rivo and my big friend were playing some sort of game resembling chess, and from the looks of it, the small blue woman was beating him with ease.

"Well, what did you find?" Slate stood up, trying to read my expression. I made it easy on him.

"We got it," I said, keeping my voice low.

"You did?" Rivo asked.

I pulled the flexible device out and showed them. "Doesn't look like much," Rivo said.

I could only shrug. "Seems to be what we were after. We'll find out."

"When do we go? Now?" Slate asked.

I glanced to the tent where my wife and child slept soundly, and shook my head. "No. We'll stay the night and head out in six hours or so. Sound okay with everyone?"

Slate had set up a few extra tents in the open space in the center of the library. "Sure. Karo and Ableen, you can take those ones."

"What about you?" I asked him.

"I already had a nap. Plus, Regnig has some serious coffee here." He smiled over at our host. "Hope you don't mind. We found it and brewed some."

That's not coffee. It's medicinal... or that's what it's meant for, Regnig said.

Slate's eyes went wide. "What kind of medicine?"

It's meant for mind stimulation. I use it when I need to concentrate for days at a time.

"Some sort of speed? I'm feeling a little funny here, boss," Slate said.

Rivo laughed at him. "You're fine. I knew what it was. I brought the coffee with me. I can never leave home without it, not after spending time with you guys on your ship, and on Haven."

Slate let out a sigh and sat down again. "See, I told you there was nothing to worry about," he said, tapping his foot repeatedly.

I rolled my eyes at him. "Sure thing. If you guys have this under control, I'm going to call it a night. See you in a few hours." I left them to play their game quietly and crept into my tent. Jules was lying side by side with Mary, whose arms wrapped around our daughter protectively. It had taken me a year to convince Mary to let Jules sleep in another room than ours, and now I could see her defensive instincts take over.

I took my boots off and climbed onto the inflated mattress beside Mary. She was warm to the touch, and I pressed my cheek against her shoulder. She moved slightly and nestled into Jules.

I let their soft breaths lull me to sleep, and I dreamt for the first time in a long while. When I woke, all I could recall of the ordeal was being trapped on a terrible world. The portals were dead, and my family was threatened.

SIX

Regnig had considered coming with us, but decided against it at the last minute, which I was glad for. He was useful, but better suited to life in the sanctuary of his library. The last thing I wanted was for him to accompany us on a mission of unknown dangers and for something to happen to our small friend. He promised to keep researching the stones among the vast array of tomes he'd uncatalogued in a distant dusty section of his shelves. He also told Ableen that he would see if there was any clue to helping the shrunken planet.

She beamed at him as he promised this, and Karo thanked Regnig as well. Then we were off, my terrible dreams a distant memory.

The ship let us off, and already we were nearing the portal room, less than a day after arriving on Bazarn. We arrived through the quiet promenade, heading down the stairs that would lead to the immense guards in the overly-decorated space.

"Rivo, I wish we had time to visit with your father. Send Garo our thoughts and best wishes in his recovery,"

I told the Molariun girl. She hadn't told us exactly what ailed him or how serious it was, but from the look that crossed her face, we knew it wasn't good.

"Thank you. He did ask for a favor," Rivo said.

"You know he's done enough for me. Anything," I told her.

"Inlorian bars. He wants to buy a thousand bars," she said quietly.

"A thousand bars!" Slate shouted in surprise. That was worth more than most planets.

"Are you sure you heard him right?" Mary asked.

Jules ran ahead, dancing on the marble floors.

Rivo nodded. "Of course. A thousand bars. He expects to have a great price at that value. He also wants to set up a meeting with the Inlor, if that can be arranged. He's considering being on the Board," she said.

"Is he well enough to do that?" I asked her softly.

Her eyes met mine. "He will be." She was leaving something unsaid, and I suspected Garo was trying to gain a foothold with the newest craze of Inlorian bars while the price was hot. If he could lock in a spot on the Board with the Inlor, he would probably attempt to make it part of the portfolio under the Alnod company, and any heir would hold the position, should he pass on. In this case, that meant Rivo. She seemed to understand this, but neither of us brought it up.

"I'll see what I can do. Thanks for coming with us." I knocked on the door, and one of the guards opened it, his hulking form stepping out of the way for us to enter.

"Your Highness, we didn't know you were coming,"

one of them said.

Rivo only laughed. "Watch the door, please. We have something to do with the portal stones."

They stepped between us and the crystal at the end of the room. "I'm sorry? How do you mean?"

"Look, we don't have time to explain everything to you," Rivo said.

They didn't budge. "We know we work for you, but we also have an obligation to the stones," the other guard said.

A shiver began to work its way up my spine.

Karo stepped forward. "What does that mean?"

The other guard spoke, his voice deep and gravelly. "We work for the stones. You stand here long enough, and you learn to hear them."

Karo's head tilted slightly. "Them?"

"I don't know how to explain it, exactly. The stone is alive," he answered.

I tried to see if I could smooth this over. "We aren't doing anything to affect them. The portals are dying; the voices you've heard are withering away, and as you know, the destinations and symbol connections are being mixed up. That's why all the portals have been closed."

"I knew it," one of them said. "It's felt off lately, weaker somehow."

I nodded. "We need to find the rest of our Gatekeepers, but we must first test a device on this stone to see if it works. Then we'll be off. Sound fair?"

They stomped away, their pumpkin-sized heads meeting in a brief huddle. "We apologize for intruding, your Highness. And...Dean Parker." My name was added hesitantly.

"Thank you. My father thanks you as well," Rivo said, and we stepped around them. Jules stayed, pointing up at one of the guards, who was at least four times her height.

"Papa. Silly man!" she told me. I scooped her up and smirked an apology, heading for the rest of our group.

Rivo followed us, likely curious to see if the device we'd found would work. Judging by our faces, we were all eager.

The stone began to glow, pulsing gently as we neared. Ableen's eyes went wide, as if she was hearing her people from inside, but she didn't say anything as I pulled the Crystal Map from my pack, setting the bag on the ground.

"Here goes nothing," I whispered, attaching the device to my tablet, the other end to the table. It latched on as if it were designed for this purpose – which, I reasoned, it was. My tablet flashed brightly before a new application appeared. It showed a series of locations across a vast array of stars, each pinprick of light clearly implying a portal stone.

Slate let out a low whistle as he peered over my shoulder. Mary clutched my arm, squeezing tightly as we all stood in awe. Seeing the network of interconnected portals from this vantage point made me realize how amazing they were. I didn't count them, but there were far more than the two hundred or so cataloged symbols in the tables.

"Are there…?" Karo started, his jaw dropping as I zoomed out, spreading fingers on the tablet screen.

"There are thousands," I said breathlessly. "More than we ever imagined."

The Gatekeepers

I became light-headed, and I placed a palm on the portal table to steady myself. Sarlun and the others had no idea these existed. How many worlds and civilizations were out there that we didn't know about? Apparently, a lot. Some of the lines led to distant dots, telling us the source stones were millions, if not billions, of light years away. It was all hard to comprehend as we remained there, blankly staring at the tablet in silence.

I zoomed in now, choosing a distant world. Its symbol appeared, a combination of a backwards check mark and a star. Light pulsed from it, stretching out in all directions, and the closer I moved to the image, the more distinct each line traveling to and from it became.

"This is amazing," Karo said.

They were each powered by the sacrifice of his people, and I glanced at Ableen, who stood solid as a statue, a sole tear falling onto her gray cheek.

I noticed a blinking icon on the bottom right of the screen, and I tapped it. A series of pathways illuminated, moving the center focus to a particular world. When I clicked it, I saw the symbol for Bazarn.

"This must be telling us the last trips from Bazarn," Mary said.

"Papa." Jules tugged on my pants, and I picked her up. She stared at the tablet with interest, her green eyes glowing in the reflection of the screen.

I lifted my arm, activating my arm console, and brought up the missing Gatekeeper profiles. "Two of our missing team members were last seen on Bazarn. Guards!" I turned to call them, and saw they were right behind me already. I jumped, causing Jules to squeal in delight. "You two are sneaky for giants… did you see these two Gatekeepers leave here a couple months ago?"

One of them nodded. "They were the last to travel through. Word came from Alnod to lock the doors shortly after. No one was allowed access to the portals, and no one tried to come through until you arrived yesterday."

I found the brightest pathway from Bazarn on the tablet. "This has to be it." I traced the line, seeing it end at a distant world. I clicked the icon, seeing an unfamiliar symbol.

Mary let go of my arm and began sifting through the portal table's symbols, trying to match it. "I wish Suma was here. She's memorized all of the symbols."

Something was off as she scrolled through pages of them on the portal's screen. "Wait. What's that?" Some of the symbols were faded blue. "I don't recognize any of these."

"Dean, I think the table is grabbing the details from the Crystal Map you've attached to it. We've unlocked the hidden symbols with this," Karo said, and Ableen nodded along, confirming his claim.

"You're right." I swallowed hard. We had access to thousands of worlds at our fingertips, most of them places no human, or Gatekeeper for that matter, had ever been. But what would we uncover? "Mary, we can't bring Jules along."

She crossed her arms. "I'm not staying behind again, Dean. She tapped my arm console screen, and I glanced at the two faces of the missing Gatekeepers. One of them was a tall, lanky alien classified as a Nix. His name was listed as Weemsa. The other Keeper was from the Udoon system, from the same planet as Cee-eight. She was listed as female and had the same short arms and deep-set eyes as the pilot we'd met a couple of years ago. Green skin was pulled tight over her face, but she had a happy expression, a look I wasn't sure existed after spending time with Cee-eight. This woman's name was Loo-six.

"Mary, we can't bring her to these dangerous worlds. We have no idea what's out there," I said.

She pulled me aside, dragging me away from the rest of the prying eyes. "Seriously? You can't ask me to stay behind, and you can't ask me to separate us. We're staying together, so either you leave this mission to these other capable people and come home with me or we all go. Understood?" Her teeth were clenched, and I could see there was no winning this argument.

"We need to help. We promised Sarlun, and then Ableen, that we'd free her suffering people," I told her.

"Then Jules comes. She's safer with us than anywhere else. Don't you agree?" Mary asked.

I glanced at our girl, who was playing with Slate beside the portal. She was so wonderful, so full of curiosity and joy. I nodded hesitantly, and Mary's stiff posture loosened. "Let's make this quick, then. We go, we track them, we head home."

"Deal," I said, and we made our way to the waiting group.

"Everything good, boss?" Slate asked without a hint of his usual jest.

"You bet. Are we ready?" I asked.

Karo glanced from Ableen to Slate; his gaze then settled on Jules, and moved to me. "We're ready."

"Then let's suit up. We have no idea what we're going to arrive into," I said.

Minutes later, Rivo had left us alone, returning to her father, and the guards moved to the edge of the portal room, standing by the doorway across the space. There was a definitive line etched in the marble floors, giving a visual on the portal's boundary. Anything within that line would transport with the stone; anything beyond wouldn't.

I raised a hand to the guards and received a grunt in return. They didn't like me much, and I couldn't really blame them. We were all wearing our EVAs, and part of me wished we'd opted for the armor suits instead of the exploratory, but they were too heavy to lug around with our supplies. I missed having Dubs with us, or one of the powerful Keppe warriors to help carry some of the burden. I briefly let my thoughts drift to Rulo and hoped she was doing well.

"Ready?" I asked, and no one said otherwise. Jules was beside Mary, eyes wide as the portal crystal shone bright. I tapped the symbol the missing Gatekeepers had traveled to, and we left Bazarn.

SEVEN

*I*t was dark when we arrived. Ableen let out a groan beside me. "They are weakening," she said.

It felt different this time, almost as if we'd taken longer to travel between worlds. I had no memory of the journey, but my body clock had been thrown for a loop. I didn't know if it was due to the sheer distance, the Theos growing weaker, or a combination of the two.

"Jules, honey, are you okay?" Mary asked. Our daughter was walking away from the table, venturing into the unknown. She turned her head, flashing a smile only a kid under three is capable of.

"This is strange," Karo said, motioning to the copse of trees around us. Symbols were carved into giant tree trunks that, in the dim light, reminded me of California redwoods. They rose higher than my eyes could make out in the night sky.

"There's no hidden portal room," Slate said. "Which probably means there isn't an intelligent race around."

"Why do you say that?" Ableen asked. Her grasp of our language was impressive.

"Because if someone knew about the stones, they'd build walls to hide it, or at least have markings to worship it." Slate ran a gloved hand over the etchings in the trees.

"Then how do you explain these?" Karo asked, pointing to the carvings.

Slate shrugged. "Every portal room has them in some form or another. I guess I hadn't really thought about how they got there."

"Hmmmm. Neither have I," I told him. "But I think you're right about the intelligent life. That being said, it doesn't mean there's nothing here that wants to harm us. Be on the lookout." I flicked my EVA suit's light features on, and went over to Jules, activating her beams too. She laughed at them, chasing the light, not understanding she wouldn't be able to catch the end.

Slate lifted his arm, keying something into his suit's console. "Scanning for any Gatekeeper IDs."

"Anything?" Mary asked.

He shook his head. "Not yet, but it can take a while."

"How about the air? Breathable?" Mary asked.

Slate checked his readouts. "It appears so." He unclasped his helmet, and for a brief moment, I expected him to drop from toxic air. He grinned and set it on the ground beside him. The rest of us followed suit.

"Should we investigate?" my wife asked.

"It's dark. I say we wait to see if this world has daylight, and see what the ID scan tells us first. I don't like the idea of walking around an alien forest in the dark." I pictured huge stalking animals, their glowing eyes watching us from above, nestled in thick tree limbs.

"I agree with Dean. Ableen, are you doing all right?" Karo asked her.

She nodded. "This is all… so new." Ableen had led a simple life among the Theos before she was taken by the Collector. And now, so many years later, she'd been rescued, and her whole existence had been thrown a curve ball. Today she was exploring a new world with us on a rescue mission. I couldn't imagine what must be going on in her mind.

"It's new to us, Ableen." She knew some of our story, but I thought now was as good a time as any to tell her everything about humans and what we'd been through.

We set up camp, and Jules quickly grew tired of chasing her lights. She settled onto my lap as we unfolded small chairs, forming a circle around a lantern. I hoped the lights wouldn't draw any local predators, and I knew Slate was thinking the same thing. His pulse rifle sat across his lap, and every few minutes, he stood up to circle our small camp, keeping a lookout.

Mary and I took turns telling Ableen about the Event and our experiences with it, and she listened with interest as we discussed the Kraski, the hybrids, and the Deltra betrayal.

"But Leslie and Terrance are your friends," Ableen said in the middle of the story.

"They are. Not everyone can be thrown into one category. The sins of our people aren't necessarily our own sins," I explained.

She nodded, as if understanding the meaning behind this. The world began to lighten around us as our tale expired.

"Thank you for sharing your lives with me," Ableen said. "It inspires me to hear that you were so oppressed and have since risen above, making things better for others unselfishly." I had to assume she was implying the Alliance of Worlds and the Gatekeepers' function to act as mediators for intergalactic disputes moving forward.

"If the portals become unresponsive, it will make everything much more difficult," Mary said.

Ableen appeared to consider this before adding, "Or much simpler. Perhaps everyone sticking to their own planets will stop the everlasting strife between worlds."

"That's been going on for thousands of years, and they don't need portal stones to fight each other. Fleets of war vessels do fine," I said, knowing war would always remain a constant. It was the one thing that would stand the test of time… and space.

"Dean." Mary was looking around, spinning her head from side to side. "Where's Jules?"

I scanned the group and stood, running behind Slate and Karo. She was nowhere in sight. Then I spotted the lights from her tiny EVA, and ran for her as she neared the portal table. It glowed brightly at her approach, and I stopped a few yards from her, wondering what she was doing.

Her hand lifted, one pointer finger raised, aiming at the blue crystal beneath the clear surface of the table. She was speaking, but I was too far away to hear the words; her voice was unable to carry over to me.

"Jules?" I spoke softly, and she turned her head to look

at me, and I saw her face in an impassive look.

Her green eyes glimmered, and she lowered her hand. "Help," she said.

I stepped over to her, dropping to a knee. "What is it, honey?"

"Papa." She clenched her little fists at her sides in frustration. "Help."

"Help you with what?"

"Not me. Theos." Jules turned around, and the hair on the back of my neck rose like a startled cat.

I heard footsteps coming up behind me, but I didn't turn, as if acknowledging them would break the spell Jules was under. "How can we help the Theos?" I asked her.

She shook her head, her gaze focused at the glowing crystal cluster. "Not Papa. Jules," she said.

Not Papa. Jules. The words were confusing. She was telling me she needed to help the Theos. Not me, but her.

"Come on, honey. Let's go see Mommy," I said, and she let me pick her up. Finally, I saw Mary there, and I passed Jules to her.

Mary spoke softly to our daughter as she led her away. Jules met my gaze, then glanced at the crystal, which slowly dimmed until it was nothing more than a sleeping stone.

When I returned, the sky was light enough to see our surroundings with ease, and Slate had stowed all our supplies away again.

"Did you track the Gatekeepers' IDs?" I asked him.

"Not quite, but I did see a flash of recognition on the map, and we have a set of coordinates to work with. Not far, which we expected," Slate said. "We leave anything not pertinent to their rescue. I'd suggest packing our EVAs and only bringing two days' rations. We're only going a couple of miles." He took the lead, and we followed him after removing our suits. We added an extra thermo layer under our jumpsuits for a precaution.

The region's temperature was mild, but since we couldn't predict the planet's ecosystem, it was better to be prepared. The Gatekeepers were trained to stay near the stones should they run into trouble like this. If a rescue mission was sent out, it made the recovery much simpler.

Seeing Jules acting so oddly around the stone and hearing Ableen's fears that the Theos were leaving quickly had me wanting to start jogging forward. We weren't going to be stuck on this planet. I wouldn't let something like that happen to us again. I couldn't.

"I feel so small," Mary told me as we continued through the immense forest. Everything was oversized; I saw that now. The rocks were all boulders; the shrubbery at the base of the twenty-foot-wide tree trunks was taller than Karo.

"It's old," I said. "Thousands of years without humans or aliens to spoil the terrain. Parts of Earth would look like this if we hadn't ever existed."

"That's a good sign, boss. Means we're less likely to run across any trouble," Slate said, and I hoped he was right.

"Then why didn't Weemsa and Loo-six stay put?" Karo asked in his ever-logical way.

I didn't answer, because there was no point.

"Dean hates speculation," Mary said with a laugh. Jules was resting in her arms, and I knew our growing girl was becoming bigger all the time. She'd only be able to haul her around for so long.

"Two miles?" I asked Slate, and he nodded.

"Little less," he replied.

There was no end in sight for the forest. From here, it appeared to go on for miles in every direction, but it was hard to know how far we were seeing in between the massive trunks. The sun was higher now, but it felt like dawn inside the thick cover. I doubted it would ever be lighter than it was now.

We walked in silence for another ten minutes before we heard it. It was so quiet, I didn't notice it at first. Ableen was the first one to sense something was wrong. She stopped suddenly, and Karo stumbled into her, nearly knocking her over.

She raised a finger to her lips and lifted a hand. We all kept still, and I turned my ear up, trying to catch what she'd heard. It was like wind, a soft breeze that kept increasing in power, gaining traction as it careened through the forest above the canopy before breaking below, soaring around the trunks, bouncing off shrubbery. By the time it reached us, the noise was a screech, a terrifying, deadly sound that turned my blood to ice.

Jules started crying, and Mary's face was pale, mirroring my own.

"Only another half mile," Slate whispered, pointing deeper into the trees.

"Are you kidding me?" Mary said. "Did you hear that? We can't go toward the source."

"We don't know where the cause is," I admitted. "Let's

keep moving."

Slate and I held our pulse rifles up, taking the lead. Karo held a pulse pistol, taking the rear of the convoy, with Mary and Jules next, followed by Ableen. Mary passed a gun to the Theos woman, but she shook her head, refusing to accept it. Mary passed Ableen Jules instead, and when I was confident Jules was happy enough to cry in Ableen's arms, I kept walking. Slate led us to the spot the ID imprint had shown on his screen, and I knelt beside a damp section beside a tree. Heavy footprints were evident all around the area.

"The tent was here," Slate said, motioning to a rectangle pressed into the leafy forest bed.

"They went this way." I pointed deeper into the forest. It was darker here, colder, but we had no choice but to keep moving.

"As long as that sound doesn't…" Slate started to say as the exact same noise carried through the trees to pass over us again. "I give up. Turn around?" he asked.

"It's only a noise. A lot of animals have sounds they use to scare off predators. It could be a type of plant, for all we know," I told him, and he shook his head.

"There's no plant in the universe that's making that sound, boss," he said.

"Slate's right. Whatever it is, it made the Gatekeepers hightail it away from their camp," Karo said from the end of the line. He was watching behind us, and I was glad someone had our backs.

"The prints are traceable. We follow them," I said, moving past Slate. It didn't take him long to catch up to

The Gatekeepers

me and jog in front.

Jules had stopped crying, but her face was buried deep into Ableen's neck. The Theos woman didn't even appear to notice the added burden of carrying my daughter. She looked comfortable with the girl, and I noticed how Karo took in the sight before focusing on his task at hand.

"Over there," Karo said, pointing in the distance. I didn't see what he meant, but visibility was deteriorating as we walked. Ten minutes later, we finally saw something different. A mist had rolled in, covering the entire region. It was hard to see from one tree to the next in the thick, soupy air.

I was glad we'd added the extra layers, because it was cooling rapidly; the damp fog cut straight through to the skin, clinging to it as we moved.

"I don't like this," Mary said in my ear. We all kept close, and I considered suggesting we use a rope to tether us so we didn't lose anyone.

Two minutes later, Slate shouted from ahead, and I could only see a brief outline of his large frame as he stopped.

"Looks like we found their camp," he said, allowing us to catch up.

We'd been heading at a slight downward slope from the portal, and the fog pooled in the flattened copse of immense trees. I saw now why they'd chosen to be near this spot. Water pooled to the edge of their neat camp; runoff from rain. Their tents were set up on three-foot-tall bases made from cut tree limbs, keeping them dry.

There were remnants of a fire in a dug-out pit, and I

crossed the camp, crouching beside the ashes, trying to gauge if there was any heat remaining. It was cold. "Doesn't look like they were here today," I said. "Or at least, they hadn't made a fire yet."

Karo apparently had an idea the rest of us hadn't. He unclasped a tent, opening the flap to see an empty space. "Not sleeping either." Both tents were empty, but there were a few meager supplies inside.

"It's been almost three months. That's a long time," Slate said, leaving the rest unfinished. Unless the two Gatekeepers had found a food source, they wouldn't have survived long.

"They're resourceful," Mary said. Their bios were strong, and both had been Keepers for some time. They'd been at Bazarn for a diplomatic meeting with some powerful people before being thrust to this remote world at the outer edges of our previously understood universe.

I peered up, wondering what type of star was in the system. Were there other worlds out there now? Did this planet have multiple moons orbiting it? I doubted I'd ever know. Finding our people was the most important thing. Any research would have to come later, and I didn't expect us to ever set foot here again, especially when the portals were all inactive.

"Do we wait them out here?" Karo asked. Ableen had set Jules to the ground, and my daughter was walking around the camp. She crawled into one of the tents and sat, staring at me with a knowing look.

"Use your earpieces. Let's split up. Two groups. One searches them out, one stays at camp," I suggested.

"Karo, can you and Ableen stay with Jules?" Mary asked, surprising me.

"We can," Ableen answered.

Before anyone could change their minds, I started forward, peering behind me as the Theos guarded my daughter and waited at the camp for our targets to return.

"Boss, I see tracks." Slate pointed to the side of the water pool. There were definite boot prints leading farther into the fog.

"This reminds me of being in Portland as a girl. My aunt lived there, and we did a hike through a coastal forest outside of town. It was magical. I remember pretending to be a princess while my consorts guided me through a dangerous goblin-infested woodland," Mary said with a smile. She glanced toward camp as we moved, and I was proud of her for being able to leave Jules with someone while we were out here.

I knew her so well, and she was torn between being the adventurous leader and coddling mother to an extraordinary girl. Even though we were going to face real dangers, I was glad to have them along on the mission with me.

"I visited something like that too when I was young. My dad hated it," I said. "He was a farmer, and getting him to leave home was a rare event. My mom could have gone anywhere that summer, but she had this idea of Oregon. Coffee and bookstores. A different outdoors than we were used to. It was a fun trip. Isabelle was old enough to miss her friends, who were home doing teenager things while she was doing hikes and visiting botanical gardens with us."

Slate laughed. "What about you?"

"I didn't mind it. Growing up in the middle of nowhere on an acreage had its benefits, but I loved seeing new things; expanding my mind," I told him.

Mary bumped into me with her shoulder lightly. "Then you chose the right career." She motioned to the misty expanse around us.

"Career," I repeated. "Is that what we're calling this?"

"Could be worse," Slate said.

"How's that?" I asked.

"You could be stuck in your home office working on some acquaintance's taxes, waiting for the afternoon baseball game to come on so you could half-listen to the announcers drone on while working," Slate said, and I didn't have the nerve to tell him how nice that actually sounded.

"You're right." We kept moving, the fog clearing slightly. We could see at least twenty yards, and every now and then, Slate would point out another imprint on the forest floor.

"What about you, Slate? Any good childhood vacation memories?" Mary asked, continuing the discussion.

Slate pondered this and nodded. "We didn't get out much, but we took a road trip to Florida when I was little. My brother convinced them to take us to the theme parks while we were there, and even though I knew my parents couldn't afford it, we spent two days on rides and roller coasters. It was the time of my life."

I knew he missed his brother. The man had died overseas on Earth, long before the Event occurred, and he was the reason Slate became a soldier in the first place.

"Sounds like a good time. I'm waiting to find an alien

world full of theme parks. That would be something," Mary said, making Slate laugh.

"Why are they all so dire? For once, let's find paradise!" he said loudly.

"Remember the lush island we found Polvertan on?" I reminded him.

"I do. It was a million degrees and had mosquitoes the size of Rottweilers. I don't consider that paradise, buddy," Slate responded.

"Good point." I thought I saw something move a ways ahead, but it was hard to tell in the fog. I raised a hand, and we all froze in silence. I pointed to where I'd spotted the movement, and we waited for the mist to roll through, only to be followed up by a denser cloud.

I took a tentative step forward, and truly hoped we'd stumble upon the Gatekeepers hanging out in the middle of the forest.

I was half right.

"Dean, stop!" Mary shouted, and the noise we'd heard earlier screeched through the air. My hands instinctively covered my ears, and Slate aimed his gun at the source of the sound.

Weemsa stood closest to us, his eight-foot-tall frame thin as a rail. He reminded me of a praying mantis, pretending to sway in the wind. Loo-six was beside him, and she turned to face us, her tight-skinned face pale as a ghost. I glanced up to see why.

All around us, the fog began to shape itself, and moments later, we were surrounded by fifty or so fog creatures, their arms outstretched toward us, each of them wailing along to the initial scream we'd heard.

EIGHT

The hunter spotted Terran One sprawled out along the ground in the windshield of the lander. It was larger than Terran Five that he'd been nesting outside of. Huge buildings jutted from the flat landscape, startling him. He'd never witnessed something like this. Until recently, he'd never seen a house, let alone structures made by animals like this.

On his planet, the mountains were the only thing that sought the stars; here, the local life attempted to reach space. *Space*. It was a strange concept to the hunter. When he was in the shapes of the local animals at home, he only thought of the stars or the sun as things to guide him during the days and nights. Now he understood so much more. There were things like the crystal that sent him here. There were space ships; larger versions of the vessel he now had the comprehension to fly.

His whole existence seemed so small, so pitiful now that he saw what else was out there. His whole life, he'd watched others like him perish on their harsh world, the land dying, hard and cracked. Now he had a chance to be among a race of… humans. He glanced at his skin, nearly hairless, long nails on slender fingers. It was not a scavenging body, but it was strong and healthy.

He briefly considered landing near the city, walking inside like he belonged. Perhaps he could trick them into thinking he was one of them. Perhaps he could live among a thriving people.

He shook his head, clearing the crazy thoughts out. No. He was destined to walk alone in this life, but he'd been granted a chance at something new. He could not only survive; he could thrive here, eating his fill, and never going thirsty. For that, he was willing to accept this new reality. There was nothing left for him at home, and he felt something he'd been unable to be his entire life: safe.

The hunter guided the lander away from the looming city. He needed to hide its whereabouts. There was a forest not far from the metropolis, but far enough to be off anyone's radar. He'd be able to hide the ship there and make a nest.

The red star had set, and lights sprang on from around the various buildings in the distance as he settled to the grass. The hunter realized he was exhausted. The process of killing and digesting, let alone transforming into his prey, always took a lot out of him. The brain of the pilot he'd consumed told him there was a transponder inside the ship. He wasn't exactly sure what that was, but it would allow the humans to search and locate the vessel if they realized what happened.

The hunter crawled to the rear seats and flipped a thin finger through a loop in the floor. He pulled the hatch open and saw blinking lights on a small black device. He unplugged it, and the glow faded. He dropped it to the floor and set about the forest, finding large branches and brush to cover the lander with. He had to hide it; only then would he allow his exhausted body rest. After that, he'd need more food, more sustenance to feed the ever-growing mind that was developing past his wildest imagination.

The hunter paused from his work and peered toward the lights of the city. There he would find ample prey.

"What the hell are we looking at here?" Slate shouted, moving toward the two Gatekeepers. I grabbed Mary's arm and fought the urge to run through the fog creatures to safety. I had no idea how ethereal they really were. We stepped backwards as one until the five of us were in a circle, facing the mist beings around us.

"We call them Misters," Loo-six said, and I nearly laughed at the reference.

"I guess you couldn't call them Misses," I joked, knowing it was neither the time nor place. Mary frowned at me.

"You're Dean, right?" Weemsa asked, her words translating into my earpiece. It was becoming more and more rare to find aliens who hadn't had the translator modification added, and I was among them.

"I am. Sorry we took so long to arrive. As you know, the portals are all haywire," I informed them.

"No trouble at all. We've only spent the last three

months scavenging for food, which, let me tell you, leaves something to be desired. Mostly rodents. And mean ones," Loo-six explained.

"What are we looking at here?" Slate asked again. "Misters?"

Weemsa took this one. His thin arm stretched out over my head, pointing at the Misters. They were in a line, hovering above the ground. They were almost humanoid in form, but like a classic ghost. White-gray and shapeless, with holes for eyes.

"We first saw them three days after arriving. We knew right away that the portal was messed up. Sarlun had been warning us they might shoot us somewhere else, and told us to stay put should it happen. Loo-six wanted to try to leave, but this place seemed as good as any. No visible hostiles, water, and to be honest, I thought it might be like camping out in the trees for a while." Weemsa spoke, and I kept my eyes fixed on the fog beings hovering twenty yards away.

"Then they arrived?" Mary asked.

Weemsa nodded. "First the fog came, much like today. Then we heard the screech. I'm assuming you did as well?"

We told them we had, and Loo-six took over. "If that wasn't bad enough, we saw one of them that night. It was late, the light all but disappeared. We were using a lantern, our fire already gone out. It was foggy, and Weemsa went to… dispose of water, and saw one of them. I ran to the scream." I glanced at Weemsa, who looked abashed at us knowing he'd screamed while being visited with his pants down.

"That's when I really wanted to try our luck at leaving," Loo-six said.

"But you didn't," I said.

"No. Despite everything, they didn't attack us. But I could feel them watching in the mist, and there were times I'd catch one forming and floating toward me, but when I turned to face one of them, they'd always dissipate into the fog," she told us.

"Then what is this?" Mary asked, motioning to the horde of Misters surrounding our group.

"We don't know. Perhaps your arrival has piqued their interest." Weemsa's real voice was low, almost a garbled sound.

"Well, I'd like to unpique it. Can we try to leave?" I asked, taking a step forward. The line of Misters moved another foot toward us.

"I'm not sure that's a good idea," Mary said.

The Misters began to screech again, a terrible and cutting sound. It wasn't until I heard a tiny voice from some distance that I realized it was Jules' cry.

"We have to go. There are more of us, and my daughter sounds like she's in danger," I told them, and Loo-six seemed to shudder at the thought. "Got it?" I grabbed her shoulders, squaring her to me. She blinked and nodded her understanding. "Slate, we shoot our way out if we have to."

"I'm not sure that's going to work against these things, boss," Slate said, but he was already moving, taking the lead. He let out a war cry and ran through the line of Misters. I saw his outline beyond them as the ones he pushed apart reformed and turned to face him.

"Come on!" I shouted, staying behind Mary as she ran and jumped through their lines. I felt cold when I passed through; a muted horror filled my veins as part of their being stuck to my skin. They were miserable, but I didn't know if they truly meant us harm. Mary appeared to have the same reaction, because she was pale too, a profound sadness expressed on her beautiful face.

Jules shouted again, and my wife moved faster than I'd ever seen before. She passed Slate, and I checked to make sure the two Gatekeepers were nearby. We all moved fast, sprinting through the foggy forest toward their camp. The Misters had regrouped, and they followed us, floating thirty yards behind. The fog around us transformed, and dozens more of them sprouted up with each passing minute.

By the time I saw camp as a bleary outline, there were at least two hundred Misters chasing after us.

"Jules!" Mary shouted, and I saw our daughter finally, her hands outstretched toward her mother from Karo's arms. Her cheeks were red and damp. Ableen held a gun, pointing it at the Misters that had the camp surrounded.

"It's a long trip to the portal," I said between breaths.

"What do we do?" Karo asked.

I tried to think. "You haven't been harmed by them yet?"

"Not yet. I've been touched by a few. It's almost as if they want to pass their pain on to someone," Loo-six said. "But look." She pressed the growing dense cloud of Misters, unable to get through the fog.

"Will they leave?" Mary asked.

"We don't know. They've never done this," Loo-six

answered.

It gave me an idea, one I wasn't happy with. "When they break apart, take everyone and head to the portal. I'll be there soon," I said.

Mary glanced dubiously at me. "Trust me," I whispered in her ear, kissing her on the lips. She was holding Jules, and my daughter clawed for my face. "I love you," I told my girl, and they were off.

I stood firmly, facing the opposite direction as my departing friends. A few Misters hovered past me, chasing after the group, but I had other ideas.

I raised my arms, silently calling them to me. I needed to draw them away from my friends; otherwise, we might not be able to escape the thick wall of them. They seemed to understand what it was I offered, and the fog surrounded me as hundreds, then thousands of the Misters connected, becoming one cloud around my body. I tried to push an arm through, but it was thick, like pressing into pudding.

I ran, away from my friends, and they followed, all of them in a horde. Before they lowered, circling me, I locked gazes with Mary, who began running with the others for the portal.

I fought to breathe, and seconds later, it didn't matter. The fog rushed into me.

I was the mist.

I hovered now, floating through the immense forest. I brushed against ancient bark, so old I didn't comprehend an age. I'd been here when the planet began. I'd witnessed the saplings protrude from the fresh earth; I'd seen them rise over the years, the centuries. I watched as life started and died all around me.

I pictured various animals in the forest, fish-like creatures in the seas beyond the trees, and I saw them as they evolved, changing to adapt to ever-adjusting weather patterns, and many disappeared from the face of the world.

Winged animals took flight, soaring through me, the mist, and I felt their freedom as they hunted from the forest floor. I absorbed the essence of the plants on the ground, and the fungi attaching to the tree trunks. I was one with the world.

I was the mist.

Thousands of years passed. Millions. I grew lonely. Was there more? Could I fade into oblivion, the way countless creatures on the ground had over the millennia? I didn't know, but I ached. Each passing day became a restless challenge. I sought ways to disintegrate. I plunged into the water, hoping to drown, but all it accomplished was killing a species of bottom-dwelling fish who needed to see to avoid predators. Even after a thousand years, I rose from the waters, more miserable than ever.

With no choice, I returned to the forests. Things had changed. The stars above never seemed to grow as bright as before. Seasons grew longer, until there was but one season for each rotation around the star far above. Was there more out there for me? Could I leave this world behind? I dared not try.

I was the mist.

Dean Parker rose inside me; his consciousness pushed away the fog of the Misters and took control of me once again. I was no longer the mist alone, but a combination of Dean and the entity.

I feel your pain. I understand. I could sense the danger from the entity. They were at their wits' end, and my friends were in real danger. They didn't intend to let another creature leave them behind. Not this time. I had to convince them otherwise.

I didn't receive an answer in return, but I could feel the oppressive nature of the Misters threaten to take over again. I chided myself for giving them a vessel. This may have been a mistake.

I fed off their biggest regret: never attempting to leave the atmosphere. They were too afraid. I truly had no idea if the mist would survive in space, but I had to try.

You are correct. There is far more than your tiny world to see. Their emotions changed. I felt it now: hope, curiosity, desire for something else. *Seek the stars. They await your arrival.*

The mood changed, and I felt them begin to unwind before half of them fought their own kind. Some of them wanted to devour me, eat me from the inside out, for I spoke lies and couldn't be trusted. I fought back, pushing images of worlds I'd seen from above, memories of traveling through space through the mist.

This went on for minutes, maybe hours, and eventually, they were convinced I spoke the truth. They started to life from the ground, and I expected to stay behind, but they carried me with them. I tried to shout, begging them to stop, but my calls went unheeded. I could see nothing beneath me and felt no ground under my feet.

Finally, one Mister broke apart from the group,

grasping on to me and tugging me toward the ground. I was clear of the dense fog now, and I fell ten feet to the ground in a heap, staring up as the fog pooled apart and lifted up from the trees. It rose higher and higher until it blotted out any sunlight. Then it was gone, past the canopy two thousand feet above.

I was no longer the mist. I was Dean Parker.

I didn't wait to see if it returned. Instead, I ran, leaving the tents behind. My legs were wobbly after the experience, and I wondered how much of that story I would tell Mary. She was already going to be angry with me for risking myself like that, but it had worked. At the end of the day, I knew that wasn't going to be a selling feature for my argument.

I didn't catch up to them, and I wondered how long I'd been there with the Misters.

Slate was on lookout, and I spotted him propped against a tree, holding his gun up. There was no longer any mist in the vicinity, and the visibility was far improved.

"Dean!" he shouted, running toward me. He clasped my shoulders and dragged me into a quick hug.

"Everyone okay?" I asked him, peering around him to see the group waiting near the portal table.

"They're fine. The Misters followed but disappeared shortly after. Should I even ask what you did?" he asked.

I didn't answer as we walked together. Jules was already coming toward me, and I waved at Mary, who had a look of relief on her face. I saw Karo already preparing the portal, adding the Modifier to it. It was time to leave.

NINE

We arrived at Haven, and when the light dimmed all the way, our entire group swayed on their feet. Weemsa fell to the ground of Haven's portal room.

"What the heck?" Slate asked. "I've never experienced a portal trip like that."

My head was spinning, and I rested a hand on the table. Jules plopped down to sit on her butt, but she didn't comment or cry out.

Mary spoke, saying what I was feeling. "The portals. They're struggling to take us where we need to go."

Ableen's gray face was whiter than normal, and she nodded along. "Our people won't last long," she said, and I thought about the remaining stranded Gatekeepers. There were three more teams out there, including Polvertan of the Motrill and Dreb from the Bhlat. They were next on my agenda.

"Dean, let's give it a night to rest," Mary told me. I could tell from the look in her eyes that it wasn't a request.

I nodded in assent. "Yes. Maybe the portal needs it too." Slate had already helped Weemsa to his feet.

"Sorry you guys have to stay on Haven for the time being," I advised the two Gatekeepers.

"We're just happy to be rescued. Thank you for finding us." Loo-six smiled wide, the taut skin on her face pulling even tighter.

"We wouldn't leave you stranded, and we aren't going to leave the others out there. Right, team?" I asked.

Karo answered. "Right." He smiled at Ableen, but she was far more affected by the Theos within the stone than the rest of us.

Jules was on her feet again, reaching toward the crystal. "Papa. Help," she said again.

"What's with her?" I asked Mary, who lifted our daughter up. Jules was stretching out toward the crystal beneath the clear table.

"I don't know. She must be able to sense what Ableen does. She wants to help the Theos," Mary said.

"Let's move out of here and call it a day," I said, following the rest of the group out of the room. With a glance at the dark table and crystal, I shut the door behind me, glad to be done with the first leg of the mission. I only wished it was over now.

---

*I*t was bizarre being filled with a mist entity one hour, and a few later, being inside your own penthouse on Haven, showering in a luxurious bathroom. I told Mary the same, and she slid her arms around my waist, pulling me close.

The Gatekeepers

"You can't keep running head-first into danger forever, Dean. It will catch up to you," she advised. She was right, but I didn't want to admit it out loud.

"I have a clean record so far," I said, wiping a blob of soap off her nose with a finger. Jules was sound asleep in the next room. I'd closed the window coverings all the way, since it was only early evening here. Traveling around through portals to strange worlds broke our regular routine. I had no idea how long it had been since we'd had a few hours of sleep at Regnig's library.

"I understand why you do it, but you worry me. You're too reckless," Mary told me.

"Is that why you demanded to come?" I asked, hoping for the truth.

"That's part of the reason," she admitted. "I thought maybe you'd be less willing to stick your neck out if we were there, but it didn't seem to work."

I laughed. "Silly Mary. You being there only makes me want to protect the group more. I'd do anything to make sure you two are safe," I said, blinking water from my eyes.

"Don't forget we need you. It won't do us any good if you're killed by an alien mist entity, okay?" I knew she was worried, joking away her true fears, and I didn't press her on it. We all dealt with things differently.

My communicator buzzed from its resting spot on the sink. I shrugged to Mary before stepping out of the shower, dripping all over the floor as I grabbed the device.

"Leonard?" I said into it, putting it on speaker.

"Dean, nice to hear your voice. Everything good?" he asked.

"We managed to rescue two Gatekeepers and are at home on Haven for the night," I told him.

"That's the best news I've heard all day."

I heard his voice catch. "What is it?"

"I don't really have any evidence, but something strange is going on," he told me. Mary was watching from the shower, craning her neck to hear Leonard's voice.

"You know that Shimmali man?"

"Yes," he answered.

"He's one of the Gatekeepers. He was on our list from the missing teams," I told him.

A pause. "Really? That makes this even more peculiar."

"Did you catch him? Was it anything to do with him?" I asked.

Leonard sighed. "We have no clue. One of Terran Five's landers went missing. The pilot and other guard are gone too. They were on patrol of the city."

Each Terran site had a ship in the air and two vehicles on the ground surrounding the cities at all times. If one went missing, then something was afoot. "Where did they track it to?"

"That's the thing. We don't record flight paths on them, because they only travel in circles. It wasn't worth the storage, and no one was looking at that data. When they realized the lander was missing, they tried to locate it, but they came up empty-handed," Leonard said.

"And you think this is related to our friend Soloma?" I asked, using the man's name.

"It has to be," he reasoned.

"We have a new device, one that allows us to track the

destination to and from a particular portal stone. We should be able to find out where he came from. It only works for a limited time period," I told Leonard. Mary was still in the shower, listening.

"Maybe it's been too long?" Leonard asked over the communicator.

"I don't think so. We tracked the first two Gatekeepers from Bazarn. I think it'll work. Let's test the theory after we've tracked the next four groups. Then we'll be done," I told him, leaving out the fact that the portals might be useless by then.

"Sounds good. I wanted to fill you in. I'll reach out tomorrow if I can… and Dean…"

"Yes?"

"Good luck with bringing everyone home. It's what you do best," he told me, and I smiled.

"Thanks, Leonard. We'll talk soon. Keep an eye out for the lander, and if you find anything else out, send word." We ended the communication, and Mary stuck her head back under the water.

"Now where were we?" I asked, tiptoeing to the shower. My hair was covered in suds, and Mary gave me a disapproving stare.

"Aren't you worried about what's going on at home? The missing people, the stolen lander?" she asked.

"If I had to worry about every detail on every planet humans are now calling home, I'd never sleep and my head wouldn't stop aching. Let me deal with one thing at a time," I said, forming an idea. "Maybe you should take Jules and head home. You know, give the New Spero police a hand with the investigation."

Mary pulled me close and kissed me. "Nice try, but I don't think so."

I briefly wondered if Magnus and Nat had landed on New Spero, before being distracted by more pressing matters.

---

*T*he sunlight shone through our floor-to-ceiling windows, illuminating Jules as she sat at the table, coloring in a paper book. Even though we had so much technology, I was glad to be able to share something basic with her. She stuck her tongue out while filling in the outline of a frog with a purple crayon. It wasn't so far-fetched any longer. I thought there might be a purple toad race in the Alliance of Worlds.

"Don't forget to eat your toast, honey," I told her, and she grabbed the slice with nut butter smeared across it and carefully ate it, making sure not to spill any crumbs on her picture. She was a troublemaker, but she sure had some particular quirks. She reminded me of myself.

"Papa… where Mommy?" she asked, looking around the room.

"Mommy's sleeping." Mary was dozing so soundly, I hadn't the nerve to wake her an hour earlier when I'd heard Jules sneaking out of her big-girl bed.

Jules appeared to contemplate this, and she set her half-eaten bread onto her plate and slid off the chair before heading down the hallway. I let her go, knowing Mary would want to be up anyway.

A screen on the wall of the kitchen chimed softly, and the edges lit up with a faint orange glow. Someone was trying to reach me. It was our system of telephones on Haven. I didn't mind the feature, but no one was ever able to hide their bedhead in the mornings.

I activated it and saw Leslie's image flash on the screen. I tapped ACCEPT, and was surprised to see Magnus' mug on the other end.

"Dean! Good to see you, brother," he said.

"Wait, you're here? On Haven?" I asked, excited they'd made it.

"You bet. Flew in yesterday, and Leslie and Terrance told us you were here. How are things?" he asked.

I had so much to tell him, even though it had only been a short while ago that we were on Volim waiting to take a Padlog vessel to Haven. They'd left a few days after me, Magnus wanting to be sure all his Keppe warriors were evacuated before he would leave. "Do you guys have time for breakfast?" I asked, knowing Mary would love to see them and the kids. We needed to take action, and find Polvertan and Dreb next, but a couple of hours weren't going to make much of a difference, not after three months.

"We'd love that. Leslie's on this health kick. Nothing but green stuff over here. Want to meet at the Diner?" he asked.

He didn't have to specify which Diner. There was only one on Haven that served good old-fashioned American cuisine, and it was quite the hot spot among the various alien races calling Haven home these days. Apparently, omelettes and grilled cheese sandwiches were now galaxy-class cuisines.

"See you there in an hour. I'll tell the others," I said.

Magnus grinned. "I'll call Randy and set up the private room."

I gave him a thumbs-up, and the call ended.

"Who was that?" Mary asked from the hallway.

"Better get ready. We're heading to the Diner to meet up with Magnus, Nat, and the others," I said, and Jules ran from the bedroom, screaming happily.

"I guess she's into it," Mary said, smiling at me from the doorway.

The Diner was busy, and I had no idea what day of the week it was. There was a calendar here, one not so different than Earth's, but I rarely paid any attention to it. I was finding that living on three different planets created a massive problem for schedules, especially when each had days of varying length. I used my arm console to keep track of any appointments and made sure they threw me reminders with ample time to reschedule if needed.

The reunion had been sweet, and after chatting outside the Diner for twenty minutes, our group took up the private suite above the dining room. The windows were pulled wide open, giving it an open-air feeling, and I was

The Gatekeepers

glad in Haven's morning heat.

Mary sat beside Natalia, and the kids were all piled in beside them. Jules and Patty were showing each other their dolls, while Dean sat there reading a paperback book. It was science fiction by the looks of it, and I smirked at his choice.

"The kids look great. I'm glad we could meet up," I told Magnus. Ableen was with our wives, and I noticed her glancing over to Karo. I wasn't sure if my ancient friend knew it or not, but she was seeking his attention constantly.

Leslie and Terrance were again visibly absent, and I knew we needed to find other people to assist them with the colony. They were putting too much strain on themselves.

"Did you encounter any trouble making it home?" Karo asked Magnus.

"Nothing too serious. Almost ran out of coffee. That would have been dangerous. Speaking of coffee, Slate, can you pass the carafe?" Magnus barked, and I pushed the cream over to the Scandinavian. After he poured a steaming cup, I filled mine up. "Tell me about the next job."

Slate poked at his food and set his fork beside his plate, taking this one. "Polvertan and Dreb left Haven right after we left. They didn't know they'd be sent to some random world."

I quickly filled Magnus in about the thousands of portal destinations, and the women stopped talking to listen. Natalia tapped her finger on the table, giving her husband a glare.

"Babe, I have to go. It's Polvertan. You know how

close we are with the Keppe now, and the Motrill are basically the same thing. We owe it to them all to rescue their prince."

"Bear in mind, Dean and I already rescued him once. Does that mean we're awarded extra kudos for doing it again?" Slate asked with a smile.

"We just got home," Nat said. "We were literally in another dimension for two months. Can we take a breather?"

Mary cleared her throat. "Tell me about it."

I could feel our wives collectively agreeing and felt pressured to react. "This is great. Magnus can come with me, and you guys can stay with the kids." As soon as I said it, I almost ducked, knowing they were both shooting daggers at me with their eyes.

"It is the best…" Karo started and I cut him off, moving my fingers over my throat in the universal "stop talking" motion. He heeded the advice.

"What if they go to find this Polvertan, and then we go retrieve the others?" Ableen said over the silence.

"What do you mean…" I started, but Mary spoke over me, a huge grin on her face.

"Finally, someone's talking some sense. What do you say? You four go on the next mission, and when you're done, you stay with the kids while we go for the next couple groups," Mary said.

Natalia nodded, taking a bite of her toast. "This I can get behind. I don't know when I last had some time away."

"Same with me. Dean was gone for a long time, and I could use the break." Mary's eyes danced as she met my stare. She was loving this.

I stifled a cough. "You're talking like this is a vacation. If you don't recall, we were attacked by Misters less than a day ago!" I set my cup down too hard, and coffee spilled onto the tablecloth.

"I know, but we were all fine. We did the job, and here we are having breakfast with our friends," Mary replied.

Even Ableen was laughing with the ladies, and I knew there was no point in arguing.

Magnus leaned in. "Dean, we know they're more than capable of taking care of themselves. It's Nat and Mary."

I nodded, not sold on the idea of them traversing the dangerous portals in search of the missing Gatekeepers.

I pushed out a deep breath. "It's settled. We track this next pair, then it's your turn." I relented and the group relaxed. Discussions flowed freely to the recent events, and what Nat and Magnus were going to do now that their time captaining the Keppe vessel *Fortune* was over.

"We're not sure. We might do it again," Natalia told us.

My head snapped to stare at Magnus, who was conveniently silent for this part of the discussion. "You were gone for three years, and ended up in another dimension. What would drive you to do this again?" I asked him. The rest of the table went silent, waiting for his answer. Jules chatted softly with Patty beside her, who was showing her how to draw an animal, acting like an older cousin only could.

"Because it was exhilarating. The kids had a wonderful time. They made friends and enjoyed their lessons. Dean, you don't understand. We were part of the community there, and you know as well as I do that the Keppe are a solid people. Plus, I love the food." Magnus set his fork on his nearly empty plate.

I had a new idea, one Terrance and I had discussed on a few occasions, mostly late at night with a few glasses of Scotch in our bellies. "What if we had our own exploratory ships?" I asked, quieter than intended.

Slate leaned in, and Nat whispered something to Mary.

Magnus had the courtesy to smile at me. "I don't think that's the same thing."

"Hear me out. We create a ship with members of the Alliance of Worlds as the crew, you as the captain. We don't work for the Keppe, but instead, we work in tandem. Surveying the far reaches of space. We know now from the Crystal Map that there's way more out there than we even comprehended." I was selling myself on the idea, becoming excited by the prospect. Before, it had only been idle talk between friends around the dinner table. Now it was gaining momentum, becoming real.

The moment Magnus glanced over at Natalia, then at his kids, I felt the entire newly-formed plan coming to life before my eyes. Mary grinned at me and wrapped her arm around Jules' small shoulders, pulling her in to kiss the top of her head.

"That does sound cool." Slate was the first one to speak, and everyone laughed.

"Dean Parker, you've done it again. Why didn't I think of that?" Magnus asked.

"So you'll think about it?" I asked him.

He shook his head. "Nope, because we've already decided. We'll do it."

I glanced over at Natalia and could tell they'd shared

some unspoken agreement with their eyes.

"That's great. We can send word to Lord Crul at once. We'll build a ship based on their specifications, but adjust it to accommodate the varying races we'll be bringing aboard." My heart rate increased as the ideas flooded my mind. I could picture a crew with Padlog, Hybrids, Bhlat, Molariuns, humans, Keppe, and Motrill. The Inlor might be interested as well, since they were new to interstellar space travel. Perhaps the Theos would be happy on board with Magnus and Nat. If the shared look between Karo and Ableen was telling me anything, they were already considering it.

I had no idea if Mary and I would be part of something like that. I felt like there was too much for us to do on our three worlds. But the idea of traveling around space for a couple of years with our closest friends on hand thrilled me.

"You better save a title for me. First Officer? Commander Campbell has a nice ring to it," Slate said, and stopped when he realized it might mean leaving my side. "I mean… if everything works out."

"I'm sure it will. Boy, am I glad we had this breakfast," I told them. "Are we ready to plan this next mission yet?"

Magnus stood. "Let's do this."

"You don't have to come. Are you sure it's okay to run away again?" I asked him out of earshot of the others.

"Your last one took less than a day. This is a piece of cake," he said.

I liked his optimism. "Let's gather what we need and move." My mind was hopeful the next Gatekeeper extraction would be as fast as the previous one, but my gut had other ideas.

TEN

*W*e'd said our goodbyes, and Natalia, Mary, and Ableen remained at our penthouse with the kids. I was having a hard time leaving the family behind. As much as I'd wanted to fight them being along on the last mission, their presence had been comforting.

I told myself that the sooner we returned, the sooner we could switch gears.

The lander touched the ground outside the city of Haven, though there were more structures out in this remote area now. It was so different from when Slate, Mary, Mae, and I had first arrived with Clare and Nick. Thinking back to that time made me feel my age. So much had happened.

"Boss, do you mind taking this?" Slate shoved a heavy pack at me, and I slung it over my shoulder. We wore our white Gatekeeper EVAs again, and headed from outside toward the portal room. Soon we were inside, and I pulled the Crystal Map from my pack, laying it beside the Modifier.

"This is it?" Magnus asked, pointing at the compact flexible device.

"It is." I attached it to the portal table, and the other end to my tablet. The now-familiar portal map appeared, and I isolated the last five trips from the stones. Some of them were ours, and I glazed over them until I found one that fit the timeline of Polvertan and Dreb's trip. They'd been trying to travel to Shimmal after their swearing in, each of them intended to be paired with an experienced Gatekeeper. Instead, the portal had sent them far away.

"Karo, do you feel anything out of the ordinary?" I asked the tall Theos, who'd stayed quiet for most of the morning.

He reached below the table and set a hand on the stone. It instantly reacted to the contact and brightened. "Nothing has changed. They are there. I fear not for long, though."

"That's what we thought. All the more reason to make this fast," I said, receiving firm nods from the three men at my side.

I zoomed in on the destination portal world, and instantly knew I didn't recognize it. This was another planet that didn't have a symbol loaded into our database. I was hoping it was something we could research quickly before going.

"Here goes nothing," Slate said as he activated the two tools we needed to safely make the trip. We'd brought more supplies than we thought we'd need. It was better to be prepared than surprised.

Magnus shot me a grim look and the portal crystal glowed hot. It flickered, and for a moment, I didn't expect it to function.

The Gatekeepers

Everything dissolved into nothingness. I floated there in my EVA, weightless in a pool of bright light. This had happened once before, when we'd traveled through a stone with Leonard, who'd been possessed by an Iskios. Only then, it was a brief pause in the journey with no light or dark, and this change made me fear we were trapped in limbo.

I took in my surroundings, unsure if what I was seeing was real or not. My hand stretched in front of my face, and I waved it across my eyes. It seemed real enough.

"Magnus! Slate!" I shouted into my earpiece, but there was no reply. "Can you hear me?"

Nothing.

I floated and tried to remain calm, which wasn't as easy as one might think. I searched for signs of anything past the thick cloud of light, but there was nothing there.

It felt like hours by the time a dot appeared in the brilliance. By then, I'd tried unsuccessfully to swim away, to use the tiny thrusters in the space suit I wore to push me from my position, and had even attempted a nap.

My pulse quickened with each passing breath as the dot grew larger. It was a Gatekeeper! "Magnus, Slate!" I shouted, seeing the familiar uniform. I couldn't make out the face quite yet.

No response.

The figure slowed about a hundred yards away, and I lifted an arm to wave, and the newcomer mirrored my movement. An odd sensation rolled through my spine, and I tested the theory, raising my other arm. The figure copied the gesture on a half-second delay.

"What is this?" I asked no one, if only to hear another voice.

"What is this?" my voice echoed into my earpiece.

"Wait. Was that you?" I asked the figure, and it started moving toward me again.

This time, it didn't parrot my words. It stopped closer now, and I understood. It was me inside the EVA.

"Dean?" I asked it, knowing full well this was some other entity copying my image to communicate with me. Karo had done something similar when I'd first arrived at the Theos home world.

"It's me," my voice said in return.

I saw his eyes now, and they were mine, but older, sadder eyes. "Why are we here?"

He shook his head slowly. "We've always been here."

If I was a cat, I'd have hissed at my doppelganger. "What does that mean?"

"Do you believe in something bigger than you? Vaster than the Iskios and the Theos?" Not-Dean asked, his voice a rough version of my own.

I shrugged. "Sure. I mean, this all came from somewhere, right? I've seen too much."

"Good. Good." Not-Dean moved a little closer, floating in the light. I could now see he was about twenty years older than me: crow's feet around his eyes, gray in his hair and beard.

"What is this?" I asked again.

"This is the end."

"That's a little ominous. Care to elaborate?" I asked him.

The Gatekeepers

"The portals are dying, Dean. But there is a way to keep everything going."

"How?" I asked.

"You'll see. But that's not why we're here," Not-Dean said. He met my gaze, and I saw a tear fall onto his cheek, a single drop shiny against his matte skin.

"Then why?" I asked, almost breathless. I was afraid of what this version of me was about to say. Was this really me, from the future?

"In eighteen years, you will have to make a choice," he said.

"Go on," I prompted him.

"Don't screw it up. You can't save them all," he said, his voice cracking.

Ice filled my veins. "What are you talking about? Why do you have to be so indirect? Just say it! Does this have something to do with Lom of Pleva returning?" That would fit the timeline.

His expression told me I was on the right path. "Don't make the same mistake I did. Don't let them die." His voice was pleading, desperate, and he reached out a hand, and I stretched mine out. Our gloved hands failed to reach one another, and he floated away, at first slowly, then faster, as if being reeled in by an immense fishing rod. "Don't let them die, Dean!"

And then he was gone, and there was only darkness once again.

"*D*ean. Dean, are you okay?" a voice asked, and I was being shaken by the shoulders.

I blinked my eyes open and saw Slate above me, his face etched with worry behind his mask. "There you are," he said, and relaxed, sinking to a seated position beside me. I glanced up, and there was Magnus, leaning over me from above.

"Gave us quite the scare there." Magnus made his way to my other side, and the two of them each offered a hand, helping me to my feet.

"Did you guys see anything?" I asked.

Slate looked around the room and shook his head. "See anything like what?"

"White light? An older Dean Parker?"

Magnus laughed. "Wow, you must have hit your head in between worlds. We arrived here instantly, and you've been on the ground for five minutes staring into space like a zombie."

So it hadn't happened. Or maybe it had, in the blink of an eye within the portal. I had no way of knowing.

"What exactly did you see? An older you?" Slate asked.

I steadied myself on the portal and peered around the room we entered into. Our packs were on the floor, and I felt to make sure the pulse rifle was intact. The space was dark rock, and the only light inside the portal room was that from Magnus' and Slate's EVAs. I activated my lights too, and saw the dim glow of the symbols on the black stone walls fade to nothing.

"The stones aren't going to last long," Karo said from

the far edge of the room. I'd forgotten he was even with us, he'd stayed so silent. He flipped his own lights on, revealing an exit. There was no door per se, only a carved-out opening in the black rock.

I ran a finger along the wall, finding it slightly damp. "Do we know if this is the right world?" I asked.

"Magnus checked when we arrived. The Crystal Map tells us we're at the same planet Polvertan and Dreb were sent to," Slate advised.

I pointed to Karo. "Have you ventured beyond the doorway yet?"

"No. We were waiting for you to wake up," Magnus told me.

"I'm up. Let's go." I shook the image of the older Dean from my mind, trying to forget the words escaping his lips. It was impossible. As I stepped forward, the phrase repeated in my mind.

Don't let them die, Dean!

Who did he mean? Was he talking about my wife and daughter? Was it any of the people around me now? I glanced at Slate, and he grinned at me. Magnus took the lead, and Karo behind him as we moved through the exit and outside.

Wind buffeted our suits, and Magnus raised a hand, silently telling us to hold our positions. He flipped his lights off, and we each did the same. I took in the landscape.

The ground was black rock for as far as the eye could see, and there was no sign of vegetation. A red star set in the distance, or perhaps it was rising. I didn't have anything to base that on. It was large and angry-looking, but my suit's readouts told me it was around twenty-five degrees Fahrenheit. A winter's day in Ohio.

"There." Slate pointed to a source of light a few miles away. Otherwise, the land was devoid of... anything.

"We search this area first. Sarlun told me they didn't have their Gatekeeper IDs yet because they were picking them up on Shimmal." I knew this was going to make the task all the more difficult. These were two missing persons we had to rescue. Our alliances were new and already only hanging on by goodwill, mostly between myself and the Empress in the Bhlat case. If we didn't find Dreb, her hand-picked emissary, I didn't know what she'd do.

The Empress was on Earth most of the time now, her home base at the Pyramids. She controlled the portal there, and I knew she could destroy everything we'd rebuilt on Earth in a handful of minutes. Even though I trusted her somewhat, it was imperative we did our part and located her subject.

"Let's pair up." Magnus was taking charge, and I was only too happy to let him lead. "Slate, you're with Karo. Dean, stick with me."

Slate didn't look happy about it. I had a feeling he and Mary had an agreement that he'd protect me at all costs. It was the same deal I had with Slate to protect my family. At the end of the day, I would protect him with my own life too, and he knew it.

Magnus pulled a drone from his pack, and we watched as it hovered above, mapping the terrain leading toward the lights in the distance. Seconds later, we had a 3D map on our consoles.

"We'll head this way, you go that way, and we'll reconvene…" Magnus pushed a pin into a local map on his arm console. "Here. One hour. If there's no sign of them or their camp, we'll have to assume they headed for the light. Three months is a long time, and this land looks cold and unforgiving."

Everyone agreed, and Magnus and I headed to the right. The ground was nothing but black rocks: some loose, but most were connected, like a sheer wall of slate. "Watch your step," I told him after almost tripping on a rock.

"What happened back there? Really?" he asked, and I saw him adjust his mic so only I could hear. I did the same, leaving the receiver end open.

"I'm not sure. I could have been hallucinating or something. It was me. Twenty years older. I was warning myself to not let them die," I admitted.

"Who?"

"I don't know. Not-Dean wasn't very forthcoming with his words. It has to do with Lom, I'm sure of it."

Magnus used his flashlight, scanning the ground to the left of us. I did the same on the right side. "I wish there was a way to know what will happen in twenty years. Or eighteen, now."

I cleared my throat, picturing Lom flailing as I shoved him through the time travel vortex. I had the device hidden away, and no one knew where it was. "We can't worry about it now, can we?"

"I suppose not. We have bigger fish to fry at the moment. Like tracking these rookies," Magnus said.

He was wearing a Gatekeeper uniform, but he wasn't

actually one of us. Sarlun wouldn't mind, I knew that much. He'd been invited but always had other pressing matters: first running New Spero's military arm, then taking over as captain of a Keppe exploratory vessel.

"I'm trying to imagine this being my first mission for the Gatekeepers," I said, letting myself laugh at the thought.

"What did happen on your first trip?" he asked.

I laughed more now. "You really don't want to know. It was… memorable."

"Slate won't talk about it," Magnus said, which told me he'd asked around.

"And rightfully so. Neither will Mary," I told him.

"Fine. But I'll pull the story out of you one day. Over a bottle of Scotch," Magnus said.

It was nice chatting with him, even if it was a walk on an alien world we knew nothing about. "Let's just say it involves a nude swim… that's all I'm saying."

Magnus laughed. "Now I'm not sure I want to hear it." I could tell he wanted to change the subject.

"What is it?" I asked.

"Are we sure Nat, Mary, and Ableen heading out after us is a great idea?" Magnus checked his map and redirected us a few degrees.

"What choice do we have? Mag, buddy, we married some strong, resourceful women. Do you think they'd let us tell them they can't go?"

"No. They wouldn't. I've spent so much time with Nat and the kids on *Fortune* that I hate the idea of splitting apart at all these days," he told me.

The Gatekeepers

I understood only too well. "I hear you. I think Mary and I have been apart more than together since we were married."

The red star was indeed setting, and the entire rock world cloaked in darkness as the last speck moved beyond the horizon. Stars in unfamiliar constellations lit the way through the cloudless sky.

Magnus turned and stopped. "Were you serious?"

"About what?

"The ship. The first Alliance of Worlds vessel."

"Why not? It would send a message that we're serious about things, about the new relationships. The more we integrate among the other races out there, the less threatening humans are," I said.

"And you think they'd be okay with a human captain?" he asked with a smile.

"I don't see why not. If it works, we can make another, and another. Maybe a whole fleet eventually," I said, dreaming big. "There's so much out there to see, Mag, and not all of it is accessible through the portals. Plus, if we lose them, we'll need other means of transportation. This could help trade, and so many other things." The more I spoke about it, the more excited I became at the possibility.

"And you, do you want to lead the ship?" he asked, quieter now.

I almost laughed but held it in. "I don't think I'm cut out for that kind of role. I do think Mary and I would be interested in joining you for the first while. Imagine how fun it would be to have the whole team around for a year or so. Clare, Nick, Suma, Rivo, maybe even Regnig.

Everyone can be part of this."

Magnus started forward again, waving his flashlight beam slowly over the rocky landscape. "Sounds like you've made up your mind. This is happening."

"I guess it is," I agreed.

"Good. Because I think our kids growing up beside each other is their destiny," he said with a smirk.

"Agreed."

Slate's voice cut through. "Boss, we found signs of someone being here. A protein bar from Haven. But nothing else."

I tapped the mic to all channels. "Then we reconvene at the rendezvous. See you two there soon." I turned to Magnus. "Shall we?"

His eyes were focused on the dim lights in the distance. It could be a small city, but I knew one thing. It was our only lead.

ELEVEN

*T*he hunter sniffed the air. It was full of amazing scents, unlike anything he'd ever come across. Here the land was more fruitful: crops grew lush from the ground, animals were penned in groups, making his feeding so simple. He moved from farm to farm, devouring one small animal from each, somehow finding his taste for what he now knew to be chickens and pigs lacking.

He'd tasted the best meat, and the shapeshifter wasn't able to shake the euphoric high he felt when digesting a human. He smoothed his long brown hair and caught a glimpse of himself in a puddle of water. It had rained, and it continued to drizzle as he leaned over the pool, catching the sight of blue eyes and a slender female face staring back at him. She didn't look like the other humans, and if he wanted to interact with them, to eat more, he had to fit in.

He needed to *become* her in order to consume and digest her body, so he could feed again.

The hunter spat out a feather and wiped his blood-drenched mouth with a dirty sleeve before standing up straight. It felt strange to walk on two legs, and he lumbered forward, each step eventually smoothing out as he went along the gravel road.

He'd been watching the farms and land, seeing who was home and who wasn't. There were two houses that appeared empty, and he made his way to the first one. It had a garden out back, and if he was desperate for sustenance, he could feed like a bottom-dweller and eat some of it for the nutrients.

The rain descended again, and he shook his head like an animal, long hair flapping wetly around his head. He was too used to being in a human body. He wanted shelter, a roof and the warmth of a fire.

He stepped up the wooden deck in the rear of the house and pressed on the door handle. It was locked. He stepped away and kicked out with all his strength, shattering the wood along the jamb, and the door flew open. He grinned, a sadistic look on his female face, and stepped in, happy to be out of the incessant rain.

The hunter pressed the door shut, and the wind blew it open again. He saw a chair in the kitchen and grabbed it, shoving it in front of the door, and this kept it in place. He sighed and felt the bones of the chicken inside his stomach begin to dissolve.

He searched through the house, making sure there was no one inside, and he found it empty. Cold. There was a fireplace in the living room, and he used it. A short time later, he peeled off the wet clothes and sat naked on the floor, the flames licking high into the hearth. The heat was nice, and he rolled onto his side, seeing his distended stomach. He'd eaten his fill and would be good for a few days.

The Gatekeepers

Eventually, the hunter rose and saw a framed picture on the mantel. The human brains he'd consumed told him this was likely the family that lived here. It was their nest. He held the picture in his hand and studied their faces. A man. A woman. A child. She was small, young, and her eyes were a bright glowing green. He'd never seen something like that before.

She must be special. The hunter imagined consuming the girl and becoming small like her, letting the parents take care of him. He could sleep and rest, and grow stronger.

Those green eyes drew him in, and he held the picture inches from his own eyes as he stared at them. Yes. He could smell her. The scent was all throughout the house. He sensed the power in her, and wondered if he'd gain that supremacy when he ate her flesh and digested her bones. He'd wait here. Wait for them to return, and when they did, he'd secretly end her and take her place.

The hunter felt good about it and settled to the floor. It didn't take long for him to fall asleep. Even while sleeping, a smile spread across his face.

"What do you think they're like?" Karo asked.

Slate hefted his pack off his shoulders and set it on the ground. "It didn't look so far from our perch by the portal."

"I'm assuming you mean the people here?" I asked Karo.

"Yes. Are we potentially walking into a hostile situation?" Karo asked.

I considered all the worlds we'd entered this way, and most of them had been sparsely populated. It made me wonder how many planets were actually full of advanced civilizations like the Bhlat, Shimmali, or Keppe.

"We're always potentially walking into hostile territory," Magnus said, swinging his pulse rifle into his hands. We were a couple miles from the city, which we now thought might be a fortress of some sort. The lights weren't spread out very far, but they appeared to be towers, with bright beams rotating around the rocky ground like search lights.

"Maybe they're looking for us," I said.

"Could be," Magnus said. "I didn't see any cameras set up at the portal, but that doesn't mean they weren't watching us with satellites or drones."

"Speaking of which. What happened with the drone you sent off?" I asked Magnus.

"Stupid me. I was so caught up with our discussion, I forgot to check." He lifted his arm, resting the barrel of his gun over his shoulder. "Looks like… it's gone. The feed is gone."

Slate stood behind him, peering over his other shoulder. "Go to the beginning. What happened to it?"

Magnus began to rewind the footage when the lights rose from our destination.

"Looks like we have company coming," Karo advised.

"Four ships." I grabbed my gun too. "Kind of hard to defend against an incoming enemy on foot. I hope they're friendly."

Slate was frowning. "I have a feeling we're about to find out." The lights moved for us now, and I shoved Magnus to the side as a red blast pulsed from the closest vessel.

"Everyone hide. Lights off!" Slate shouted, and we obeyed, flicking our EVA systems to dark. We scrambled away from the ships, which were hovering around us now. We each moved apart, not wanting to risk being fired at in a group.

"What do we do?" Karo asked quietly.

No one had time to answer. A bright light enveloped me, reminding me of the bright space Not-Dean had communicated with me through.

My body went weightless, and I scanned for the others, unable to see anything in the vastness of light.

"Slate! Magnus! Karo!" I received no answer as I floated, my pack left behind on the ground.

We were moving now, the ship carrying me in its tractor beam. It wasn't long before it stopped and I was spat out, propelled violently from the beam onto the ground. I spun in the air before crashing to the ground, which, luckily, was grass-covered instead of rocky like the rest of the landscape we'd seen.

I tried to sit up, to defend myself, and saw that my gun was missing too. I cursed and rolled to the side as Karo's tall form came tumbling from another ship. Slate was next, and we weren't able to move in time. He crashed into us, and I was grateful for the EVA's layers of protection. My ribs ached where his knee hit, and Slate lay on his front, groaning.

"You okay?" I asked him, and his helmet moved enough for me to know he was alive.

Karo was on his feet, fists clenched, ready to defend himself and us. I was right behind him, pushing myself up and feeling lightheaded as I did. My neck ached from the fall, and I feared the strain wouldn't end there.

We were in a courtyard, beyond the walls we'd seen from two miles away, and I looked up to see one of the towers the lights had been cast out from. The barriers were tall, at least a hundred feet, and made of the same black rock as the ground beyond the fortress.

"I think we answered whether the locals were hostile or not," Slate said, finally standing of his own volition. His lip was bleeding inside his helmet, and he shook his head as if trying to clear his foggy mind. That was never a good sign.

"What is this place?" I was trying to understand, then I saw the forms walking along the wall, and the guns. Drones hovered in the air around the courtyard, and I noticed the many outbuildings. It hit me, and I answered my own questions. "It's a prison."

Slate looked around and nodded. "It is. Damn it."

Karo took a step ahead and gazed into the dark sky. "Where's Magnus?"

He was right. The big Scandinavian hadn't been tossed inside with us. I scanned for a ship, but none were visible. "Hopefully, he hid before they saw him," I said.

Slate grimaced. "Or else, the worst might have happened."

We were alone in the courtyard, and I scanned around,

trying to see if there was any escape. I couldn't find one, and even if there was a way to scale the walls, the guards up there would make quick work of us. "Does anyone have weapons on them?"

Karo patted his suit and shook his head. I didn't either and told them so. Slate smiled and pulled a blade from his suit. "I have to hide this. They're going to search us." He knelt down and tore a chunk of grass out. We stood around him, blocking his silhouette from the wall's view. Seconds later, the knife was gone from his grip and the patch of grass was flush with the ground. Slate stepped on it for good measure.

It was the perfect timing, because a door from one of the stone-carved buildings opened, and five beings rushed out, each with a slender harpoon-shaped gun in their hand. They spoke in rushed phrases, and the translator didn't relay their words.

"I think they're telling us to get on our knees, or raise our hands or something," Slate said through clenched teeth.

I did both. They neared us, with weapons aimed steadily. They were short, only three feet tall, but I wasn't about to equate that with capability. It was their home, and they were the ones with the guns pointed at us.

One of them took the lead, standing at the front of their group. It spoke again, this time slower, less threatening. The translator clicked in, and I glanced at my arm console to see the device attempting to calculate the dialect.

The being spoke again, and this time, I heard English words in my ear. It had found a language similar enough, and I knew the translator technology was already piecing it together. The leader tilted his head over to the others and said something else, his tone less hostile.

"Quite the collection we have now," the translator said for the guard. He was wearing all black and appeared to be shielded in armor. I could only see the eyes, which were bulbous and red-veined behind a slit visor. Its head was too large for its skinny body, and I glanced down to see tiny hoofed feet balancing it out.

His words made me bristle. He called us part of their *collection*, and after seeing the Collector on the other side of the dimension where we'd found Magnus, I didn't want to end up on display somewhere, frozen in time.

I flipped my speaker on and spoke, hoping the translator would function in their recently learned language. "Hello. I'm Dean Parker from Earth. I represent the Alliance of Worlds, and am part of a collective including the Keppe, Bhlat, Motrill, Molariuns, Shimmali… you get the point, I could go on for a while with this list."

I waited on my knees while the words translated. Karo and Slate were in the same position as I was, and the Theos locked eyes with me, concern etched all over his face. I forced a smile at him, trying to convey that we'd be all right.

The leader heard me and spoke. "Those names mean nothing to us. Wait. Bhlat; that is what the large one called his people. Ulpo, am I mistaken?"

One of the others stepped forward, this one even shorter than the first. He was stockier too, almost round. "He is Bhlat, you are correct."

Dreb was with them, and they were speaking in present

tense about him too. That meant he was alive. "Can we see Dreb?" I asked, and their eyes flicked to meet my gaze. Ten bulging red eyes, behind black visors, all focused on me. I wanted to break the stare but wouldn't let myself.

"You will see Dreb, and the other." Then a sound that I could only assume was laughter.

Slate cleared his throat, and I saw that his hand was near the patch of grass where he'd hidden the knife. I thought about our odds and didn't like them, so I shook my head. He nodded his understanding.

"Get up." The lead alien gestured with his slim weapon, and we stood now as three guards came to stand behind us.

We followed two of them, with guns pressed against us, toward the far left corner of the courtyard. They were leading us to an entrance, and I had a sick moment where I feared if we went inside, we'd never see the sky again. With a last glance at the wall, I hoped Magnus was alive. He might have escaped before they lashed him into their beams. *Stay strong.* I willed the words to him, and was the first of our small group to enter the prison within the fortress.

TWELVE

I sat in the corner of my cell, trying to modify myself so the hard rock floor didn't cause as much discomfort. It didn't matter what I did; it hurt after a few minutes. I scanned the room, hoping to notice something I'd missed over the first two days of isolation.

The initial night, I'd run my fingers over every inch of the walls, trying to feel for weakness, but found nothing. The energy barrier at the far end was impenetrable, and I decided there was no way out, at least not from inside the cell. Someone on the outside would have to release me.

I'd been transported to the end of a corridor, and was in the only cell in this wing. Were Karo and Slate okay? Were they as isolated as I was?

Our jailors were less than friendly with me. My suit had been removed, and I now sat in a dirty white jumpsuit, finding gratitude that my human lungs were able to breathe the musty air here. It wasn't perfect, and I had to fight for the odd breath, but as long as we weren't here long-term, I thought it would be fine. *Long-term*. Even after two days, I was beginning to doubt we'd ever be rescued.

Magnus had likely been killed, and no one would be able to track us through the portals. We had the devices, or at least our captors did now. I considered this and remembered that Magnus was the one who'd held on to the Modifier and Crystal Map after we arrived. There was hope, albeit a small chance. I clung to it as the day went on. Endless nothing transpired.

Finally, like the first day, one of the prison guards entered the hallway, his small hoofed feet clacking against the hard rock, warning me he was coming. He spoke to me, but without my translator, it meant nothing to my ears. He touched a screen outside the barrier, and a compact slot opened in it, framed by green energy. He slid an archaic tray inside, spilling half the food onto the floor.

This was my life now. I waited until he stopped staring at me and his footsteps had clopped away, and I forced myself to rise and scoop the food onto the tray. I wasn't going to give them the satisfaction of watching me eat floor slop.

It was terrible, but I had to stay energized. There was a cup with gray liquid in it, and I tried not to think about what it might be. I closed my eyes and swallowed it quickly, feeling tiny chunks pass into my throat. I fought my gag reflex and drank it all.

When I was done, my belly finally stopped growling at me, and I crept to the edge of the room. I settled to the ground and tried to sleep.

Sometime later – maybe hours, because the tray had been cleared away – I heard a noise from behind me. The walls, floor, and ceiling were all fabricated from the same black stone this world had everywhere. Dust fell from several feet up the wall, and I peered into the newly-formed hole, seeing a pupil on the other side.

A voice spoke in a language I didn't know. It was quiet and feminine.

"I'm sorry," I said, speaking for the first time since I'd been thrown inside. "I don't know what you said." Another whisper. "I can't understand you."

"English?" she asked.

I was startled. "You speak English?"

"Yes. I have the ability to speak many languages," she said.

"Who are you?" I asked. The voice modifiers weren't that new, but I knew that English and other languages like Mandarin and Spanish had only recently been added to the software updates. I wondered about allowing something to be implanted in me that needed constant updating. But I was trapped in a terrible prison cell, so it probably didn't matter.

"I am Loweck from Udoon," she said.

"Udoon." I pictured the strange four-legged locals, their heads not unlike those of hippopotami, and their flowing colorful clothing.

"And you're from Earth, or one of the other human settlements?" she asked.

"Earth," I said, adding, "originally. Kind of all over the place now."

"You seem to know Udoon," she said quietly. I had to strain to hear her voice.

"I've been there. To the Udoon station, at least," I told

her. That was where we'd caught the scared Kraski as he'd tried to meet Lom of Pleva with Karo in hand.

She made a noise. "Depravity, if you ask me. I know the locals love the station, but I never understood the point of a place where all one did was drink, gamble, or associate with illegal activity."

"I see your point," I told her. I needed to learn more about my surroundings. "How long have you been imprisoned?"

"Five of your years," she told me.

"How did you end up here?" I asked. "We're in the middle of nowhere. Aren't we?"

"You're correct. I was part of a team specializing in experimental ship drive technology. We were stranded after our core exploded and sent us to the far reaches. Our life support failed, and everyone died," she said.

"I'm sorry," I said. My body was pressed to the wall, and I leaned over, hovering near the hole that allowed us to communicate. "You made it, though." It wasn't a question.

There was a slight pause. "I did. I flew a pod to the surface. I saw the lights and continued to them on foot. They opened the doors to let me in, then shoved me in a cage."

"Are you ever able to leave your cell?" I asked.

"Yes. They're assessing you first. Trying to see if you're a danger. If you play along, you should be able to walk about in a few rotations of their world," Loweck told me. This was good news. Maybe I could see Slate and Karo again, perhaps find Polvertan and Dreb.

This woman might be a mole, though, and I had to keep some of my questions strategic, especially about my connection to the others. "Do they give you any indication that you'll be released?"

Another pause, then Loweck spoke again. This time, her voice had a hint of sadness to it. "No. No one is released. At least, not as far as I can tell."

"What do they do with the prisoners, then? Why are we here?" I asked, angry at the entire situation. My only objective was to secure my crew and head home to Mary and Jules. This had already taken too long, and I tried not to imagine how worked up Mary and Nat would be by our lack of communication. In another day or two, they'd be ready to single-handedly tear apart planets to find us.

"We work the rock. Six hours a day. Bashing stone with pickaxes," she said.

Great. That was what I had to look forward to for the rest of my life. "How many prisoners are there?"

"I don't know. We're only one side of four. The workers are in shifts, and I see the same thirty faces every day. Other than that, I could only guess," Loweck said.

"I'll take a guess," I told her.

"Two hundred. Maybe more."

"And guards?" I hoped she wasn't a mole, because this wouldn't look good.

"Maybe twenty. There are usually four along the walls, and two watching the workers in the pit. But they have drones, and other means of keeping everyone in line," she said.

I didn't ask what that meant, not yet. I was about to

bring up Pol and Dreb when she spoke again. "They're coming. Fill the hole with something. Clothing, dirt, a small pebble."

I scrambled around, searching for something to shove in the tiny opening, and found a piece of rock the right size. "Thank you, Loweck."

"Don't thank me yet," she whispered.

"Why?"

"Because you're going to help us escape." The voice muffled as she covered her end, and I heard the guards barking at her from beyond. I stuck the stone in on my side and leaned against the wall, her last word echoing in my mind.

Escape.

Three days passed by with the same routine. Terrible food. No discussions. No bed to sleep on. I was so glad at that moment that Jules and Mary weren't here with us. I wouldn't have been able to live with myself. They were safely on Haven, warm and protected. It was the only solace I found while lying on my back, staring at the black ceiling, counting grooves in the stone.

It was the worst. On the fourth day, after first talking with Loweck, someone different approached the cell. This local guard was shorter yet, but he moved with dignity, a sense of self-confidence the others didn't relay. He tapped the barrier off, stepping inside. None of the others had done this. I stood straight up, ready to defend myself, though I kept my arms loose at my sides to not appear aggressive.

He was without a gun, but the little guard didn't seem to care. He stomped over to me, reaching up to grab my jaw. I let him touch my face with his black-gloved hand, and he assessed me as if I were a show dog on display. It was unsettling.

I could end him there, I knew it, but I restrained myself. Killing this guard would only kill me, and with me, the others' chance at escaping with Loweck's help. I clenched my hands in fists as I thought about my daughter and Mary's smile.

The guard turned his back to me and motioned me forward. I followed cautiously, past the lowered energy barrier and into the corridor. After nearly a week locked in the cell, it was strange being on the other side. I refused to glance over at it. I expected they'd return me here at some point.

"Where are we going?" I asked, my throat dry and rough.

He didn't answer. We finally passed other cells that held all kinds of beings. How many of them had arrived through the portals? Why did this prison have a veritable zoo of aliens at their disposal? I wasn't sure if I'd ever find out, but I hated this place with a fervor. A few of them peered up at me with sad eyes. They were beaten, hungry, and desperate.

I was led out of the cells and into an open room with twenty-foot ceilings, windows carved out of the roof, allowing natural light to seep through. This was the chow hall, for lack of a better term. Most of the people milling about were in black jumpsuits, and many were the local race. These ones didn't have on masks and uniforms like the guards. They were pale and bald, their large eyes jutting from their heads like they were trying to escape their sockets. A few of them glanced up at me before returning to the brown piles of food on the trays in front of them.

The guard brought me to the line, and I understood he wanted me to eat. Once I had a tray in my hand, he left my side, heading for the door, where he paused and whispered at the one watching the dining room. And with that, I was now part of the general population of the prison.

There were twenty tables, each allowing for ten prisoners. I found the only one devoid of anyone and sat at the edge of it, my back to the wall so I could see everything in the room. Slate stumbled in. He looked like crap, his hair a mess, his beard sticking out at all angles. His red eyes met mine, and he gave me a slight nod. A few minutes later, he was bringing a tray to me, and he sat beside me, not across.

"Thank God you're okay," I told him.

"Me? I was worried about you. You're too dainty for this kind of place," Slate said, ever the joker.

"Have you seen Karo?"

He shook his head, scooping up some food with something resembling a spoon. At least they gave us utensils here. He was looking around grimly. "This is my first time out. You?"

"Same." I told him about my encounter with Loweck in the cell behind mine.

"Can we trust her? I haven't seen any other women

here, have you?" he asked.

"I don't know. These aliens could all be females," I told him.

He took another spoonful and shuddered. "You're right. What's the plan?"

"The plan?"

"Yeah, how do we break out of here?"

"We haven't seen outside yet. We have to do some recon first. Loweck mentioned escaping with us. I'll need to explore that. She's been held for five years. That means she has a much better lay of the land then we'll ever have. We need her." I tried the food and gagged at the taste. Maybe it was eating at a table with a spoon instead of my hands, but it did taste better than in the cell.

"What about this work detail? A pickaxe can make a good weapon," Slate said.

"Sounds like they have the firepower to blast you on the spot. We'll have to see," I said.

"We might be given the chance sooner rather than later." Slate nodded to the exit, where the prisoners were lining up.

"We need to find Karo. Loweck said there were other complexes connected. Other wings to the prison. If we don't locate him here, we're going to need to extract him," I whispered.

Slate nodded his agreement and finished his tray of food. I ate as much as I could and washed it away with a glass of murky, tepid water.

We were the last ones seated, and a guard came behind us, kicking my chair. He motioned for me to stand with his harpoon-shaped gun.

"We're up," I told him, and my big friend and I followed the line outside. It was bright, everything with a red tinge to it, reminding me of New Spero.

The rock wall shimmered, and I saw that it was an energy barrier projection. I made a mental note of the location of the keypad, ten yards to the left of the opening. I did a quick count and saw there were indeed thirty of us, like Loweck had advised.

The guards lifted in the air, soft propulsion from thin packs harnessed to them.

We were led a mile, then two. I was sweating through my jumpsuit by the time we arrived at the pit. When Loweck had mentioned it, I was picturing a minor area, contained and guarded. This was massive. Steps were carved out of the hard black stone, and we advanced into the maw of the ground here. By the time we hit the bottom, my legs and calves were burning fiercely. It had to be three hundred steps underground. The guards were down there waiting for us, and one cut his jet pack inches above the ground and landed on the rock, kicking up a little dust.

"This is no joke," Slate said, running a hand through his damp hair.

Above us, silent droves hovered as a reminder they were watching. There were only the two guards who came with us, each with weapons strapped to their backs, but not in their hands. They were complacent, and maybe that was a crack in the foundation we could exploit. Only time would tell.

The line began to spread out, these people knowing

what their tasks were. One figure stood at the front, and she turned to us. She was a dark orange tone with wavy long hair, somehow not greasy. She lifted a hand at her side in a hidden greeting.

"I think we've met Loweck," I said.

Slate's voice was low. "She's beautiful."

THIRTEEN

We made the trek to the pit again, my fourth day in a row. This time, my legs didn't burn as badly once we neared the bottom, and Slate and I escorted Loweck to the far edge of the fenced-off area.

"What do they do with all this rock?" I asked, searching for an answer.

Loweck shrugged. She was humanoid, though we'd never heard of the race she was part of. She was clearly not a local from Udoon. She'd told us her people were called Rescaps. Slate glanced over at her, and I shook my head. Leave it to Slate to remain solo for years after Denise betrayed him, then find someone he was interested in at a prison millions of light years from anything we knew.

It was as if the universe had a strange sense of humor.

"I know what they do with it," Slate said.

"And?" I prompted him as he used a laser to cut into the stone. Apparently, it went on for a few miles of the planet's surface, and everything around there was built with it. The prison had to be there for cheap labor. I wasn't expecting a judge and jury any time soon.

"They throw it in a pile. Probably make a mountain to counter the crater the prisoners have made over the years. What else could they do with so many tons of rock?" Slate wiped sweat from his brow. It wasn't warm out here, but the journey mixed with the endless labor was enough to make us perspire.

Once we were done, the moisture quickly cooled, and by the time we ended up within the high prison walls, I was shivering.

"They must have a reason, but I really don't care what it is. Loweck, we can't keep doing this forever. We need to find a way out," I told her.

She lifted the visor she was using to protect her from rock chips jutting in her eyes, and met my gaze. "If you haven't noticed, your friend has been watching us every day."

My pulse hurried, and I searched for the man, trying to not be obvious about it. She hissed at me quietly, "He's not there right now. He's quite stealthy at avoiding detection."

It had to be Magnus. So he'd eluded capture after all. That was a good sign. He'd also salvaged enough supplies to keep going, along with weapons. He had the option to leave through the portal and bring reinforcements, but with the volatility of the stones, I wasn't sure he'd risk it.

We worked for another two hours, cutting away rock in even chunks, then transporting them with the aid of a robotic hover lift. It was strenuous, even with the advanced tools. It was far from the old mining days on Earth.

Everyone was lining up, ready to move, and the guards were lazily standing near the stairs, chatting to each other, when I heard the falling rock. It bounced along the walls before landing ten yards away from my feet. I jumped in reaction and set my sights to the ridge above. I thought I saw Magnus' form for a brief moment before there was nothing. The drones were up in the air, focused on inside the pit, not the ground around it.

I crouched, as if I was tying my shoelace, and picked up the flat rock.

The others are in pit 3. Karo with them. Four days. End of shift. Be ready.

The words were engraved into the rock face, and I grabbed the cutter, slicing the evidence into pieces, then kicked the remains around.

The guards barked at me, and I set the tool onto the rocky floor.

"What is it?" Slate asked. He and Loweck had been talking, and neither even noticed the drop.

"Magnus sent a message. Four days. He said the others are working pit three." I grinned at him.

"Four days. Then what?" Slate asked.

Loweck took the answer. Her orange skin darkened, and her bright blue eyes danced as she spoke. "Then we escape."

---

*W*aiting for another few days was excruciating. We kept our heads low, eating before and after our shifts before being relegated to our cells. Loweck and I talked each night, deciding how to disarm the guards. We agreed they would be tired and disinterested by the end of the workday, as they always were, and we'd be able to attack easily.

It was the night before Magnus' planned extraction, and we were beat after the long shift. It had been warmer, and I really wished we were supplied more than a bucket of water to rinse off with after the pits each day. It was also disturbing washing off with the rest of the local prisoners staring at me. They were strange creatures.

"So how good is this friend of yours?" she asked through the secret hole between our walls.

"He's the best. Military, captain of space vessels, husband and father." I knew the last weren't necessarily prerequisites to most people, but they would be to anyone with children.

"How will he deal with both pits at once?" she asked.

I didn't know and told her so. "If it were me, I'd rescue us out first, then head to pit three as a unit. Are you ready if it comes to a fight?"

There was a slight pause before she answered, "I'm ready."

"Good. I hope we can pull this off. Truth is, we've been in stickier situations than this one." I had to laugh.

"And look at you now," she said with a hint of mirth.

I glanced at my filthy uniform, my black rock-dust-covered hands, and shook my head. We were going to escape tomorrow, and with the two rookie Gatekeepers at our side. It was already decided; we only had to follow the steps. I told myself this a few times, fighting the doubt creeping into my mind. We were bringing them all home.

The Gatekeepers

"What's the deal with Slate?" she asked quietly.

I'd been waiting for this. I didn't know how compatible the two races would be, but from everything I could tell, we were very similar. "He's… complicated."

"He doesn't seem complicated," she said.

It wasn't my place to tell her his past. I couldn't tell her about his brother being killed overseas long before the Event. About Slate signing up for the military with a head full of revenge, only to never find peace from it. He'd been by my side since we'd arrived at the base in New Mexico, and had traveled all around this great universe, helping me save people and saving himself in the process.

I definitely couldn't tell her about the woman Slate considered his one love, the very same woman that was working for Lom of Pleva, and that I'd shot dead at point blank. I couldn't tell her any of that, but I could tell her something. "He's the finest man I know. He's my brother, and he deserves the best." I closed my eyes, thinking about how much we'd all been through.

"I can tell. I didn't mean to pry," she told me.

"Where will you go when this is all over?" I asked her.

"I don't know. I don't have a home to return to. My home was our ship, my family the crew. They're all dead now. Perhaps…" She stopped.

I had a feeling where this was heading. "Go on."

"Perhaps I can come with you. Live on this Haven you spoke of. Would they let someone like me live there?" she asked.

Someone like her? "Of course. Haven is a refuge for the unlikely and outsiders. It has been since Kareem of the

Deltra started it. It may be turning into a regulated planet, but the heart of the place hasn't changed. You'd be more welcome there than you can imagine," I told her, and meant it. Leslie and Terrance were building something special.

It had only been ten days, but I was feeling the itch to resist authority. The sheer idea we might break free the next day had me vibrating with anticipation.

"Good. I'd like that," she said, and we settled into silence. We closed the hole in the wall. It was late, and we had a lot of work to do tomorrow.

Tomorrow, we were escaping from prison.

"Stop working so hard, Slate. You're drawing their attention," Loweck told him.

He had twice as many stone slabs piled near him as any other worker, and he was pouring sweat as he chipped away, beating out the frustration of captivity.

Slate wiped his brow and set a hand to his hip. "Sorry, I'll slow down."

The other prisoners were staring at him with bulging eyes.

"Nothing to see here," I said to the ones nearest us, knowing full well they had no idea what I was saying.

It was almost time, and as expected, the guards were at their usual spot, feigning interest in what we were doing, but after who knows how many hours a year spent standing in the pits without altercation, they weren't too worried about an uprising. That was going to be their demise.

We were a good distance from the prison here, but they had ships: the ones that had locked on to us and dragged us beyond the walls. I'd seen them on occasion, moving around the landscape on our trips to and from the pit, but only once had I seen the lights activated. I wondered if that was what they did. Search out for roaming people, only to force them into servitude. It was terrible.

"I hope Magnus has a plan. You know him, he's a little 'shoot first, deal with consequences later'," Slate said.

"I thought that was you." I chuckled nervously. It was almost time, and we had no idea what to expect.

The line began moving for the stairs, and the guards noticed us lingering in the pit.

"Come on, Magnus. If you're doing something, do it now," I said through gritted teeth.

"There. The light." Loweck gestured above, where one of their square vessels lowered. The drones lifted out of the way, clearly programmed to defer to the alien-driven ships.

The beam cut from the bottom of it, shooting to the floor of the canyon we stood inside. The guards raised their guns, unsure of what was happening. They stared up into the sky and pointed at their own people's ship as it entered the pit.

"That's the plan! He's going to beam us out!" It reminded me of the Kraski ships, and memories of every human being lifted from the surface of Earth rang through my mind. James being pulled from my house. I had to shake the feeling of dread. James was okay. He was on New Spero safely, with my expecting sister.

"Stay closer," Loweck ordered, and we listened. The guards were coming for us, and I hoped the ship would arrive first.

One of them skidded to a stop twenty yards away and fired the slim gun. A blast shot toward us at the same moment Magnus' ship ripped us from the ground. Seconds later, we were lifting from the pit's floor. We moved quickly, and five minutes later, we were settled on the rock miles away.

The ship landed, and I saw it was smaller than I'd thought. A hatch opened on the top, much like a tank, and Magnus' head popped up. "Quick, they're going to be looking for us. Pile in," he said, and Slate pushed Loweck up the side of the boxy ship. It was only ten feet tall, and she clambered up. There was a wet spot where she'd been, and I let Slate shove me up the ship's edge. Magnus lowered his hand and Slate jumped, clasping arms with the other man.

A minute later, we were all inside the cramped space, and Magnus lifted the ship high into the sky, carrying us far away from the prison.

"Loweck, are you okay?" Slate asked, and I saw the blood leaking from her arm.

She nodded, but her blue eyes faded to gray as she slumped to the floor.

FOURTEEN

*W*e settled to the surface roughly a hundred miles away. The cockpit of the ship was the size of a small bedroom, screens and computers lined the walls, and a single seat close to the floor sat along the main controls. It was meant for the aliens, whose average height was three feet. Magnus hunched on the seat; his knees in proximity to his ears would have been a comical sight at any other time.

"Loweck." Slate said her name again, but she was out. I lifted the injured arm, reaching for Magnus' pack. There was a first-aid kit inside, and I grabbed it, searching for something to help.

Her arm wasn't bleeding any longer. I threw on gloves and touched the blood pooling on the floor between the metal grates, and felt it between my fingers. It was viscous, smooth like oil.

"I don't think this is blood," I told Slate.

"What do you mean? She was shot," he replied.

I showed him, and his brow furrowed.

"Where are we, Magnus? Will they come for us?" I asked.

He was standing now, ducking from hitting his head on an overhanging console. "No. I removed the tracking system and found a place at the edge of the rocks. They don't seem to venture this far."

"They might after what happened," Slate said.

Magnus shrugged. "Maybe. Honestly, they're not very tough. I kicked this one's butt."

"Where is he?" I asked. "The one who flew the ship?"

"Don't ask," Magnus said, answering my question indirectly. "Who is this?"

"Loweck. She's with us," Slate said defensively.

"Settle down, slugger, I was only asking. Why was a robot in prison?" Magnus asked, crouching beside us.

"Robot?" Slate's eyes went wide, and it all became clear.

The fact that she was from Udoon, yet looked nothing like the Udoon race. Her ship had failed, and life support ran out. Her crew had died, but she hadn't. She asked if they would let "someone like her" live on Haven. I felt foolish for not cluing in before.

Slate mopped his face with a hand. "Oh man. Story of my life."

"Don't tell me…" Magnus started, and I shot him a look, shutting him up mid-sentence. He cleared his throat. "Let's get out of here. Come on."

It was dark out by the time we settled into the camp Magnus had been living at for the last while.

"How did you visit us without being detected?" I asked, glancing over at Loweck. She was lying on the ground, and the liquid had stopped flowing from her injury. She made a few whirring noises, but her eyes remained gray.

Slate was eating something and pouting. There was grass here, but not much else. The ship was concealed under a sheet of the same material we used to cloak our ships. Magnus was pulling out all the stops here. That explained how he'd come and gone with ease.

"Like I said, these guys are pretty dumb, and the cloaking stuff helped. But they do seem to have some serious commerce going on here. There were some large transport vessels lowering through the atmosphere, so I had to check it out. It looks like they're selling the stone slabs to outsiders. The whole operation is happening about a hundred miles from the other side of the prison." Magnus fumbled through his pack and pulled out a bottle of Scotch.

"Are you kidding me?" I asked, rolling my eyes at him.

"Could you imagine if I was stuck here alone for ten days without it?" Magnus asked, and I had to laugh. Even Slate cracked a grin.

"That's a new one, Mag." Slate kept eating, but he was warming up a bit.

Magnus unscrewed the cap, and I was actually surprised to see it was unopened. When he saw my expression, he laughed. "You don't think I brought just the one bottle, do you?"

That had us all in stitches, and it felt good. He took a swig and passed it to Slate. "Here you go, pup. Sorry your girlfriend's a bot." The words, while a little harsh, were sincere.

"All good. I hope she's okay. She wouldn't have been

hurt if it wasn't for us," Slate said.

"She'd also still be trapped at the prison," I told him, and he nodded slowly as he passed the bottle to me.

I held it in my hands and turned the label to face me. "You can't be serious."

Magnus smirked. "The very same."

I couldn't believe it. "You kept bottles from the liquor store we visited the day you bartered for Nat's engagement ring?"

"I do. There may be one or two safely at home."

I lifted it to my lips and drank. I wasn't much of a Scotch man, but after being in prison for the last ten days, it tasted like liquid gold.

"You, my friend, are a nutcase." I passed it over to him and changed the subject. "What's the plan? We have to figure this out."

"They may be on the defensive after what we did today," Magnus said. "I was thinking of waiting it out a few days before striking. They may think we left."

I considered this, but hated leaving Karo and the others there any longer than we had to.

"I can help." The voice startled us all, and Magnus almost dropped his bottle to the grass.

"Loweck," Slate said, moving to her side. She sat up.

"I guess you know now," she said.

"That you're robotic?" Slate asked.

"I'm a cyborg. Not quite organic, not quite robot," she explained.

"Were you made this way?" Magnus asked.

She accepted Slate's assistance up, and he unfolded

another seat for her. "My city was invaded. They destroyed everything. I was left alive, but barely. Someone happened up on me after they left, stripping us of everything valuable. I was saved, but at a price," she said, head lowered, looking at the soft light of the lantern.

"I'm sorry." It was all Slate could say, and he wrapped an arm around her, pulling her close. "Are you okay now?" He nodded to her arm.

"I'm fine. This arm is mechanical." She used her other hand to knock on it. "This one isn't." She smiled. "I have to power off to fix any major issues, but there are essentially small nanobots inside me that attend to any issues. It has its benefits."

"No kidding," I said. "You told us you could help save our friends. How?"

She explained, and we huddled around, listening until late into the night. By the time we were ready to sleep for the night, we had our plan.

The star rose over the horizon, and my eyes blinked open. Slate was already up, packing things away, and I glanced over to see Magnus' chest rising and falling slowly. Loweck was standing on the edge of the grass patch staring toward the prison, which wasn't visible from this distance.

"You good, boss?" Slate asked me as I rose to my feet. My neck hurt, and the lack of food and water as well as good sleep was catching up to me.

I stretched my arms out, feeling my spine pop. "As good as I can be. I'll be better when we're getting the hell off this rock-covered world."

"Me too."

"Do we have enough firepower for this?" I asked him.

"Probably not, but when has that ever stopped us before?" he said with a grin.

He was right, but these little prison guards didn't seem like the type you could negotiate with.

We had a quick meal and, an hour later, we were inside the ship again. Magnus attached the cloaking sheet across it, connecting it to the outer sides. We knew it wouldn't hide us fully, but if the others were outside in pit three, we'd have a good shot of rescuing them. If they weren't, it was on to plan B.

The trip didn't take very long as Magnus moved us over the great shield of bleak black rock.

"Two pulse rifles, a pistol, and…" He held up some tool we'd found inside the ship. "Whatever this is."

"I'll take the pistol," I said, knowing the other two preferred the rifles. They were also better marksmen than I was.

"Maybe Loweck should stay in the ship. You know, our getaway driver," Slate said.

"I don't think so. I'll be more help out there," she said confidently. Her long hair was pulled into a ponytail, and she appeared ready to go. Her orange-tinged skin was flushed, like a blistering sunburn.

I stood beside Magnus, watching the live camera feeds from below the square ship. We were nearing the prison, and we moved over pit four, heading for three. Inside it, thirty prisoners went through the never-ending cutting of stone, stacking the slabs only to mine more. I felt bad for them, having experienced a few days of the hard work and monotony. I couldn't imagine a lifetime of it.

"Everyone ready?" Magnus asked, and when we all shouted our answer, he lowered toward pit three. It was empty. "I had a feeling," he said, raising us up.

"We have company," I said, pointing to the main viewer to my left. "Drones. Five of them."

The ship shook lightly as the drones attacked. Their shots were feeble, but with enough of them, they'd be able to take us on.

"Plan B," Magnus said, moving us faster now, this time toward the prison as we'd discussed.

Drone fire shot out, but with our cloaking device, they were having a hard time tracking us, especially with Magnus' erratic flying.

We were tossed around inside the compact ship, and Slate caught Loweck as she tumbled across the floor.

"Will you ease up a bit?" I urged Magnus.

"Hold on to your hats." The warning came too late, and he drove the ship toward the prison. My feet lifted, hovering me inches over the floor. I tasted my stomach as we lurched, and soon we settled into a straight line. "You know the drill. Go go go!"

I opened the hatch, and Slate shoved me up; the rope was clasped to my belt, and I jumped. The sky was gray, and a few drones blasted toward me, hitting the roof instead. "You're making this easier on me," I said to the drones. Slate was at my side a second later, then Loweck. Magnus must have changed his mind about coming with us, because he lifted away as soon as we'd detached our tethers, leaving us alone on the prison roof.

We watched as the drones duplicated Magnus' actions, chasing after him. "Okay. We know Karo, Polvertan, and Dreb are in this building. We find them. We extract them into the courtyard as planned. Magnus will find us." I took the lead, but before I finished my quick speech, Loweck was placing the explosives on the stone roof.

Slate and I stepped into the shadows, hearing guards shouting from the ground. They couldn't see us, but it sounded like they knew we were there. "I hope these bombs have enough kick. Magnus sure came prepared," Slate said, and as Loweck neared us, she pressed the detonator. The entire roof shook, sending us off our feet. When the dust settled, a hole the size of a bathtub had been blasted into the rock.

"Looks good to me," I said. If each of the four quadrants of the prison followed the same footprint, we'd be blown above their kitchen storage. The guards were rarely inside there, since the prisoners did all the food preparation. Slate grabbed my arm, and I climbed through the hole, wishing I had armor on, or at least more than my dirty old jumpsuit. He let go and I dropped the last seven feet, bending my knees to absorb the landing.

He was beside me in a second, and Loweck jumped, landing softly and impressively without assistance. Apparently, there were advantages to being a cyborg.

One of the local prisoners stood there, five feet from us, his eyes close to popping out of his head. He blinked, eyelids slowly arcing over his pupils.

Loweck said something in their language and he raised his hands, crouching to the ground. She said something else, and the prisoner pointed out the door, and then right. He gibbered something I couldn't understand.

"The layout is a mirror of ours. They're detained in the cells. He says they weren't sent to the pits today because of what happened yesterday," Loweck said.

Pit four remained in operation, but I was willing to bet it had far more security than two lazy guards. That might mean there were fewer guards stationed here at the prison today. Things were looking up.

We ran, Loweck in the lead. Slate struggled to keep up with her, and I took the rear. The pulse pistol was tight in my grip, and when I felt more than heard the volley of fire from the harpoon lasers, I ducked, rolling through an open doorway. When the shooting dissipated, I could hear their slow footsteps from the hall. Slate and Loweck hadn't stopped, and I hoped they were already at the cells.

The shadow of a prison guard entered the dim room, and I didn't hesitate. I fired, hitting him squarely in the chest. The other returned fire at me, and I stayed low, aiming at his legs. I hit, and he buckled. They were writhing in pain, and I crept over to them, peeking out the door to make sure more weren't hiding there. When I saw the coast was clear, I kicked away their guns, and flicked my pistol to stun.

"You don't deserve this." I fired once, twice, and they both went limp.

I heard more fire from the direction of the prison cells, and I ran, tapping my earpiece. "Magnus, you okay?"

He screamed, an exasperated cheer. "These little dorks don't know who they're messing with. I've managed to confuse and crash most of the drones. You have the targets?"

"Not yet. Working on it." I moved slowly, keeping close to the wall. I turned the corner in the hall and saw the solitary guard creeping up behind Slate. Before I could aim and fire, Loweck shoved Slate to the side and kicked out, knocking the harpoon gun from the alien's tentative grip. She kicked again, this time a sweeping roundhouse, and he spun to the ground, unmoving.

I didn't want to fight with her and was happy to have her on our team. "Karo!" Slate shouted. "Pol! Dreb!" A few aliens in cells shouted, and over the sudden influx of voices, I heard a familiar one.

"I'm here! I'm here!" Karo's voice carried to me loudly.

I ran past Slate and Loweck, and saw the Theos standing behind the energy barrier. He looked terrible. His thick white hair was long and lanky, greasy. He was thin, like he hadn't eaten in weeks, and I wondered how bad I must appear to him.

"We're taking you out," I told him, and Loweck was there. She typed something into the control panel, and it flashed red. She tried again, swearing in another language, before it repeated the red notification.

"Damn it. This should do the trick." Her finger pointed toward it, and a tiny rod extended toward the panel. It stuck inside, and I saw a blue current course from her hand into the controls. The red light turned green before smoke rose from the device, and the barrier dissolved. Karo stumbled out, and I gripped his arm.

"Where are the others?" I asked, and he pointed down

The Gatekeepers

the hall to the left.

A dozen guards stood between us and our Gatekeeper friends.

FIFTEEN

Loweck didn't wait for us to make a plan. She held a pulse rifle, the one she'd taken instead of Magnus, and fired a succession of quick shots at the ground. Two hit the walls; one hit the ceiling, where rocks crumbled around them. What it did was send the guards scattering, unsure where the next shot would end up.

Slate was right behind her, and I stayed with Karo, keeping watch. Two guards made it past Slate and Loweck and ran toward us. Slate shouted to me, and I fired at the lead one, striking him in the facemask. Slate intercepted the other and quickly returned to firing at the ones in front of him.

Seconds later, the halls were quiet, even from the stunned prisoners. Loweck kicked a prison guard's head and waved us forward. I noticed Slate watching her with impressed eyes.

Karo moved with more speed than I expected, and he grabbed a gun from one of the dead guard's sides. "This way." He led us past three more cells, and there he was: Polvertan, the Motrill prince. He stared at us with disbelief.

The Gatekeepers

"You're really here. When Karo told me…" Pol stopped. He was a tall Motrill, thinner than a Keppe, although much larger than a human. His gray armored skin was bulkier than I remembered it, but his waist was thinner. Three months in this hellish prison would do that to anyone. It was the combination of unrelenting work and an absence of calories. His snake eyes blinked at me.

"Where's Dreb?" Slate asked.

"I'm here," his low voice said from across the corridor. Loweck was already at work on Pol's energy barrier when alarms rang out through the prison.

"Took them long enough," I muttered. There were at least ten or so dead guards. With the alarms notifying the rest, I expected we'd have company very shortly. "We have to hurry."

Pol's barrier evaporated, and our new cyborg friend set to work on Dreb's control panel. He shuffled from foot to foot. He was wide, a real Bhlat guard. His hair was long; thick dreadlocks swung side to side as he moved. The Empress had claimed him as her own, and what that exactly meant, I wasn't sure. Either way, I knew I needed to bring him home or suffer her wrath.

His barrier disappeared, and he let loose a warrior's challenge to any enemies listening. The sound was like the roar of an angry bear, and I stepped away from him as he reached for a dead guard's gun.

"Everyone's here. Let's move outside to the extraction point," I shouted. The other prisoners were all yelling now, desperate for our attention.

"Where's the main control room?" I asked, a new idea

forming. If I could let all the prisoners out, they'd take the target away from us, giving enough time for Magnus to swoop in.

Pol answered, "I saw a building out in the courtyard. It was guarded by two of them, and not the usual dummies you see every day. These ones were watchful. Bigger guns," he told us.

"That has to be it. Everyone to the courtyard. I'll locate the control room," I said.

We rushed through the corridors, finding another three guards. Dreb and Loweck were at the front of the line, and they dispatched them quickly, nearly fighting over who would take the last guard on. In the end, they each shot him. A fair bargain.

The outside air felt cool as we emerged from inside the prison. Alarms rang out here too, red lights flashing along the huge stone walls. A bullet hit the side of the rock behind me, and I glanced up to see the guards atop the wall in the towers.

"Magnus? Can you take out the tower nearest us?" I asked into my mic.

"On it," came the reply.

"When that tower is hit, you all regroup into the center of the courtyard," I said, and ran for the building Pol had spoken of. No one tried to stop me, and I was glad for it. The usual guards were vacant, and I found the eight-foot-tall door unlocked.

It was quiet inside, save the whirring electrical motors and cooling fans of the immense computer system the room held. I stayed close to the door, sliding my back along the wall. I fully expected someone to be here; perhaps not a warrior, but someone familiar with complex systems that would control the lights, power, and utilities of the prison.

In the end, the room was empty. I slid another of Magnus' special explosive devices from my pack and placed it in the middle of the room. Everything told me the largest piece, with the most blinking lights, was the key to overthrowing the prison. I hoped I was right as I stuck the device on it and ran for the door. Right before I pressed the detonator, a guard stepped into the building, pointing a harpoon gun in my direction.

"Do you know where the little boy's room is?" I asked him, trying to look as innocent and lost as possible.

He stood up, a full three and a half feet, and tipped his visor, covering his bulging eyeballs. In the moment he took to look flabbergasted, I had my pistol in my hand. I shot at him, running toward the guard, at the same time pressing the detonator. The bomb exploded, throwing me and the guard out into the courtyard. Another second or two slower, and I would have been torn apart.

Magnus was shouting into my earpiece, but the explosion had sent my ears ringing fiercely.

The guard was up, and he kicked me in the ribs, surprisingly hard for such a small foot. He struck again, and his gaze scanned for his dropped gun. I took the blows.

Magnus was across the way, using the square ship's beam to pluck my friends from the courtyard. The tower was in shambles, rock spread out like an avalanche around everyone.

The alarms were ringing endlessly, adding to the noise

in my head, and as Magnus lifted them away, I reached out, grabbing the guard by the leg. I pulled him towards me and punched him in the visor, bending the slots. I hit him again, and he went limp, my hand aching.

More guards were pouring from the outside walls. They'd arrived from the pits. These ones had the jet packs, and I formed an idea.

"Over here, you scum!" I grabbed my pistol and fired at the group of half a dozen or so. I struck one and felt one of their bullets slice into my thigh as I dropped another two guards. My leg burned, but I pushed the pain away. If I was going to live another day, to see my wife and daughter again, I needed to forget the injury. It wasn't even there.

I ran behind a large chunk of rock that had fallen from Magnus' attack on the tower, and felt a half dozen shots hit the stone from the other side. I crawled along the ground, dragging my injured leg, and fired at the remaining three guards. I hit two: one a death shot, the other grazed a leg, but he dropped his weapon. I shot again, hitting his chest.

I had to steal one of their jet packs.

"Over here!" I yelled, trying to coax the last standing guard to come to me. I pressed myself against the rock, and finally, the ringing in my ears subsided.

"Dean! We're coming for you," Magnus said, and I forced a smirk.

"I'll meet you in the sky," I said, pushing to my feet. I fired the pistol, but nothing came out. It was spent. I guess it needed some Inlorian coil cores, because the charge hadn't lasted very long.

The Gatekeepers

The guard arrived, grinning at me. He lifted his visor, displaying strained red eyes. I peered to the ground, seeing the grass patch Slate had tucked his knife under when we first arrived. The guard fired, and I rolled, my hand pressing under the earth. I felt the cold steel of the blade and pulled it out, throwing it at the guard with every ounce of balance I could. It struck him in the center of the forehead, and he dropped.

With great effort, I stood up on my leg again, which was bleeding profusely at this point. "Almost done, almost done," I kept saying as I rolled the guard over, removing the jet pack from his shoulders. I strapped it on myself and fumbled with the controls. I'd used something like this before, but usually in space, where the rules of gravity didn't hinder me.

I lifted slowly, tilting too far forward. I tried again, only to find that I was angling too far sideways. I wondered if I was too heavy for the device, since the guards were all so small. I was two feet off the ground when more guards arrived. They searched around, trying to understand the destruction and dead bodies in the courtyard. Then they spotted me.

I wasn't even armed and felt the cold clutches of death coming closer. I fought the controls and lifted higher, and just as the guards took aim at me, prisoners rushed from inside the walls. My explosives had done their job. The prison cell's energy walls had failed, and the courtyard now flooded with angry inmates. They rushed the guards, taking the ten or so down in seconds. They cheered me as I slowly rose from the ground.

I waved at them as Magnus arrived, his tractor beam aiming for me.

"I'm in the air," I told him through the earpiece.

"Of course you are," he said with a laugh. Seconds later, he had me nabbed, and we lifted high into the sky, safe from the prison.

Smoke poured from the prison as we moved toward the portals. "What about the factories?" I asked, wishing we could affect the little buggy-eyed aliens even more. They were horrible people, imprisoning innocents for free labor. Loweck stared at the prison. She'd spent five years there. I couldn't imagine what she was feeling right now.

Slate put an arm around her and pulled her close. "Let's get out of here. Head for Haven," he said.

Pol and Dreb stayed close: new best friends, from the look of it.

My leg was wrapped up, and already I felt the skin healing. I didn't talk about it much, but I consistently healed faster than the average human, ever since Mae had transfused her blood into me after I'd been shot on a Kraski cube ship. Magnus had brought a medkit and the pain-dulling shot was working its magic too. I hobbled toward the portal stone and set the Modifier on the table.

"It's time to go home," I said, and Pol smiled widely. Even Dreb managed a grin, and he clapped Pol's back.

"Looks like you owe me a drink," Dreb told the prince.

The Gatekeepers

"Why?" I asked.

"I bet him you guys would come for us," Dreb said.

I was honestly a little hurt. "Pol, you didn't think we'd come?"

"It had been a month already. I was in a bad place," Pol said. He didn't even look like the same man we'd found in Fontem's collection, searching for the time-travel device.

"Fair enough, but you're one of us now. A Gatekeeper. We don't leave our own behind. Ever," I told him, and he nodded with resolve.

"What a start," Pol said. "What about the rest of our missing people? We want to help," he said.

"Spoken like a true Gatekeeper," Slate told them, and I pressed the icon for Haven.

SIXTEEN

"You didn't see anyone on the portal trip to Haven?" Mary asked. We were side-by-side on the couch in our penthouse, and Jules was fast asleep after running me ragged for hours after I returned home. I didn't mind spending time with my daughter. She'd almost been as worried about me as her mother had.

"No. What do you think it means?" I drank my cup of coffee and kept it cradled in my hands. I'd told her about the other version of me, the older one who'd warned me of things to come.

Don't let them die, Dean! My own voice echoed in my head, and I tried to shake the bad energy off.

"I think it might have been your own subconscious. Do you think you really time-traveled and spoke to yourself through a portal transition?" Mary asked. She wasn't judging, only asking, and I knew I was in a safe place beside her.

"It might have been. It looked like me. It felt like something I'd do." I laughed at my own comment.

"It does sound like you. Save who, though?" Mary's

eyes told me she knew.

"I think it involves you or Jules, or someone else very close to me. That's what Not-Dean told me." I took another sip of coffee. After ten or so days without it, the hot beverage was even better than I remembered it. It was also going to keep me up all night.

"I don't like you calling him that," she said.

"What? Not-Dean?" I asked.

"Exactly. It's creepy."

"So should I call him Old Dean, then?" I laughed again, and she slapped my arm.

"This is serious. If he… you… made it through the portal to talk to yourself, maybe the portals don't end up dying out," she said.

"I hadn't thought of it like that. Who knows? I'm beat. Do you think we could change the subject?" I set my cup onto the table, and she leaned into me. I accommodated, wrapping my arms around her as she relaxed. I kissed the top of her head. She smelled like home.

"I'm just glad to see you. We were so worried about you guys. Ableen was a wreck. She just met Karo and then he was gone. It's clear how she feels about him," Mary told me.

I lifted my eyebrows. "Is that so?"

"It is."

"You know Loweck?"

"The orange woman Slate couldn't stop praising?" It was obvious Mary knew what I was going to say.

"Slate's in love with her. At least, I think he is. Also…" I paused for dramatic effect.

"Go on."

"She's a cyborg," I finished.

Mary didn't reply for a second. "A cyborg? What is that, exactly?"

"Part Rescap, that's her race name, and part robot. Her story is amazing." I told Mary about her village being invaded, and how she was found and repaired. Years later, her ship from Udoon was debilitated outside the prison world, and she was the last of her organic crew to survive.

"She's been through a lot. I hope we can give her some peace at Haven." Mary always had a huge heart, and I pulled her in a little tighter as we lay there on the couch.

"She can also kick some serious butt. It was like watching Bruce Lee beat up three-foot-tall ugly aliens," I told her.

"Another reason for Slate to like her. You think he'll do anything about it?" she asked.

"Who knows with that guy? I think it's time. But a cyborg? I'll talk to him," I said.

"What's tomorrow? We bring you to New Spero with the kids, then head out on our trip to the next two missing Gatekeepers?" Mary asked.

I hated the idea of them leaving us behind and heading into danger.

"Can you and Nat do me a favor?" I asked.

Mary spun around slowly, looking up at me from my chest. "Depends on what you're asking."

"Can you bring Dreb and Pol with you? Or at least Dreb?" I didn't know if this would go over well. "They want to help."

"They can help by learning from you. Plus, all they managed to do was get captured by the prison guards and thrown behind bars," she said, implying the two rookies would be more in the way than helpful.

"If you recall, Mary Lafontaine-Parker," I started, and used her old last name hyphenated in there for emphasis, "Slate and I were also captured and thrown into cells."

"That doesn't help your cause. You're basically saying that you're all ineffective." Mary was prodding me, but in a playful way.

I nodded and smirked at her. "True. Good thing we had Magnus with us… and…" I had an idea, and hoped Mary would run with it.

"I know that look. I can literally see the cogs spinning behind those eyes of yours, Dean," she told me.

"Take Loweck with you."

"Dean…"

"Hear me out. She's a woman, and if you're doing this No-Men-Allowed club, she fits the criteria. Honestly, I'll feel better knowing she's there with you three. Magnus will too," I admitted.

"What about Slate?"

"He can wait until you return to ask her out on a date. He's waited this long, what's another day or two?" I asked.

"And if it's longer? What if something happens?" she asked, her face turned serious.

"Then we'll come for you." I kissed her on the forehead, and she relaxed into me again.

"I know."

"Then it's settled? Loweck goes with you?" I asked.

"Fine. As long as the others accept her, and she wants to come. We can't force her to do this. Plus, she's only been free from prison like, a day."

"Technically two."

Mary didn't take the bait. We lay there for another hour, talking about the little things that meant so much to us. It was the best time I'd had in a while.

The trip to New Spero had been uneventful, and as discussed, Loweck was heading out with Natalia, Mary, and Ableen for the rescue of Bee and Da-Narp from the Oryan system. Ableen didn't sense the same disturbance as before when we used the portal, but she also said it was almost as if the Theos inside weren't there. She felt none of their energy or attention. It didn't feel like a good sign.

"You know how to use the Crystal Map and Modifier, right?" I asked from outside the caves at Terran Five. "I wish we'd held on to the other end of the communicator." It had been lost when our belongings were confiscated at the prison, along with our custom EVAs. Good thing we'd had the common sense to have alternates made.

"Me too. We need to check with Clare on a few priorities. Communication across millions of light years is something we desperately need these days," Mary said.

The four women appeared ready for battle in their EVAs. They carried pulse rifles and supplies for three weeks' survival with them. Loweck and Slate chatted for a moment to the side, and Jules was standing beside her mother.

"I want go," she said, sticking her lower lip out in a classic pout.

I scooped her up and stood beside Mary. "Mommy will be right back. And you get to stay with Daddy," I told her.

Jules' eyes were welling up with tears. "But Papa go and no come back."

"Honey, I'm here now. And Mommy will be home soon," I said.

Magnus and the kids were seeing Nat off, and soon the women were all gathered. Karo reached out and grabbed Ableen's hand. "Be careful."

"I will," she told him, and with that, they were off.

We watched them as they entered the caves, and Jules let out a whimper. I stroked her hair and knew what would spruce her up. "Let's pick up Maggie, and then we can go home. Do you want to see your doggie?"

She squealed that she did, and I told the guys I'd meet them at Terran One.

My trip to Isabelle's was uneventful, and when we arrived, my sister greeted us. Maggie was thrilled to see me and Jules, and she wiggled around like only a cocker spaniel could.

"You were gone longer than we thought," Isabelle said, without a hint of scolding.

"I'm sorry, sis. Was Maggie good?" I glanced at Isabelle and couldn't believe how far along her pregnancy was.

"She was fine. Have you spoken to Leonard yet?" she asked, and I saw the worry in her face.

"No. Why?"

"The killer seems to have moved on. He's in Terran One. There have been at least five people missing since the lander was taken. This is bad, Dean," she told me.

Terran One. I hated the idea of a killer on the loose near my home. I forced a smile. "We'll figure it out. I'll talk to Leonard and see what they're doing to catch this guy."

I thought of the footage of Soloma the Gatekeeper waltzing through our portal from a few months ago. I needed to find out if he was ever located. In my head, the two distinctly different issues were possibly related, or he'd also been murdered by the killer.

We talked for a few minutes longer over a cup of coffee, and Jules and I left with Maggie in tow. She was only too happy to be heading home, and so was I. If Mary had been with us, it would have been better. They swore they'd return after rescuing Bee and Da-Narp, leaving only one group of Gatekeepers left stranded. We'd bring them home too, then I'd have to settle my deal with Ableen. We'd find a way to release the Theos from their commitment.

As I lowered the lander toward our home in Terran One, I thought about Not-Dean's words about the portals. *The portals are dying, Dean. But there is a way to keep everything going.*

Perhaps it would come clear soon enough, but I wasn't so sure. Tonight, we planned on hanging out. The kids could watch a movie, and Karo, Slate, and Magnus could come over and eat a steak at my house. I'd invite Leonard too. As much as I didn't want to think about work, or portals, or killers on the loose, I knew it was inevitable. It was my destiny.

We settled to the ground, and I instantly knew something was wrong.

The hunter had been well-fed over the last few weeks. His nest was perfect, but he knew he'd have to clean it up. The owners would eventually show up, and then he'd be able to take the young girl. He'd consume her flesh and embody her. Yes. Those green eyes. He stared at the picture in the frame every day and didn't know why he sought her vessel.

She was small, weak, but he sensed the power behind her. She was different. Special. He scratched at his beard. His latest kill was tall, broad-shouldered. He'd been working at a construction site two miles away; building a barn, from the looks of it. The man hadn't expected the hunter to kill. He now used weapons, which were a new concept to him.

Through the minds of his victims, he'd determined a knife could puncture skin and disable a person quickly. That was what he'd done to the large man, whose eyes had sprung open as the steel entered him. Surely the slender female in front of him couldn't really be doing this?

The others had been more for sustenance, but the hunter wanted a big vessel for the time being. He felt strong and oddly comforted in the shape of the last kill.

The hunter attempted to clean his nest and was satisfied he'd done a fair job. It was time to stretch his abilities and enter the city. He'd put it off for too long.

He stood in the house's doorway and tested his voice, which was functioning better with each day. "Hello. I am Stan," he said, attempting to smile. He bared his teeth and thought it was a good representation of a human interaction. "The sun is hot."

He kept saying short phrases he'd picked up from the brains he'd consumed, and from listening to a pair of farmers a mile over. He hadn't killed the man and woman. Instead, he'd used them to comprehend speech patterns.

With a glance at his new nest, the hunter – or Stan, as he now thought of himself – strolled down the gravel driveway, and onto the road. The city was huge, reminding him of the mountain ranges at home, but with peaks and valleys of man-made structures. It was beautiful to the hunter, but also unsettling and terrifying. He wasn't meant to be here and wondered if there was any way for him to ever go home.

Home was bleak. Food was hard to come by, his race all but vanished over the years. Here, he could thrive.

His instincts made him place one foot in front of the other, and he directed himself toward the tall buildings. The sun had moved a great deal by the time Stan arrived at the edge of the city. The changes were subtle but obvious. The roads went from dirt to gravel to a hard surface. The houses grew closer together along the outskirts, no longer farmland.

Parks were erected, and small children played, their noises unsettling to Stan's ears. At first, he thought they'd seen him and knew that he was a predator, that he'd eat them, but then he realized they were playing. His people didn't play, even as small hatchlings.

He kept walking, ever toward the center of town, to the tallest of structures. He was curious to see them in person, up close.

Something beeped at him, a soft honk of a horn, and he spun to see a four-wheeled vehicle. He scanned Stan's mind to determine the word. A woman sitting in the jeep waved him to the side. Stan ushered himself to the sidewalk and waved at her in a friendly gesture. Existing among humans was going to be a trial.

From the looks of the children, it would be easier to hide among them. They were tended to, fed, and cared for, and their parents didn't expect them to speak or interact on a normal human level. The girl with the green eyes was going to be perfect.

Stan moved toward the downtown core, and the further he went into the city, the more people were on the sidewalks, walking from place to place. They walked with beverages in cups, some talking to one another, others passing by without a thought for the people around them. Stan tried to emulate those people, but their clothing was different. *More formal*, he heard Stan's brain tell him. They worked, held "jobs," a concept he didn't quite understand.

"Excuse me," a voice said as a man bumped into Stan. His first instinct was to rip the man's throat out and consume his flesh and bones. He held it in and attempted a smile. The man stepped away as if afraid.

"Hello. I am Stan," the hunter said, and the man straightened black frames around his eyes. Glasses. He was shorter by half a head, and had thick, dark curly hair.

"I'm Leonard. Are you okay? Do you need help?" Leonard asked him.

Stan shook his head. "The sun is hot today," he said, using a variation of his practiced phrases.

The man glanced up to the sky. "Yeah. It's a nice day out. Have a good one, Stan." Leonard stepped around him, leaving Stan alone on the sidewalk.

Maybe he could get used to this. Be a human. Live among them and stop feeding so much. Become a friend to people like Leonard.

He sniffed the air, spotting a woman entering an alley. His instincts took over. No. The hunter knew he'd never be one of them. He was something far different. And he was hungry.

He followed his prey, where the two of them could be alone.

SEVENTEEN

The door was ajar, and Maggie ran out from the lander before I could stop her. She made for the house, barking the entire way.

"Maggie!" Jules shouted at the dog.

"Maggie, stop!" I yelled now, but she kept going, pushing through the doorway. "Crap." I searched the trunk of the lander and found a rifle. "Jules, Daddy will be right back," I told her, leaving her in the modified car seat. Her green eyes were wide, scared, and startled. Maggie's barking stopped, and I feared the worst.

I ran for my house, calling for Maggie. The porch had muddy footsteps caked on it, and the door didn't appear to be broken here, but it wasn't closed. I scanned the windows and didn't see anything shattered. "If anyone's inside, come out now. I have you surrounded and I'm armed." I waited two minutes, and when no one replied, I pushed the door open with my boot.

Maggie barked once, running for me, and I jumped as she startled me. The dog was fine, but she let out a whine and turned to face the inside of the house, emitting a low growl.

It was clear someone had been inside. It was filthy. There were fragments of bones on the floor in the living room, and at first I thought maybe an animal had made its way inside. The entire place smelled musty, like the stink of rotting meat and a wild beast. I stepped slowly through the small farmhouse, glad none of us had been home when something invaded our property.

I found the rear door open too, the frame and handle busted. This wasn't the work of an animal, at least not a four-legged one. Maggie stayed close now, her growl non-stop as we explored each room. It was a mess, but there was no sign of anyone currently inside. I reached the wall and used my screen to call Magnus. I needed backup.

I lowered the saw and lifted the safety glasses, admiring my straight cut. "You know I always wanted to start a woodworking side hustle on Earth," I told Slate.

He laughed. "Dean Parker making furniture. Sounds hilarious."

"It's not that funny. What about you? Any hobbies I don't know about?" I asked my friend. I was pretty sure there were no surprises left there.

"I didn't have much time to think about it. I joined the military so young," he said, picking up the door jamb. He used the air compressor gun to tack it into place, and stood to appreciate the repaired entrance. The smell in the house remained, but we'd opened all the windows to alleviate some of the stench.

"Drones are all set up." Magnus arrived from the front of the house. "Anyone or anything shows up within two hundred yards of here, you'll know it."

"Good. Thanks, Mag." I clapped him on the shoulder. He passed me a tablet that showed the active drones hovering in the air above our complex.

"This is messed up. You leave for a couple weeks and your house is being lived in by… whatever the hell did this," he said.

The tablet chimed, and an image appeared of a white SUV approaching the driveway. That would be Leonard.

I tapped it to silence the alert. "Leonard's here. Maybe he has some insight."

Karo exited the door from inside the house. His long white hair was braided, and he was wearing lipstick and a botched job of eye liner. "What was that alarm?" he asked, glancing around. The cords on his neck were tight, and he appeared ready to fight.

The three of us stood there gaping at him, and Slate broke first, bending over in laughter. "What happened to you?"

Karo appeared confused before realizing Slate meant the makeup. "The kids were playing." He wiped at his lips, leaving red streaks on his gray hand. "Never mind this. What was the alarm?"

I peered inside the house to see Jules with a tiara on, and Patty was walking around in one of Mary's dresses. It dragged behind her as she strutted around. Little Dean was doing his best to ignore what his sister and cousin were doing.

"Leonard's here, Karo. Mag has the drone system set up so we'll know if this… invader comes again," I told him.

Karo nodded, and I heard the SUV door shut. Seconds later, Leonard was walking toward us, smiling wide. All three dogs ran out from the house and toward Leonard, barking. Carey was last, trudging along, but looking five years younger than he really was. Maggie and her brother Charlie ran circles around Leonard as he neared, and my friend stopped to pet each of them in turn. He smiled widely as he approached.

"Guys, so good to see you," he said. "And that was quite the greeting." His face went somber. "I tried to reach you every day, Dean."

"My communicator was taken when we were imprisoned," I told him.

"What? Imprisoned?" Leonard asked.

Slate waved a dismissive hand. "No biggie. I did lose those five pounds I've been meaning to shed," he said, and Karo shook his head.

I focused on Leonard. "I'll tell you about it later. For now, I need to know what's happening with your search for the missing Gatekeeper. The Shimmali named Soloma."

Leonard was in the newest version of a suit. The pants were made from a local tree, Proxima's version of bamboo. The material was breathable, and he looked comfortable even in the mid-afternoon heat. No one wore a tie any longer, and that was a tradition I was glad to be rid of. "We never found him."

"Do you think he's gone?" Mag asked.

"Gone?" Leonard shifted on his feet.

"Dead," Magnus clarified.

I cut in. "I have a theory."

Everyone went quiet, and the five of us moved from the doorway inside. Mag went to the fridge and grabbed a six-pack of locally-brewed Terran Fourteen beer, sliding one to each of us.

"Go on," Slate urged.

I wiped my sweating brow and took a drink. "It's going to sound a little insane, but hear me out."

When they all nodded, I continued. "Soloma comes to New Spero. We don't know where he traveled from, but we could probably find out using the Crystal Map, right?"

Karo nodded first, following along.

"Sally wasn't seen with him, so I'm going to assume she didn't make it," I said.

"We could look for her," Slate suggested.

"And we will, but first, we need to figure this out. Soloma ends up here… it had to be randomly, since the portals are all haywire. He stumbled around, wearing what appeared to be an undersized uniform, which we've identified as Sally's from the footage. There was blood. I imagine we won't find Sally in one piece.

"Soloma looked possessed." I glanced at Jules, who was on the floor of the living room, coloring in a book beside Patty. The two of them were so cute together. I couldn't believe she'd been carried by Mary as she was possessed by the Iskios.

"Dean?" Karo tapped my shoulder.

I shook my head, returning my attention to my story. "Sorry. Where was I?"

"Possessed," Slate offered.

"Right. Soloma was messed up, which tells me he arrived here by accident. Then people and animals started going missing around Terran Five. We can assume he might have something to do with that. Then," I started, my voice going an octave higher, "you have a lander go missing, with two of our people vanished. The lander tracking is cut, so there's no way to find it."

"We did find it," Leonard said.

"Let me guess. Not far from here?" I asked, and Slate's eyes jumped open.

"Wait… why didn't you tell us?" Slate asked.

"I wasn't sure."

It was Leonard's turn to be confused. "What are you talking about? Sure about what?"

"Someone was living in my house while we were gone. It was… like a nest. There were pieces of animals, or possibly humans, near the fireplace. It was so pungent in here. I kept the remains so we can have them tested," I told him.

Leonard sat on one of the island's stools, running his hand through his thick curly hair. "This is crazy. There have been at least another five missing persons reported around here over the last few weeks. One of them…" Leonard stood straight up like his pants were on fire.

"What?" Magnus asked him.

"Stan. One of them was named Stan. The missing person. He lived about four miles from here," Leonard told us.

Magnus frowned and rubbed his forehead with a big hand. "Stan? Stan Weaver?"

Leonard nodded.

"Crap. I know him. He helped me dig my cistern years ago. Great guy," Mag said.

"His wife reported him missing eleven days ago," Leonard told us. "Then today, I was downtown heading to the office when I stumbled into this man. He was tall, thick dark stubble, wide as an ox." Leonard glanced at Magnus, then Slate. "Kind of like you two," he said.

"Sounds like him," Mag said. "That's good. He's alive."

"No. Something was wrong with him. He spoke in a strange accent, and he walked…" Leonard's gaze went distant.

I finished for him. "He walked like Soloma had when he emerged from the caves at Terran Five."

"Yes. Exactly. He said the strangest things. He told me his name was Stan, like a kid might tell you how many fingers old he is," Leonard said. "And his smell. It was… overwhelming. There are a few people living on the outskirts that live a little… differently, so I didn't over think it."

"Musty, like the den of a bear?" I asked, recalling the powerful scent when I'd first stepped into my violated home.

"Yeah, like the den of a bear. He also said something else… what was it?" He sipped his beer, deep in thought. "'The sun is hot today'."

"The sun is hot today?" Karo asked. "Isn't the sun

always hot?"

"Yeah, but that's why it struck me as so strange. The whole thing was weird," Leonard said.

"So we have a better idea now. We're dealing with a virus, perhaps?" Magnus suggested.

I tilted my head side to side, cracking my stiff neck. I took another sip of my beer as I considered this. "I'm not sure. It appears to have some sort of a learning personality. Maybe it's more of a parasite than a virus." The three dogs were sleeping on the cool floor, all in a row, on their sides. It had taken them a while to calm in the house, where they could still smell the intruder's presence.

Karo chimed in, "I've heard of something like this before. Rubic III had a race of small, peanut-sized bugs that would crawl into the mouths of sleeping animals, fixing themselves to the creatures' brains and effectively taking over, like a puppeteer."

"They *had* a race like that? As in, past tense?" I asked.

"Yes. We ended up destroying every last one." Karo averted his eyes, as if he was ashamed of his people's actions.

"You don't have to apologize to us. I'm sure the universe is better off without brain-sucking aliens," Slate said. "You guys did the right thing."

"We know some made it off-planet on space ships, and they could have expanded out there, propagating. Could you imagine a race like that being loosed somewhere like Udoon Station, or Bazarn Five for that matter?" Karo asked.

I shuddered, thinking about one of the parasites being

inside my house. "We did a clean sweep of the house and didn't find anything. But now you have me worried about the kids." I glanced at the three of them and smiled as Dean picked up a crayon and showed Jules how to color a duck properly.

"I have an organic sensor Clare gave me years ago somewhere in my garage. I'll find it in a bit," Magnus said.

"Of course you do." I laughed, clinking my beer bottle to his. "Where does this leave us? If this is a parasite, why is it killing so many?"

"We don't know that he's killing them," Leonard said.

"But so far no bodies, right?" Slate asked.

"Right."

"That means he's killing them. Consuming, perhaps?" I asked.

Karo tapped a long finger on the countertop. "These parasites didn't do that. They could live in a vessel for as long as the body functioned, which could be years and years. The vessel only ate what they would normally eat to stay strong."

"Then it has to be something else. Something dangerous," I said. I hated that the thing had been inside my home, of all places. But at least that gave me the drive to find it and kill it. "Leonard, can you call your friends in high places and ask them to find the footage of Stan? You remember where you were, and what time it was?"

He nodded. "Yeah, close enough. I'll call the city office now. Clay has access to all the cameras. He'll shoot it right over." Leonard crossed the room and used the console to contact his friend.

"As if we don't have enough on our plate," Magnus said, looking at his kids playing with mine. "All while the wives are off on a fun excursion."

"The wives?" I glanced at Slate, who took the comment in stride. "You do realize our last two trips of gallivanting ended with us being chased by Misters, then being imprisoned? I mean, Slate, Karo, and I literally worked in a rock pit for weeks."

Magnus nodded. "And you seem like you're almost rehabilitated now." He punched me in the arm and guffawed. Only Magnus could pull off a true guffaw.

"What's the deal with you and Loweck anyway, Slate?" Magnus asked the younger man.

Slate shrugged. "I don't know. I like her."

"You do know she…" Magnus started.

"I know, she's part robot. But she has her own mind." Slate focused on his beer.

"I was going to say that she could kick your butt. I don't really care if you're dating a cactus, as long as you're happy," Magnus said, surprising even me. These two were always quick to get on one another's nerves, and it was rare for Magnus to say something so kind to Slate.

"Thanks, Mag. Appreciate it." Slate took a drink.

"Sure. I'll stand by my statement. From what I hear, she'd give Van Damme a show," Magnus said.

Karo remained noticeably quiet. "What about you, big guy?" Magnus turned to the Theos man. "Ableen is quite a catch. Do I hear wedding bells?"

Karo smirked at me and took the bait. "The Theos do not partake in such barbaric ceremonies."

"Barbaric?" Magnus asked, standing up straight like he was about to defend the sanctity of our tradition. He broke into a laugh and loosened up. "You're probably right. Plus, the Theos would know better. You've been around a lot longer than us."

I saw Karo's face change. He was upset about being the last of his kind, and even having Ableen around wasn't enough to cheer him up for long. His people's life forces were inside the portal stones, and we'd promised to release them. "It's going to work out," I said quietly.

Leonard ran over, holding a tablet in his palm. "Clay found it. Check this out." He set the device on the countertop, and we all leaned over it. "There he is." Leonard pointed to a big, lumbering man. His shirt was filthy, his pants torn. He walked how I imagined Frankenstein's monster would carry himself through the streets of Terran One. People shifted out of his way on the sidewalk, and he stopped every now and then to peer at the buildings.

The camera changed, and we saw him from the front, dark bags under his eyes. Then he stumbled into Leonard. We watched the incident without volume, but knew enough from Leonard's recount of the story.

Then Leonard was off, leaving Stan alone. "Where did he go?" I asked.

The camera showed Stan sniffing the air, and he headed into an alley.

"Any cameras positioned there?" Mag asked.

Leonard shook his head. "No. They lost him after that. Clay's searching, though."

I used my finger, sliding the bar on the bottom of the

tablet back half an inch. I played it at half speed. "I think I saw something." I paused it, zooming past Stan to the entrance of the alley. "A woman went into the alley. I think he followed her."

Leonard went white. "I know her. That's Amy from Human Resources."

"Call the office. Find out if she's there." I had a bad feeling she hadn't returned from lunch.

"Looks like we have a job to do." Slate clenched his fists, and I nodded.

"Who's going to look after the kids?" Magnus asked, and all of our gazes landed on the Theos man beside us. His hair remained braided, and his lips held a tinge of their former red glory.

He raised his hands in the air and shook his head. "Dibs out."

EIGHTEEN

The last piece of pizza sat cold in the box on the coffee table, and we sat around, music softly playing in the background. If we weren't discussing finding a killer staking Terran One, with an ancient alien in our midst, I could have sworn we were on Earth, shooting the breeze after watching the Yankees win a playoff game.

Empty beer bottles littered the kitchen countertop, and I was amazed how far New Spero had come. We'd actually ordered three pizzas and had them delivered via drone to my home. Karo had watched the incoming food with a vested interest that made us all laugh.

"I think humans are one of the most evolved beings out there," Karo said from his spot beside Slate on the couch.

"Why do you say that?" Slate burped, reaching for his beer.

"Despite your... belching and unusual traditions... you have found a way to outsource pizza production, and then a robot brings it to your home. That is far above anything the Theos accomplished," Karo said, with only a hint of a joke.

"You found a way to power crystals that allow people to traverse the stars with the blink of an eye," I told him.

"Yes, but... pizza." He reached for the last piece, and I shook my head.

"I don't know where it all goes," I told him.

Leonard was in the kitchen, trying to find out more about the city office's missing HR person. Amy hadn't returned, and we knew why. The kids were sound asleep in Jules' room. We decided sticking together would see us through the next couple days. The children were happy about it – even Dean, who was used to being outnumbered by his little sister and Jules.

"Wait... they found her," Leonard said, rushing into the living room. He flipped the tablet, and showed us.

"That's her?" Slate asked, squinting.

It was dark, and the camera was giving us a feed of night vision. "It's her. I think" – Leonard zoomed, and there was a dark blotch on her shirt – "that's blood."

"So what? It kills the next victim and takes her over? Then there should be remains of Stan somewhere, right? If it hops bodies?" I asked.

"Presumably," Magnus said. "I'll make some calls. We can meet the local PDs tomorrow morning first thing."

Magnus used to run the New Spero defense force, and his name still carried a lot of power around here. He'd claimed mine was even more mystical, and was probably right.

Slate cracked his knuckles. "So we search the city center tomorrow, locate its whereabouts, and take it down?"

"Exactly," I said. "Speaking of which, I think we'd better call it a night if we're going to stop a killer in the morning. I'm sorry the house isn't larger. Someone can share my room with me, but I have to warn you I have cold feet."

No one laughed at my joke, and Karo said he'd sleep there as long as Mary didn't mind. We settled on pulling a cot out, meeting halfway. I offered to take the cot, since Karo was far taller than I was.

Slate found a home on the couch, and Magnus had brought cots from home, laying them out for Leonard and himself. Carey and Charlie stayed in the living room with Magnus, and Maggie followed me to my bedroom.

Minutes later, I was on the cot, staring at the ceiling, wondering what strange things had to occur in my life to end up chasing an alien murderer on a colony world, with a seven-foot-tall alien sleeping in my bed instead of me. Dean Parker's story was one even I couldn't believe at times. Maggie curled up between my legs near my feet, and was already breathing deeply, the day too much for her. Somehow the two of us still fit on the compact bed.

"Dean, are you awake?" Karo asked, his voice a quiet whisper.

"Can't sleep?" I asked him.

"No. I'm worried."

"About what?" I asked, knowing there were a few things on the man's mind.

"Ableen. Then the Theos in the stones. We really don't want to lose our method of moving between our worlds. There's so much to see out there. Now that we have the Crystal Map, we've found so much more than we ever knew. How can we lose that?" he asked.

"I don't know. Ableen can feel their need to move on. And I think I can too," I admitted.

"You're right. I wish there were another way. Will you be there when we disable them? Will you help us?" he asked.

"I will."

"Good," Karo said. "Dean, there's something I haven't told you."

My heart raced, but I didn't let him know that. "What is it?"

"I know how to release them. I wasn't sure I wanted to do it before, but if we're going to, there is a way."

"You mean we won't need to hit every stone to do it?" I honestly had been dreading the logistics of the mission. In my head, it could have taken a lifetime to release the Theos, especially if we needed to fly between portal worlds.

"The control crystal is on my home world," he told me. "You remember?"

I'd visited his planet once, when I was searching for the Theos' help to rescue Mary from the clutches of the evil Iskios. "I remember, all right. We can shut it off from there?"

"Yes." Karo's voice was low. "The apex of the crystal cluster lies high in the mountains. That is where a highly concentrated number of Theos poured themselves into the stones. We can shut off the entire system from there, freeing every last bit of their energy. The whole map as we know it will cease to exist."

"Then you and I will go there and release them when

we have the last of our Gatekeepers. Deal?" I asked.

"Deal. You're a good man, Dean Parker," he said.

"So are you," I told him. "But whatever you're thinking, I'm not singing you to sleep."

He laughed, and moments later, Karo was snoring softly. It wasn't long until the sound lulled me to sleep.

Slate stood with the shortest straw in his grasp, and he frowned. "I'm not staying here!"

Magnus barked a laugh. "Slate, you drew the short straw. That means you're the sitter."

"What about Karo? He's much better at this kid stuff than I am," Slate argued.

"Jules loves you. And maybe you can teach Dean some fighting techniques," I told him, and finally, he calmed and nodded slowly.

"I do like the idea of shaping his young mind," Slate said.

Magnus poked a finger at Slate's chest. "Make sure you don't hurt him. And don't let Patty eat any dairy."

Slate scribbled his instructions on a pad of paper. "Anything else?"

"Yeah. Keep them alive," Magnus added. "You have the drone system set up, so you'll know if anyone's returning to their nest."

I shuddered as he called my house the creature's nest. "Let's avoid naming it that. Thanks. Slate, you're going to be fine. And don't worry about us. What I need from you is to watch the kids for us. We're counting on you. Okay?"

"I won't let you down, boss," Slate said firmly.

Jules ran up to him and tugged on his finger. Maggie followed behind my daughter, hoping the girl would drop a piece of the toast she was slowly eating. "Zeke," she said. "Play dollies."

Slate's eyes met mine "Zeke?" he whispered at me, and I smiled widely.

"Fine. But we're going to play Gatekeepers, not tea party," he said with finality, and set off toward the living room.

Dean appeared in the kitchen and was wearing a deep frown. "Dad, I want to go with you." He crossed his arms.

Magnus shook his head. "Kid, we're going somewhere dangerous. You have to stay and watch over your sister and Jules." He jerked a thumb toward Slate. "And keep an eye on this guy too."

"But, Dad…"

"No buts. Your mother is away, and I'm in charge."

Magnus led the way outside, and Leonard, Karo, and I followed. It was chilly out this morning, the sky overcast, and light rain fell as if an ominous portent of what was coming. I pushed the worry aside. With any luck, we'd track the thing Amy was carrying by lunch time, and we could go home.

Maybe the women would even be finished saving the next twosome of Gatekeepers by then. One could dream big.

"We ready?" Leonard asked. Instead of taking his SUV,

he'd opted for calling in a police transport. It landed in the back yard, the lights and siren turned off.

Jules was on the porch with Dean and Patty beside her, Slate standing protectively behind the three kids. Maggie started to follow me onto the pathway to the police vehicle, and I had to tell her to stay. She cocked her head to the side but understood, running over to Jules' side. The other spaniels were hiding on the porch in the shade, staying out of the already hot sunlight.

"Ready as we'll ever be." The lander door opened, and a woman stepped out. Her hair was cut short and she was wearing oversized aviator sunglasses.

"Which one of you is Leonard?" she asked.

He raised a hand and stepped forward.

"Good. I've been instructed by Mayor Patel to make sure your group is provided with whatever they need. I understand you have a line on the guy that's been going around killing people?" she asked.

"We think so," I told her.

She lifted her sunglasses and stopped a foot away from me, entering my personal space. I forced myself to stand my ground. "And who are you?"

"Dean Parker," I said, seeing the flash of recognition.

"Never heard of you," she said, and Magnus laughed.

"What about you, big guy?" the policewoman asked. I saw her name etched into her uniform. Reed.

"Magnus," he said.

"Just Magnus, no surname?" she asked, standing before the large Scandinavian.

"For today, Magnus will do fine," he said with a big

smile.

I had the feeling she knew exactly who we were; she was just toying with us. I wasn't sure if I appreciated that.

"And who's this piece of work?" she asked Karo, who glanced over at me.

"Look, can we go?" I asked, moving past the introductions. "You're supposed to help us, then fly us into the city. We have a killer to find."

"Fine. Have it your way, Parker," she said, and I saw the hint of a smile. "I'm Reed."

"What, no first name?" Magnus mumbled as he entered the police transport.

"Very funny. How does that lovely wife of yours put up with you?" she asked.

So she did know who we were. "Reed. Nice to meet you. Downtown?" I urged, and she moved to the front of the ship and sat in the pilot's seat.

I peered out the side window and waved at Jules, who was waving both hands to see us off. I loved that little girl with all of my heart. She was the perfect blend of Mary's grace and beauty, and my stubbornness and curiosity.

"Downtown it is," Reed said. "What do we know about the perp?"

Leonard took this one. "We think the *perp* is from another world. They might be transferring from one vessel to another."

"Vessel?" Reed asked as she raised us higher from the surface. The skyscrapers of Terran One were already visible in the viewer.

"Bodies. The target is killing its prey, then taking the

bodies," I explained.

"Then there has to be a corpse, right?" Reed asked. She was catching on quick.

"That's what we're going to find out. The local PD did a quick scan last night, but they came up empty-handed," Magnus said.

"And you expect to find more than they did?" Reed pressed.

"No. But they didn't have all the information," I said.

"You're the boss," she told me, and Magnus frowned.

"Leonard, they didn't find her on any other feeds?" Magnus asked, indicating Amy, the missing HR woman we'd seen emerge from the alley.

"No. She must have avoided the cameras," Leonard told him.

"She could be anywhere," I said.

"Dean, if this is the same creature that was living in your house, do you think it would return?" Karo asked the question everyone had been thinking.

"I don't know. I can't presume to understand its motivation. I'd have to speculate, which can be a dangerous game," I said.

Karo leaned forward. "And if you were going to speculate?"

"I'd think the creature used my place as a nest to grow stronger and be sheltered, but then moved on. If no one from the city had been missing before yesterday, that means it was living in my house and feeding. Now it's migrated. I doubt it'll risk such predictable behavior. And we have the drones activated, and Slate's with the kids," I said.

Magnus rubbed his forehead. "We should have parked them at my house for the day. Should we call Slate and suggest it?"

I didn't know. My gut was telling me there was nothing to worry about, but the others seemed concerned enough for all of us. "I don't think that's necessary." I tapped Reed on the shoulder. "Reed, can you send another transport to my house and have them stay until we arrive?"

Reed nodded and tapped on her console as she directed over the city.

"Where do we land?" I asked, looking out the side window to see birds we'd brought from Earth flying high over the spires of our civilization.

Leonard smiled. "City Hall. You're going to love the view."

We settled onto the highest building in sight, and the lander's door hissed open. A cool breeze pushed into the cramped vessel. "My partner's on the way to watch your house and kids."

"Thanks, Reed. I appreciate it," I told her, and she waited for us to exit before standing up.

I gasped as I saw the view of Terran One from here. It wasn't often I was surprised, especially after having seen views from so many worlds, in orbit, from space, from mountaintops, and below ground, but this was spectacular. An ocean expanded in the distance on one side, and from the other, the metropolis spread out beyond the horizon.

"It's amazing," Karo said from his spot beside me. The wind blew his long white hair as he neared the edge of the rooftop landing pad. I joined him, holding on to the glass

The Gatekeepers

railing.

"That's the symphony hall, there's the medical research facility, and the biggest library on New Spero." Leonard pointed out landmarks, and I realized how little I knew about our new home.

"You've all done such a great job bringing this to life," I said. "I remember when we first arrived here, years after you, Magnus." He grunted, likely remembering those years he and Natalia thought Mary and I were dead. "The roads were gravel, and we were only beginning to build three-story buildings. We went to the store and used credit to purchase supplies for our garden." I gripped the railing tightly. So much had changed, and not only in our lives. The lives of all humanity had transformed at the same time, and being away for most of it, I was detached from New Spero.

Reed was behind us, and she set a hand on my shoulder. "Dean, this would be impossible without what you guys did for us all. I remember hearing your name whispered on Vessel Thirteen."

I turned to her. "Wait, you were on Thirteen?" That was the vessel that Katherine Adams had saved. "Did you know Kate?"

"Kate… she was Mrs. Adams to us, and she was the only reason we made it long enough to be rescued. I volunteered to be on the police force she created. I was only nineteen." Reed stared out at the view.

"Thank you, Reed. You did a great service," Magnus told her.

"Nothing compared to what you all did. Wasn't there

another of you? A fifth?" she asked.

She had to mean Mae, but I shook my head, not wanting to discuss it. "We only did what we needed to, like you did."

She nodded, her eyes hidden behind her dark lenses. Her personality snapped into place, the character of Officer Reed. "If we're done with the sightseeing, let's put you on the trail of this alien killer."

Leonard took us to the elevator and set a thumb on the screen, accessing it. The elevator accommodated all of us, and Karo and I stood beside one another, watching through the glass wall as we descended from the top of City Hall to ground level.

I honestly had no need for days of the week any longer, but I saw the streets emptier than I expected. "What day is it?" I asked.

Reed answered, "Saturday. To the right, there's a market going on. Handcrafted stuff, local produce, that kind of thing."

I glanced over, seeing people setting up booths across the City Hall courtyard. It felt so natural, but so foreign on New Spero. A farmer's market. I'd have to recommend Leslie and Terrance start one on Haven. It could be an intergalactic farmer's market. It would be a great way for the different races living amongst each other to learn about foods and culture from their neighbors.

The four of us were in street clothes, Karo in tall jeans and a long-sleeved shirt to attempt to blend in. He still looked like a gray giant with a white mane, but it was better than a Gatekeeper jumpsuit or something even more conspicuous. Magnus wore a t-shirt and jeans, and I was in an old pair of jeans and a polo. Leonard had his work clothes on from the day before, but seemed comfortable enough in them to walk through the hot morning in a blazer.

"Let me take the lead here. If people see you four wandering around with weapons, they might panic," Reed said. She was in her full New Spero police uniform, and I was suddenly grateful Slate wasn't here. She'd remind him too much of Denise, the police officer that had stolen his heart, then betrayed us to Lom of Pleva.

"This is the alley," Leonard said, pointing to the space between two tall structures. A café adorned the corner, and a few patrons watched us from the patio as we walked by, heading into the alleyway. I nodded at a couple, and they whispered to one another, obviously recognizing me.

It was strange to be out and about in a place where everyone knew you by your face. I wasn't used to it, and Mary claimed it was one of the reasons I preferred to isolate us at my old childhood home on Earth, in our farmhouse here, or at the penthouse on Haven, where we were nothing but a few more humans among the plethora of alien beings.

Reed pulled her gun out, an old Earth Glock. Bullets always did the job, and that was what the police were issued. I grabbed my pulse pistol, and Magnus and Karo unslung their rifles. Leonard stayed unarmed, but he held his tablet, marking out our path.

A hundred yards into the side street, police tape was wound around two light posts, but there were no officers in sight.

It didn't take long to see the markings left by the team. Reed pointed to a yellow plastic label on the ground. "This is where they found the blunt object, a rock."

"Where is it now?" I asked her.

"At the forensics lab," she said.

I didn't bother telling her it was pointless. We knew Stan had assaulted Amy, but now we needed to see if we could find either of them. We would detain Amy and find out what was living inside her, and study Stan to see what kind of damage the parasite had done to him.

We kept going, the trail of blood dripping for fifty yards; then, suddenly, there was no sign of anything nefarious. "He couldn't have disappeared," Magnus said, looking around the sterile alley.

I pointed to a doorway, the only entrance to the side of this particular building. "There," I suggested, and found the doorway unlocked. I nodded to Magnus, and he took the lead, entering first, his gun raised for a kill shot if needed.

"Nothing here," he said, and I followed him inside. We immediately descended a small flight of stairs and saw we were in a storage facility under a residence. Rows of half-empty cages were here, built for the occupants of the above suites to keep their possessions in. It was forward thinking, because most of the people on New Spero didn't own much, and what they did have was government-issued.

Capitalism was emerging, though, and slowly the world was returning to the greed-fueled one we'd left behind years ago after the Event. I couldn't say I loved that, but there was no other way to change a majority mindset. It was a balancing act, and I did think the government was doing a fair job.

I scanned through the storage cages and didn't see anything of use.

"We don't know they came in here," Karo said.

"You're right. Call it a hunch," I said. It had been the only doorway, and I was surprised the police hadn't looked in here. Or maybe they had, and we were wasting our time now.

Reed was halfway across the long room, dimly lit by the ceiling fixture, and she called for us. She was standing there pale as a ghost, and she pointed toward a golf cart stored beside a staircase leading up to the main floor.

"Dear God," Leonard said, moving his left hand over his mouth.

I sniffed the air. "That smell. It's the same one from my house. This is it." My gun was up, the steel pressing into my bare hand as I moved toward the crawlspace under the stairs.

Pieces of clothing were torn, and we saw Stan's stained shirt chucked to the side of the space. I expected to find his corpse, but there was no sign of it. "They're not here," I told the others.

"Where's the body? If Stan came in here with Amy, and only Amy left, with her new host inside her, where's his husk?" Magnus asked.

It was so simple. "Leonard, bring up that footage again. The one of Amy walking away last night."

He blinked a few times, as if trying to comprehend

what I was saying. "Sorry, sure." He tapped the tablet, and seconds later, he played the video. I grabbed the device and paused it as Amy turned toward the street. I zoomed, and pointed at her stomach.

"Was Amy expecting?" I asked.

"Expecting? Was she pregnant?" Leonard asked.

"Yeah, was she pregnant?" I asked, growing impatient.

"No. She…" Leonard's eyes widened as he stared at her image. "Look at her stomach. It's bulging."

"Exactly. Stan isn't here, because he's inside her… or whatever that is. I don't think this monster is a parasite," I said, and Karo nodded beside me.

"Where do we go?" Magnus asked.

I glanced at the spot under the stairs and thought about the nest that had been inside my house. "We have to find its new nest. And fast."

NINETEEN

The hunter turned his attention toward the city. His new body was fresh, limber, and stronger than it had initially appeared. Amy, as he understood her name to be, was lighter, easier to manage, and he could only imagine how freeing it would be to become the girl with the green eyes.

He'd always appreciated becoming the smaller animals, rather than the big, bulky ones. They were easier to hide with, and prey always found them less suspicious.

Her bones were still digesting inside him, and the transformation had taken longer last night than usual for some reason. Perhaps he'd fed too much lately, altered too many times for his own good, but here, with cameras and humans watching him, he didn't want to be tracked.

It was far different than home, where he could stay one creature for extended periods of time. Here, he was an outlaw, one being searched for. He finally understood this.

The hunter moved along the forest edge as Amy, trying to keep his movements smooth and normal to any passerby. So far, only a few vehicles had driven by him, one stopping to see if the "young missus" needed any help.

He'd told them that he was okay, that he was going for a walk. The man had squinted and shaken his head as he drove off.

Humans. They were a complicated animal, and a deep-rooted part of the hunter wished he were home, where life had been simpler in some ways, but desperately more difficult in others. Here, he was well-fed, and that kept his spirits up.

The roads would take him several hours to walk, but he'd eventually make it to the house with his nest once again. Maybe the girl would be there. Maybe she'd never come. He didn't know, but he would wait and find out. He continually pictured the green eyes, and the power they promised. Amy's legs moved faster as he considered the young girl.

As he moved, the sun beating onto his skin with ferocity, he hoped his nest was untouched. He wouldn't be able to feed yet; his stomach was too full, too distended, and he definitely wouldn't be able to transform for a few more days.

He kept moving toward the acreage he'd been staying at, wondering what the day held in store for him. The anticipation was killing him.

"Now what? We only have the single video feed showing Amy walking away from the downtown core," I said. We were on the main street, out of the alley, with only that small detail to go on. It didn't help us track her, but we did understand what we were up against a little better.

"Then we follow her trajectory. She was heading north. That's where we go," Reed said.

Magnus nodded. "This is an animal, by all accounts."

"How do you think?" Leonard asked.

"It came to New Spero in Soloma's body. It didn't look sure of itself on two legs. Ten bucks says it was used to walking on four or more, perhaps. It's making nests where it can consume its victims, perhaps changing into them or using their bodies to move around in. I don't have that quite figured out. The smell alone… it's musky… like a hibernating bear's cave," Magnus said.

His points were all valid. "And I supposed you know what that smells like?" Leonard asked.

"Yes I do. It's the same smell I inhale when I head into your room to wake you up in the morning," Magnus said, cracking a grin.

Leonard shrugged, not disagreeing.

"Then we go north. It was living in my house, so chances are, it'll head to the country, where fewer eyes are on it," I said.

"Why did it go into the city in the first place?" Reed asked.

Karo started walking, and spoke as he took the lead. "Because it's curious. It becomes its prey, to an extent. It feels what they've felt. It knows their thoughts… or memories," he said flatly.

He could be right. My stomach dropped. "If that's the case, it might go back to the nest."

My pocket vibrated, and it took a second to realize what was causing it. The communicator, the same one that Mary had the other end to. She'd contacted me the day before, saying they'd arrived and were working on tracking the duo.

I flipped it out, anxious to see what she had to say. "Dean?" Mary's voice sounded like honey.

"I'm here, Mary." I stepped away from the others, who remained huddled into a group on the side of the alley, discussing monster theories.

"We have Da-Narp… and Bee. She's hurt, but we'll be able to help her." Mary's tone told me the woman was worse off than she was letting on.

"I'm so glad. Are you coming home?" I asked.

"It went smoothly. We found the last missing group, and we're full of supplies. We were thinking of heading out and tracking the next duo on the list. We'll stop and see Sarlun quickly too, since that group left from Shimmal. We'll need to head there anyway," Mary said quietly, as if worried how I'd respond.

I wanted to tell her to come home, that leaving again was risking too much, but I wasn't ready to tell her about the creature living in our house, or the fact that it was on the loose. I relented and hated myself for withholding the details from her. "Go on. We'll stay with the kids. We're in the middle of something."

"Are you sure? I was… I don't know… expecting some resistance," Mary said.

"Do you want some for old times' sake?" I asked with a light laugh.

"No. Is everything okay? What are you in the middle of?" she asked, and I knew I had to give her some of the information.

"Do you remember Soloma? The one Leonard told us about?" I asked, walking farther from my group. The sun was bright, and I squinted against it.

"Of course," she said.

"We think something's taking over victims and killing. Again and again. We've tracked it to Terran One, and we're on its trail now." I waited for her to reply.

"Why are you doing this? Don't they have police and detectives for this kind of thing?" she asked, exasperated.

"I know. Leonard asked…"

"Tell Leonard we have enough going on. Where's Jules?" Mary asked, and I wished I'd kept the whole story to myself.

"She's at home with Slate," I said.

This seemed to calm her. "Fine. We'll be home as soon as we can. Let Magnus know Nat's okay. And Dean?" Here it was: she was going to lay into me. "Loweck is awesome. She's saved our bacon a couple of times. Tell you about it when we're home," she said.

"Glad to hear. Mary…" I thought about telling her about the monster nesting in our house, but it would only worry her.

"Yes?"

"I love you. Come home soon," I said, changing my mind.

"I will. Love you too." And in the blink of an eye, the communicator's lights dimmed as it powered off.

I headed toward the others. Magnus raised his eyebrows, searching for news in my expression. "Everyone's fine. They found the two from the Oryan system, and they've decided to keep going. They're heading for Shimmal and then to the last portal world to extract the final team."

Magnus looked infuriated. "You let them go?"

I laughed. "Let them? Have I ever *let* Mary do anything? Have you *let* Natalia?"

He sighed and shook his head. "No, I suppose you're right. We better deal with this before they're home. I don't think our wives will like it if we leave a psychopath predator wandering around our neighborhood," he said. I wanted to add: *or my living room,* but kept it to myself.

"North. Let's go," Reed said, taking the lead.

We walked through the city, and I tried to take it all in. The blocks were neatly laid out, the streets labeled with a clear and concise number pattern that made it easy to navigate. Cars and SUVs drove in the roadways, and it was still strange to see only a couple models of vehicles. Production for all vehicles was being done out of Terran Seven these days, and they were slowly adding in different colors. For the first few years, black had been the shade of choice.

People meandered along the sidewalks, idly out for a weekend stroll, and we received a series of odd looks as our ragtag group strode through the city armed. At least we had a uniformed police officer with us; otherwise, we might have drawn even more attention.

I heard my name whispered a few times, and someone shouted to Magnus. He waved and smiled, but didn't stop to talk. The sun was rising higher in the sky as we moved past the tall skyscrapers and into the outskirts. Here, there were many small distribution stores: hardware, fabric shops, beauty supplies. It was like being back home for a moment, and it gave me a sense of loss at what used to be, but also a sense of pride at what humans had accomplished. Many races would have crumbled after what we'd been through, but here we were: thriving, living among each other on a new planet. It was amazing, and I'd been taking a lot of *this* for granted.

Businesses turned to residential walk-up apartments, some of these the originals from the start of the colony. They'd been updated, and the smell of barbecue burgers wafted through the air. Kids played in a park, screaming and running around the bases at a baseball diamond. I stopped for a moment, watching as a girl no older than ten lofted a softball toward home plate. A boy took a big swing, narrowly missing the ball.

"Oh, to be young again." Magnus stopped beside me and rested his hands on the chain-link fence lining the park.

"Were we ever that young?" I asked him.

"I was. I never played baseball, though," he admitted.

"Seriously? That's all I did for a few years. We'd ride our bikes out to the field every day after school, and play until dinner time." I wondered what had happened to those friends. Were any of them around on New Spero, or even Terran One?

"You'll have to show me sometime," Magnus suggested.

"Deal. I'm holding you to that." I almost laughed,

thinking about our gang playing baseball.

"Wait, I have a message from Clay. Looks like they spotted Amy leaving town." Leonard was tapping away at his tablet.

"Where and when?" Reed asked. She was frowning, peering over Leonard's shoulder to see the screen.

Leonard pointed to the northwest. "There. Five blocks." He touched the screen again. "An hour ago."

The woman's stomach remained distended, and she was walking fast, a predator trying to escape the confines of the dangerous city.

"We have to catch up to it," I said, and Reed spoke into her earpiece, requesting drone coverage for ten square miles north of the city. The region covered our house and Magnus'.

"If she's out there, they'll find her," Reed said.

"Let's not call it a *her*. We can't think of this as Amy," Leonard said. He knew the woman, and it was easy to forget this was a person, not just an alien entity we were following. Was there any way to separate the two and save Amy? Only time would tell.

Karo sniffed the air, his green eyes dancing as he stared into the sky. "Rain's coming," he said, but I saw nothing but clear skies.

"You have to be kidding, Karo. There's not a cloud in the…" Magnus stopped mid-sentence, the wind blowing in hard enough to push Leonard off balance.

Behind the wind came black clouds from the west. They were plush and angry, ready to emit their precipitation on anyone below.

"Great. This is going to complicate things," I said.

Reed tapped her earpiece and gave me an apologetic look. "Sorry, Dean. They've grounded the drones. The wind is too much, and the radar's showing a serious storm out of nowhere."

"Come on. It has an hour's head start." I ran in the direction of my house. It had to be moving that way.

The nest was there, half a mile across the yard, and the hunter waited for signs of life. A form moved across the window inside the home, and the hunter felt trepidation creep into his mind. He'd hoped the girl was there, but this was a man, a big man. Still, he'd overpowered a lot of humans so far, most of them big as well, and armed.

The hunter saw the door open, and three children emerged, laughing and playing. The boy sat on the steps, staring up, making the hunter do the same. The sky had turned black, and he smiled, a sick and malevolent grin that twisted his host Amy's face into a contorted version of herself.

He felt his pocket and found the steel knife he'd killed Amy with, and felt stronger for it at his side. He preferred the old way, tearing out a warm throat with his teeth, but humans weren't built right for that method.

Wind rustled the trees around him, and he dodged a falling pinecone. For a second, the clouds stilled, the breezing ceased to blow, and everything went silent. Then it hit.

Water drenched the ground in seconds, and the hunter basked in it. The drones he'd seen hovering around were no longer in the air, and he scanned the area, seeing a vessel at the end of the driveway. A man with a rifle perched on his shoulder moved for his transport ship and stepped in: a refuge from the rain.

The big man inside the hunter's nest house was on the porch, urging the children inside. The small girl stared out toward him, but he knew she couldn't see him. He was too deep into the trees, but he shivered as she looked in his direction. The hunter saw the glint of her green eyes glowing even from here, and a thrill coursed through him. He would devour the girl, today. His hand found his stomach, and felt the round protrusion full of flesh and bones.

He growled, knowing he couldn't eat today. He'd take her. He'd keep the prey and feed when he was able. Yes. It was happening.

Lightning flashed, and thunder clapped applause for the show seconds later. Fat drops of rain blew in sideways, and the hunter made his first move. He crouched, hugging the treeline until he was closer to the rear of the house than the front. The police vessel, as he now understood it to be, was sitting there with the officer inside. When he was out of sight from the house's windows, he ran toward the ship. A woman soaked and in need. From Amy's memories, he knew this would work.

The man appeared to be shocked as he ran for the window, knocking on the glass of the compact ship.

He opened the door, which hinged upward. He was older, smelled less fresh up close. "Can I help you?" he asked.

The hunter found Amy's voice. "My head. I hurt my head," he said in his most feminine octave.

"Come in," he said, moving over. The hunter stepped inside and gripped the knife behind his back as he entered. He kneeled low, letting the officer look at his head. It was an exact copy of the woman he'd consumed last night, and the man finally spoke. "Looks okay from here. Did you bump it?" the officer asked.

The hunter raised his head with a snap of his neck and felt the impact as it crushed the man's nose. "Son of a …" The knife entered the man's throat, and the hunter shoved the officer into the petite cockpit.

He didn't feel the need to eat this one, so he stood a moment, watching the life bleed from the man. He couldn't believe there had been a moment where he'd considered acclimating to their ways. He was so much more advanced than these pathetic creatures. Surely they were at least ten steps below him in the evolutionary charts.

He nudged the man's arm with Amy's black flats and found him lifeless. Good. One man down, one more to go.

The hunter wiped the blade on the officer's shirt and slid it into his belt, covering it with Amy's tunic.

There was no time to waste. The longer he waited, the higher the chance of being caught.

He exited the police ship and paced toward the house. His long black hair was dripping everywhere, and he wiped the water away with his left forearm. The porch was solid under the hunter's steps, and soon he was at the door.

He breathed once, twice, three times, and knocked.

As the door opened, a muscular blond man with a beard answered, and a voice behind him was shouting.

"Slate! Lock the doors. If someone shows up, don't let them in!" a man's voice shouted through a speaker on the wall of the kitchen.

The hunter could smell his own scent throughout the home and found he already missed the place. It took a second for this Slate to comprehend the voice from the speaker and the woman standing in front of him. The hunter didn't wait. He lunged forward with the metal knife, sinking it into the prey.

TWENTY

"Slate! Do you hear me?" I shouted into my earpiece, but I didn't receive an answer.

"This is bad," Karo said. We were all running now. Reed had called for backup, but they hadn't arrived yet. If Slate wasn't answering… I couldn't let myself think about it. My legs kept pumping, and my chest was beginning to burn. I hadn't run this fast since I'd run the slopes of Machu Picchu years before, hoping to stop the *Kalentrek* from being turned off. Karo was making quick work of the roads, and Reed was holding her own, but Magnus and Leonard had fallen behind.

"We'll stop it," Karo said, his breath steady.

I didn't reply, only kept running. It was at least ten minutes before we passed Magnus' house, which sat in darkness, lights off in the downpour. I kept moving. The police lander Reed had promised to send was there, and she broke away from behind Karo and me, heading for the ship. I gripped my pistol in my hand and slowed. The front screen door flapped in the wind, and I blinked the dripping rainwater away from my eyes. I wanted to shout, to yell for

Jules, but I also knew I might need the element of surprise.

———————

The hunter stepped over the lumbering body and moved toward the children. Acting in the form of Amy, they might not be as scared of him. He hid the knife and lifted his hands, using her calming voice. "It is okay. Your father sent me," he said, glancing at the small girl with green eyes. She was wearing a dress with flowers on it, and she wasn't crying like the other two. There were three dogs inside, each of them growling and barking at him. Them, he understood. He felt more akin to the dogs than the human whose shape he wore.

The boy put on a face of bravado and stood in front of the two girls. "Don't come any closer! I'll hurt you!" the boy said, and the hunter had to smile, baring his teeth.

The hunter moved forward with startling speed and slapped the boy. He flew to the side, an angry red welt already forming on his face. "I'm not here for you."

He moved for the girl with the green eyes and heard footsteps on the front deck. "Carson's dead," a woman's voice said over the thunder, the sound carrying into the living room. He had to be quick. They'd tracked him. The small dogs were underfoot, and he shoved one off with a light punt. Another grabbed his ankle, biting the pants. He ignored them. They couldn't hurt him.

The hunter grabbed for the small girl, the one from the pictures, the one that lived in the house, but something terrible happened. She didn't attempt to evade his grasp.

She let him take her tiny arm. She smiled, a devious look, and pressed her hand to his chest. Green energy shot from her palm in a steady flow, shooting him across the room. He screamed in pain and torment, and it was only when the girl's father stepped into the house that she broke her concentration for a moment.

He had to escape, but he wasn't leaving empty-handed. The green-eyed girl was running now, heading toward the front door. That left the other girl standing there, eyes as large as boulders, tears flowing like the rain outside. The hunter snatched her in his grip, and she bellowed as he exited the house.

Lightning flashed as he hit the ground on two feet, and he pushed through the agony in his chest and morphed his legs and one front arm so he could gallop away on three legs, holding the prize to his chest with the other. He heard shouting behind him as he entered the treeline, and didn't stop until he returned to his secondary nest.

"*J*ules!" I shouted and saw my little girl arrive instantly. Slate was on the floor, unmoving. I heard Reed call it in, requesting assistance urgently.

"Papa! Monster!" She pointed at the back door, and I scanned the room, seeing little Dean crumpled on the floor, but no Patrice.

"Honey, where's Patty?" I asked. Karo went to Dean's

side and helped the boy up. He appeared to be okay, considering. The dogs were in a frenzy, all of them barking in synchronicity.

"Papa! Monster took Patty!" Jules' eyes were glowing brightly, but her cheeks were dry, flushed with anger like my own. I glanced at Slate and felt rage fill my veins. This creature had been killing with no remorse all over New Spero, and now it had entered my home, stabbed my best friend, and taken Patty. It was going to die. Today.

I didn't wait for anyone else. I ran through the house and out the door, which was left ajar. I followed the muddy footprints, which changed from two legs to something else, something alien.

"Dean! Where is she?" It was Magnus. They caught up to me at the treeline, where the evidence of footprints ceased to be so easy to spot.

I turned to my friend, my chin dipping toward my chest. "She's gone. It took her."

Magnus entered the trees, and I went with him. Karo and Reed joined us, and Leonard stayed behind with the kids. Already I heard sirens as two police landers arrived, followed by an emergency medical lander. If there was a chance for Slate to live, it was imperative they transport him to a hospital in minutes. I pushed the dread aside for now. I couldn't help Slate, but I could help Patty.

Magnus moved like a man possessed. Karo pointed out prints on occasion as we jogged through the thick brush, and I was sure we were on the right track. It was booming above, the rain relentlessly dripping on us, even in the deep forest behind my home. By the time we broke from the trees once again, I was shivering, both from a chill and from my fried nerves.

If anything happened to Patty, I wouldn't be able to forgive myself. I'd only started to know Magnus and Nat's kids again, since they'd left for three years, and they were an absolute dream. Magnus and Natalia were the best parents I knew, and we had no options here. We had to be fast.

We stopped, scanning the farmer's field. It was yellow canola, fully bloomed, and the scent was overwhelming mixed in with the rainstorm.

"Over here," Reed said. The same odd three-footed tracks aimed across the field.

We ran again, this time faster than inside the dangerous forest. It only took a few minutes, and we were at the far edge. We passed another home; this one had lit-up windows, and a woman peered from behind the door. When she saw us approaching her land, she stepped out onto the porch, arms crossed over her chest.

"It went that way!" she shouted, pointing toward the barn a half mile away. "We've lost a few animals this week, but Philip thought they snuck out the fence."

"Are you saying something is living in that barn?" I asked, coming closer. Magnus and Karo were moving for the structure.

The woman was old, and she shook as she hugged herself. "I think so. It wasn't natural. I think it was carrying something. Hard to get a good look from here."

"Thank you," I said, and Reed nodded to her. She called in the location and requested more support. They'd be here in minutes, but I wasn't sure Patty had that long.

Once again, I pressed away the ache in my side and legs and ran for the barn, trying to catch up to Magnus. He was like a bear protecting his cub, and I fully understood the feeling.

The nest was comfortable, and the hunter thought about how lucky he'd been to escape. That girl, he knew she had power; he'd been able to tell from the scent of the house, and from the picture as well. How strong he could have become consuming her. It wasn't to be, at least not yet.

"I want to go home," his consolation prize said. He eyed her, morphing his legs to their human length, his arm bending and skin stretching as he popped it in front of him. Once again, he appeared to be Amy. The effort exhausted him, combined with the trauma of whatever green energy the other girl had sent through him. He wanted to sleep, but he had to deal with this one first.

He considered eating her, but he was full of his last meal, his stomach protruding. The hunter looked down to see a piece of bone from inside protruding through his skin. He groaned and pressed it back inside, blood spilling out through his soaked and tattered clothing.

He'd almost forgotten about the quiet girl, whose only noise was a muted sobbing. Her hair was muddy, plastered to her head, and he thought she might pass out. That would make things easier. He didn't want to kill her yet – he preferred his meals fresh — but he wasn't sure he had a choice.

"Why?" the girl asked, and he couldn't answer, because she would never understand.

Because this is what I am, he thought as he moved across the room.

Magnus arrived at the barn first, and he flung open the door. I was right behind him, and Karo sidled up beside me, ready to attack, but all we found was an empty space. Hay bales lined one wall, and Reed ran up to the loft; shortly after, she stood at the railing, shaking her head.

"Damn it, where is she?" Magnus asked.

Then it hit me. "I saw a storm cellar behind the house. She couldn't have seen it enter from the front window."

Reed took the lead, and I took a last glance around the barn to make sure we hadn't missed anything. Outside, the storm raged on, and my pocket vibrated as we made for the back of the house. It was Mary, but I couldn't talk to her right now. I couldn't tell her what had happened until we resolved it. I let it ring, and eventually, the call ended. I hated leaving her hanging like that, and I began telling myself stories.

Mary was dying, the last remaining of their group, and she wanted to tell me she loved me one last time before she went. Mary was happy, successfully returning from her trip, she wanted to warn me she'd be home in an hour and that she was feeling like lasagne for dinner. The stories went on, a constant stream of possibilities as I neared the storm cellar doors.

The police landers were there, but without sirens, as Reed had requested. Half a dozen officers ran for us, and I knew it was time.

Magnus crouched low, his rifle in one hand, the other on the wooden door's handle. He flung it open and didn't hesitate. I saw him take the stairs, and I followed without question. It was musty here; it had the same scent as my house had held when I'd found the nest. This was it.

I heard the scream before I saw Patty. She was against a wall, and Amy's form loomed over Magnus' daughter, clutching her arm.

Magnus didn't risk shooting the monster, not with his girl so close, so he lowered an elbow and charged the thing. It howled, a terrible noise, and let go of Patty as Magnus bowled it over.

Patty was already moving for me, and I grabbed her, passing her behind me to Karo, who rushed her up the steps.

It only took Amy a few moments to rebound to her feet, and already she was changing, shifting. Her face grew longer, the skin stretching out. Magnus kicked her in the side, and she howled again. Her arms grew thicker as her stomach shrank. It looked like the monster was storing spare parts inside its gut and using them to transform.

The monster, no longer resembling Amy, swung at Magnus and knocked his rifle to the ground. It kicked up dust from the dirt floor, and I grabbed the gun, tossing it behind me.

The room was dark, my flashlight giving the only illumination. Lightning flashed from outside, momentarily lighting the cramped space. I held the pistol in my hand, aiming toward the monster, but Magnus was too big, and he blocked my view.

Magnus punched it in the face, its snout shooting to the side, blood spilling from its face against the wall.

It lashed out, and I held the gun up, hoping for a clean shot. It struck Magnus in the head, then a quick shot to his stomach. He lurched over, his breath shooting out with a *woof*, and I had my chance.

Thunder boomed, and another flash of light coursed into the room. The monster's eyes met mine for a second, slowing time. I almost understood it at that moment. It was an animal, doing what it had to do to survive.

Regardless, it had to die. I pulled the trigger, my pulse blast hitting it in the chest. I fired again, this one a head shot. The monster that had plagued New Spero for too long fell to the dirt floor, and Magnus didn't scramble away. The monster let out a horrifying roar, then went silent, and Magnus pulled a knife from his boot and shoved it into the thing's head.

"You okay?" I asked him. He took my outstretched hand, and I helped the big man to his feet. His head almost touched the ceiling.

"Where's Patty?" he asked, his eyes wild. I hadn't seen him so out of control before, and it was a terrifying sight.

"She's fine. She's outside. We did it, Mag. We did it," I told him as he ran up the steps. When I emerged, three police officers went the opposite direction, and I stopped one of them. "This thing is dangerous, and we don't know where it comes from. Don't assume it's dead. Contain it. And it can shapeshift, so don't let it out of your sight."

"Shapeshift?" The policeman's eyes were wide.

"My suggestion… burn it." I left them to it, and stepped outside to see Patty in her father's big arms, crying into his neck. He was petting her wet hair, and softly whispering that she was okay.

TWENTY-ONE

"Mary!" I said into the communicator.

"Dean, you didn't answer. I always go to the worst place," she said.

"You and me both. In this instance, you were almost right," I told her.

"What do you mean?" she asked, her voice tense.

"You first. Where are you?" I asked.

"We found them. This world is amazing. I think if we ever figure this whole portal thing out, we have a new vacation spot," she said, warmth in her tone.

I kicked my feet up on the coffee table. Jules was on my lap, sleeping soundly on my chest. "Vacation. I could use one of those. Tell me about it." Maggie was on her side, snuggled up against my leg. Everyone had been through a rough day.

"Turquoise oceans, white sand beaches, it's always eighty-five degrees, and the sun is just right. Mark my word, Parker, we're coming here. How's Jules?" she asked with a hint of concern.

"Sleeping on me as we speak," I said.

"What happened?" she asked.

"Where are you?" I diverted.

"Shimmal. Dean, Ableen passed out during this last trip. I think the portals are at their end. Sarlun is coming with us to New Spero. He wants to talk to you, and fears the worst," she said.

I thought about this. "If the portals go while he's here, it will take him years to make it home," I reminded her.

"He knows this. But he doesn't want to risk us coming there with the Modifier, then using it again to bring you here. The fewer uses, the better at this point," she said, and I couldn't argue with the logic.

"Good. You're coming home, then?" I asked, my heart fluttering a bit. I was nervous to tell her what had happened, but didn't want it to be a surprise.

"Yes. We should be at Terran Five in a few hours," Mary said. She knew something serious had happened. "Dean, tell me."

"Slate's in the hospital," I told her.

"What? Is he all right?" she asked.

I hesitated, and she didn't wait for me to answer. "What happened to him?"

"You remember the killer Leonard told us about?" I asked her. I wanted to do this in person, but I could give her part of the story. It wasn't my place to worry Natalia about Patty being abducted.

"Of course."

"It came to Terran One. It…" I didn't know how to say this part. "It was living in our house while we were gone."

The Gatekeepers

A pause. I checked the device to make sure we hadn't lost the connection. "It…was living in our home? How? Why?"

"I don't know. It stole a lander from outside Terran Five and made for here. We think because we're north of the city, straight from Five as the crow flies, that it landed and came to our house, seeing it was empty. We aren't sure," I said.

"And Slate?"

"He was stabbed."

"What kind of creature was it? Was it Soloma?" she asked.

"Some kind of shapeshifter. I saw it transform." Jules stirred on me, and I wrapped my arm around her, pulling the blanket up.

"Transform. Slate's going to be fine?" she asked.

"He should be. The doctors are confident he'll be good to go. We can visit him tomorrow," I said. He'd lost a lot of blood, and it had taken some real next-level medical attention to revive him. I was so grateful for all the new technology we'd uncovered over the last decade.

"Don't come for us. We'll come home, and everyone can gather at the hospital tomorrow," Mary said. It wasn't a suggestion, it was an order.

"Yes, ma'am," I said.

"Don't get smart with me, Dean," Mary said with a laugh. "This shifter. It *is* dead, right?"

"It's dead," I admitted.

"Were you the one to kill it?" Her voice was soft, hopeful.

"I was. Well, Magnus did stab it, but I think it was dying."

"Good. I'm glad it was you," she told me. I wasn't sure why, but likely because I'd avenged Slate, our good friend and ever-loyal guardian. Sometimes the strongest around us needed to be protected as well.

"Me too." And in truth, I was glad I'd shot the monster.

"See you at home."

"In a few hours," I said. "Mary. Good work out there. When this portal business is resolved, let's stop going on solo missions for a while, okay?"

"Haven't I been saying that for ages?" she asked, and I agreed she had been.

"Maybe this exploration ship isn't such a bad idea. What do you think?" I asked, knowing this wasn't necessarily the time for that particular discussion.

"I think it's a good idea too, as long as we're all together. See you soon."

She'd actually agreed with the concept of setting sail into the great unknown on an exploratory vessel. "Love you, Mary."

"Same."

The communication ended, and I stroked Jules' hair softly, and in minutes, I was sleeping, dreaming of watching space through the viewscreen of our newest venture.

I awoke hours later. Light seeped through the windows, the start of another day. The doors were broken, propped shut with boxes, and I set Jules aside. She came to, green eyes sparkling as they blinked away the sleep. I sat up, my back cracking from the uncomfortable position I'd slept in. My legs were sore, and my hip ached as I stretched.

"Papa," Jules said. She rubbed her eyes and stood up, tottering over toward the bathroom.

"Yes?" I asked.

"Potty," she said, and I laughed. I was so happy she could do that herself already. She was truly a quick learner.

"What do you want to eat?" I asked her.

"Fluffy eggs!" she shouted from the bathroom.

"I want fluffy eggs too," Karo said from the hallway. He'd slept on a cot, instead of trying to fit on Jules' tiny mattress.

I heard the lander lowering to the ground and rushed to the front of the house. Maggie barked, and I kicked aside the box keeping my door shut and let her out. She ran at full speed toward Mary. The full entourage emerged from the lander. Sarlun waved, Suma beside him. Ableen was there, with Loweck walking behind her. Seeing them all lifted my spirits. I glanced at the hardwood beside the door, and even though I'd worked for half an hour to scrub Slate's blood out, it was still stained dark brown, the color of rust.

"Mommy!" Jules was running past me, arms outstretched as she hit the grass. She was barefoot, her hair a mess of brown curls, and she had on her space ship pajamas.

Mary scooped her up and spun her around, kissing her repeatedly on the cheek. Jules giggled, and Maggie sprinted around the group in excited circles. It was quite the homecoming.

"We dropped Nat off at home first," Mary told me.

I waved to them all as they neared the porch. I hugged Mary, and Karo was wrapping Ableen in his long arms. He whispered to her, things I couldn't hear, but she smiled widely and embraced him in return.

"Sarlun, good to see you," I said to the Shimmali man. He stared at me with black eyes, and his slender snout twitched from side to side.

"You as well, Dean Parker," he said in English.

I stepped down, hugging Suma. "How are you doing? Keeping busy?"

She grinned. "I'm doing okay. How's Slate?"

Everyone was watching me, collectively holding their breath. "I haven't heard anything so far. There were no messages from the doctors." I set a hand on Suma's arm. "I think he'll be fine. It would take something more than a maniacal shapeshifting alien to take down our friend."

"Anyone hungry?" I asked, taking Mary's pack from her shoulder.

"I could eat," Sarlun said.

Loweck was the last to enter, and she was the first to notice the horrible stain on the floor. "Is that his?"

I nodded. "He'll be all right. He was worried about you, you know."

"He was?" Loweck met my gaze, her orange skin looking a little flushed.

"Yep. He's going to be so glad to see you at the hospital," I told her, and she nodded her thanks, entering our small house.

Mary sat with Jules at the kitchen table, chatting with

our daughter as she drew on paper with crayons. Sarlun joined me by the stove as I prepared breakfast for our group.

"I'm worried about things, Dean," Sarlun said quietly.

"When are we ever not worried?" I asked him.

"You know what I mean. Ableen said they're in pain, they need to be released. What are we going to do? The Gatekeepers are old, established. Can we remain Gatekeepers without a gate to keep?"

I wasn't sure if his question was rhetorical, so I answered it. "We can be anything we have to be. Planet keepers, peacekeepers, unity makers, I don't know. A label is sometimes meant to be torn off," I told him as I turned the gas burner off. "Eggs are done!" I slid the hash browns into a bowl and dropped a large serving spoon into them, setting it in the middle of the table.

"But how will we move around?" he asked.

"I have the portals from Fontem. We'll figure out how to duplicate them. Clare will find a solution. At the very least, we can use one end from Shimmal to New Spero," I told him.

He shook his head. "That's too much to ask. You must have one from New Spero to Haven. That's the only way. Haven needs to have the Heroes of Earth around. You, Dean Parker, are special. A Recaster, an inspiration, and, I hate to say it, a figurehead," he said.

"You mean a guy they make statues of, even though he never does anything himself?" I asked, not loving the term *figurehead*.

"You misunderstand me. A symbol, then, of

something more than wars and mistrust. You are the linchpin on the success of the Alliance of Worlds. Shimmal will survive without contact. We all need Haven to be the center of it all," he said.

"Earth will be on its own then too," Mary said from the table. Apparently, we'd raised our voices enough for the others to hear us.

"Earth is fine. They're thriving there," I said.

"Until the Empress decides to dissolve our deal," Karo said.

"She won't," I said. I honestly believed that.

"Then it's settled. Until you duplicate the portal sticks from Fontem, we link New Spero with Haven," Sarlun said.

I wanted to tell them I had another set, that I had it locked away under my farmhouse on Earth. It led to the ship I'd fought Lom of Pleva on, the same ship that held my time-travel device.

"I want to stay on Haven," Suma said from the table.

Sarlun's dark eyes went wide. "Suma... we've talked about this."

"But they're building a Gatekeepers' Academy there. I want to be part of it," she said.

"A lot of use a Gatekeepers' Academy will be without the portals," her dad said.

"Sarlun, we'll build an institution regardless. A place for any member of the Alliance of Worlds to send their children. We'll unify through our children, building stronger bonds than us old guys could ever do," I told him, getting a nod.

Sarlun sat with humility. "Very well. Suma, I won't hold you back."

Karo passed Ableen a plate and cleared his throat. "Dean, have you told them where we have to go?"

I realized I hadn't yet. "No." All eyes met mine as I stood there, about to tell Mary I was going to leave her side once again, one last time. "Bear in mind, we'll have the portal device to transport home when I tell you this."

Mary grabbed for Jules' hand. "Go ahead," she urged me.

"Karo said the main portal power source is on their home world." I stopped when Ableen gasped. "We have to shut it off there. We'll use the methods we utilized on Sterona when I pulled them out to help me fight the Iskios. It should disable the entire series of portals, freeing the Theos once and for all."

"When? When will you go?" Sarlun asked.

"As soon as we're done with the hospital. We'll bring everyone to their final destinations first, so no one is stranded here when the portals are deactivated," I said.

"If you bring the portal device with you, how will we link it to Haven?" Suma asked. She was a smart one. "One end will be anchored to New Spero, the other to the Theos world."

She had a good point. I couldn't disable the one where the Theos lived. Tough choices. "Then Karo and I will await a vessel to pick us up."

Mary stood up, nearly knocking her plate over. "No way. You are *not* waiting out there for a space ship to come get you. Do you have any idea how far away their planet is?"

Truthfully, I didn't. Karo answered, "The wormhole drives could move there quickly."

"But then you risk the time dilation on the way home. No. No way." Mary's arms were crossed. "What about Dubs? Can we send him through to release the Theos?"

"Someone organic has to bring him across, plus I don't think it would work with a robot anyway. I promised I'd do this, and I have to stick to my word," I said.

Ableen spoke up for the first time. "Karo and I can do it. We can go, and fulfill your promise."

"But you'll be stranded there," I said.

She shrugged. "Maybe that's our purpose. Karo waited for you to show up for centuries. I was frozen in time aboard the Collector's ship. We were meant to be here together to release our people. Perhaps we can start again." She slipped her hand into Karo's, and he smiled dotingly at her.

"I don't like it," I said, poking at my eggs.

Mary glared at me. "You don't have to, Dean."

"Ableen is right. It's up to us to make this right," he said.

"Well, let's eat and meet Magnus and Nat at the hospital. Slate needs to see us." I changed the subject. I hated to think about Karo leaving our lives for good. He'd become a great friend: someone to rely on, and I'd miss our late-night discussions over cold pizza.

Jules ate a few bites of her breakfast and continued drawing a picture. I tried to understand what I was seeing, but couldn't. It looked like blue squiggles coming from a planet, or maybe a rock. Mary glanced at the paper and smiled at our daughter. She still didn't know about Patty. I had to tell them, knowing Magnus would have told Nat by now.

"There's something else I need to tell you about last night," I said, and everyone stopped their quiet chatter and eating. All eyes focused on me standing at the kitchen island. "Slate was stabbed by the monster, but we didn't catch it here. It took Patty and escaped."

"What? Why didn't you tell me this already?" Mary asked.

"Because you were with Nat and I didn't want to freak her out. It wasn't going to help anyone," I told her.

"Is Patty okay?" Sarlun asked.

I nodded. "She's going to be fine. She's shaken up, as you can expect."

"I assume this means our friend and fellow Gatekeeper Soloma is no longer alive?" Sarlun asked.

"No. They're doing the autopsy today, but we think this creature eats his victims, and then shifts into them. It's really quite amazing…" I stopped. It was an interesting biological trait, but this wasn't the time or the place to discuss it. "Anyway, we killed it, and Patty is safe."

Jules smiled at me. "Papa. Lady wanted me."

Mary leaned forward. "What did you say?"

"Lady wanted me. Bad lady." Jules' attention returned to her coloring.

I crouched beside her. "What are you telling us?"

"I stop her." Jules stuck out a palm and smiled. She wasn't making any sense.

"Who knows what's going on in there?" Mary rubbed Jules' head lightly. "I'm glad you're all safe."

Breakfast ended, and Karo and I took turns getting ready. When I emerged from the bathroom with fresh pants and a polo on, Mary was on the couch combing Jules' hair. The others were outside.

"I can't believe this thing was in our home. I feel so… violated. I'm not sure I can stay here," Mary said.

I glanced around, taking in our first real home together. We'd lived at my old house on Earth after the Event, and even in her small apartment for a while, but neither had felt like *our* home. This… this was a Godsend after we arrived at New Spero. We'd grown our first garden here. We celebrated anniversaries, birthdays… we were married here.

I peered outside, seeing Sarlun in my yard, and I recalled the moment he'd asked us to become Gatekeepers. This house was us, and I wasn't sure I could part with it. "We can talk about it," I said. We had a home on Earth and one on Haven too, but I knew Mary loved this house as much as I did. Jules too.

Maggie was beside Mary, and she set the brush down and stroked Maggie's coat. "I can smell it. Can you smell it?"

I could. "It'll go away." I saw the bloodstain and pictured Slate's big body on the floor, the dogs barking, Patty missing, and sighed. "Maybe you're right. This might be too much."

"Let's go make sure Slate's fine. Come on, Team Parker," Mary said with a smile, and we brought Maggie. Everyone filed into the lander, and we headed for the city.

TWENTY-TWO

*T*he lights were dim as Mary and I headed into the hospital room with Jules between us. Maggie tried to follow us in, but Suma took hold of her leash, keeping her in the hallway. We were the first to visit Slate, or so we thought. Reed's shadowy form was slouched on the chair beside the bed.

I cleared my throat, waking her up, and she stood up fast, ready to defend herself or Slate, I wasn't sure.

"Dean! I must have fallen asleep." Her short hair was wild, bags under her eyes. She peeked over at Slate, who was still out. Machines beeped softly and consistently.

"Reed, this is my wife, Mary. And you remember Jules," I said.

"Pleased to meet you." Reed stuck her hand out, and Mary pulled her into a hug.

"Thanks for looking after my brood while I was gone," she said, letting the policewoman go after a few seconds.

"Anytime. They're a good bunch," Reed said. "I'll let you guys have some privacy."

"You should get some sleep. We'll make sure to keep

you posted," I told her, and she nodded.

"Thanks," Reed said as she left the room. I heard Magnus' booming voice greet her from the hallway.

"Slate, buddy," I said, standing beside him on the bed. He seemed older lying there unconscious. The door opened, and a nurse stepped in.

"Hi. Any news?" Mary asked her.

The nurse smiled. "He's had a good night, but he's not out of the woods yet. We managed to give him a transfusion, and he's taking to it," she told us.

"Don't we have things to speed this up?" I asked. Slate was too weak, too helpless. It was weird seeing people you love in the hospital. No matter the circumstances, they always seemed like a shell of their real selves there. Slate was a larger-than-life hero, not… I couldn't finish my thought. I turned from the nurse, too ashamed to let her see me upset.

"We've stitched him, and the wounds are clean. He should be fine, but as I said, he lost a lot of blood. Last night, his heart stopped beating for almost a minute, but we were able to revive him," she said. This was news to me.

I grabbed his hand and gave it a squeeze. Jules snuck up beside me and reached for Slate too. She found a finger and held on. "Zeke. Zeke, wake up. Play."

Mary cried now, and I couldn't help but feel the onslaught of emotion. After everything the two of us had been through, there was nothing I could do for him.

Jules looked up at me, not understanding why Slate wasn't responding.

"He's sleeping, honey," I told her, but she seemed to comprehend there was something else going on. She glanced at the machines, and then at me and her mother.

"We can help," Jules said, reaching for Slate again.

Mary picked her up, scooting her away. Jules kept reaching for Slate, but she held our daughter at a distance. "He's sick and sleeping. We can't wake him."

There was a knock on the door, and Magnus peeked his head in. "Come on in, we're heading out." I stayed beside Slate for a moment, watching his chest rise and fall. He was my brother, and I couldn't bear the idea of losing him. It wasn't his time.

"Papa. We can help," Jules said again, big fat tears dropping down her round cheeks.

"I know we can. I know," I said, letting Magnus and Natalia by. He stopped and grabbed hold of my arm.

"Dean, Patty said she saw Jules do something at the house," he whispered so no one else could hear.

My heart raced. "What?"

"She doesn't know. She thinks the monster was after Jules, though, and your girl stopped it," he said.

"How, Magnus? How?" I asked, and he shook his head.

"You know what it's like asking a little kid to describe what she saw. I just wanted you to know," he said.

Nat was angry, I could see it in her eyes, but they softened as they lay on Slate's form. We left them alone in the hospital room, and joined the others in the waiting area.

I didn't think there was anything my Jules could have done to prevent being attacked by the shapeshifter. It was too powerful, and she was only a tiny girl. I set the worry aside. It was over.

Leonard sat beside Suma, chatting with her. Sarlun was speaking with Loweck, and Karo and Ableen were farther down the hallway. Reed was gone.

Ableen waved and walked over, stopping in front of us. Karo spoke for them. "Dean, it's time. We have to go. Ableen can feel them from here," he said.

I was exhausted. My best friend was in critical condition on the other side of the door behind me, and my wife had only been home for a day. I nodded and saw Mary do the same.

"We'll see you off," she said, holding Jules protectively in her arms.

It was far too soon to be heading to the portals. Karo didn't bring much with him. I remembered the home he'd lived on at the Theos world, and the fact that he'd been able to make pizza there. They had technology that read minds, and even Karo didn't fully understand how he'd survived for so many years in solitude.

He was going home now, no longer alone. He had Ableen, the tall white-haired woman, at his side. Magnus and Nat stayed at the hospital, along with Leonard and Loweck. It was only Mary, Jules, and me to send Karo and Ableen away.

We kept pace with them through the tunnels outside

The Gatekeepers

of Terran Five, and stopped at the portal room doorway. I passed the Crystal Map and the Modifier to Karo, holding in the emotions coursing through me.

"Wait. Dean, you need to set up the other end of your device at Haven first," Karo said, eyes wide. We'd almost forgotten, amongst all the day's stressful events.

I turned to Mary, pursing my lips. "I have to go do this. Can you wait for me? Hopefully, it only takes a minute."

"I know. Go ahead. Please hurry," she told me.

Karo leaned toward Ableen. "I'll accompany Dean, then we can leave for home." *Home.* Her eyes brightened at the word.

The last male Theos and I entered the portal room. It was the first place I'd been drawn to all those years ago. I remembered the fever, the near-possession driving me to enter the caves and find the thrumming portals. The Theos had called to me. They'd directed me to them that day, and Regnig thought it was because of his label for me: a Recaster. Someone who changed the universe and had events bend around. It wasn't always good, nor always bad, but things altered wherever I went.

Ableen whimpered from the entrance as the crystal began glowing. The symbols on the walls illuminated, and the table powered up. We attached the devices, and I fought the urge to go don an EVA. The stones hadn't failed us yet, not with the use of the Modifier we'd received from J-NAK on the robot world.

I smiled at my family, and Karo at Ableen, and we activated the portal. This would be the last return trip I took through them, and I wondered how many times I'd used the tools.

We arrived at the room on New Spero, and I was glad this time there hadn't been a version of myself floating in white light, giving me ominous messages from the future.

"Will you set it up here?" Karo asked.

I pulled the one end of the portal device from my pocket and stepped out of the room, making for the hallway. This would make more sense. A smaller area.

My arm console buzzed. Now that I was within range on Haven, half a dozen messages flew into my computer, and I opened the window. Five urgent notifications from Leslie, three from Terrance. They would have known I couldn't reply from home, but I would have received them eventually, even all the way at New Spero.

"What is it?" Karo asked, peering over my shoulder to read them as I opened the messages.

"The school. It's been bombed," I told him.

"The Gatekeepers' Academy?" he asked.

"The very same." There were no details about injuries or damages. "Karo, do you mind if we take a moment to divert your mission? I need to see what happened."

Karo nodded toward the exit. "I want to know too. My home world will be there in an hour," he said, and we left the halls, emerging into a chilly autumn-like day on Haven.

I grabbed the communicator and relayed the information to Mary. She told me they'd wait for us outside the tunnels on New Spero.

"Leslie. Come in. Terrance. It's Dean." I tapped my earpiece.

"Dean? Thank God. There's a lander there waiting for

you," Leslie said.

"How did you know I was coming?" I asked.

"We didn't. We've sealed the portal and knew the only person coming through would be you." I glanced over to see the door shut and a blue energy barrier around it. We couldn't leave if we wanted to. "Don't worry," Leslie said. "We'll give you the biometric code to leave after."

"Where do you want to meet?" I asked her.

"At the school. We're there already," she said, and I could detect the panic in her voice.

I ended the call and looked over at Karo. "This isn't good."

He didn't speak as we entered the lander, but waved me into the pilot's seat. I was glad I'd learned to fly these things, because I'd needed to use them on a few occasions. The trip didn't take long, but the damage was evident as soon as we neared the outskirts of the main city. We'd placed the school close enough to the growing city, but far enough to keep it away from the expansion, which meant it was ten miles from the city limits.

The ground was pocked with holes: big ones, carved into the grassy fields behind the structure. From here, it appeared that the Gatekeepers' Academy was intact, but as I came closer, I saw the entire east wing had been decimated. It was nothing but rubble and charred rocks. My stomach sank.

We'd been doing so well lately. The planets had been thriving. We'd had peace for a few years, other than the odd run-in with some powerhouse, and we'd even delivered *Fortune*, the Keppe ship Magnus had been captaining, from another dimension. Now the trials and tribulations of attempting to expand into a dangerous universe were rearing their ugly faces.

"Who could have done this?" Karo asked as we lowered toward the main building. There were half a dozen landers outside the front of the school, and I recognized Leslie and Terrance standing at the stairs leading to the Gatekeepers' Academy. A Kraski ship sat at the edge of the parking pad. I was sure I'd been in that ship before.

"I don't know, but I expect we're about to find out." I settled the lander to the concrete pad, beside the other vehicles, and soon we were outside, the cold wind biting at our faces.

"Dean!" Leslie shouted, waving us over.

I hadn't visited here in a long time, but the progress was impressive. From here, you couldn't tell the school had been attacked. I recognized the structures from the model image we'd pored over for the last year or so. Even now, drones hovered around the region, and I expected these ones were security rather than worker drones.

Leslie appeared tired, and we hugged. For a brief moment, I saw my ex-wife in her eyes, the sick one on her deathbed. Leslie's eyes were sunken, her skin taut. I leaned in and whispered, "Are you okay?"

She gripped my forearm and squeezed it. "I'm fine. I haven't been sleeping much, that's all."

Terrance shook my hand, and then Karo's. "Glad to see you two. Everything good?" He studied me, then Karo, who shrugged.

"We're about to shut off the portals," Karo told them

point-blank.

Terrance hung his head and let out a deep breath. "That's… unfortunate. We knew it might come to this, though."

"I'm going to place my portal device inside the halls so we can move between New Spero and Haven." Their eyes lit up at this piece of news.

"Good. We need the trade. Out here, we have access to a few other worlds, some of our Alliance members. The Padlog are close enough to trade, as are the Inlor. Even the Bhlat to some extent, if we count their colonies," Terrance said. "This can work. Dean, tell me this is feasible."

I clapped him on the shoulder. "This will work." I turned to the school and marveled at the lettering spelling out the words *Gatekeepers' Academy* in blue crystals. It was amazing. "What happened here?"

Leslie perched on the stone steps, and we joined her, sitting in a row, looking out to the fields beyond. "They came in the dark of night. Somehow they disabled our perimeter alerts in orbit. Their ships lowered, blasting the school. Good thing we had a Bhlat envoy visiting. They were preparing their vessels for takeoff when the attack hit."

I gulped. "Does this mean we fended off the incursion?"

"There were three ships. The Bhlat lost one in a dogfight, but we took them down. No survivors," Terrance said.

"Then who were they?" Karo asked.

"We don't know. We ran the specs from our camera

feeds through every system we have, and they're an unknown. None of the Alliance knows where they come from, or have seen their type before. We have bodies, but they're hardly in one piece. We're trying to determine their origin," Terrance told us.

"Seriously? No one has a record of these guys? They're organic?" I asked.

"Yep. Like I said, the Bhlat did quite a number on them. We have samples, but it wasn't much more than blood by the time we got to them," Terrance finished.

"So what now?" Karo asked.

"Well, we've set up some serious defense in orbit. The Inlor, the Bhlat, the Padlog, and the Keppe have offered a war vessel each to stand guard. I doubt anyone would be foolish enough to come without expecting a battle they'd struggle to win. We've also added ground defenses from the Molariuns. We can shoot a rock the size of your head from three thousand kilometers away," Leslie said, smiling.

I patted my head. "Please don't tell me that. When was the attack?"

"Two nights ago," Leslie said.

"How much damage?"

"The east wing is gone. That's the arts section." Leslie stood and walked over to a double bench golf cart-type vehicle. "Come on, we'll show you."

I glanced at Karo, hoping he was okay with the delay. He didn't seem overly concerned, so we jumped in, allowing Leslie to drive us onto the roadways, through the school.

"You think they were targeting the school because of

its purpose?" I asked through the wind. My cheeks were red and tight in the chilly air.

"We have to assume that's the case. They don't want the Gatekeepers' Academy to exist," Terrance staid from the front bench.

"Well, we're going to have to rethink things now that the portals will be dead," I told them.

"There will be need for shared education. And our purpose was higher than the Gatekeepers alone, right?" Leslie asked.

"That's right. It's about the children of our Alliance of Worlds learning and growing up cohesively. It's the first step to a new universe. One with less hostility and borders," I said, knowing it was only a small step. As with old Earth, there would always be differences among people, aliens, and anything in between.

The school was made from earthy materials: stone, brick, crystals, and it was done with the expertise of an architect from Shimmal. The work was so tasteful, and I squinted, picturing my own daughter around ten years old, walking the sidewalks with a backpack, giggling with Patty as they headed to classes for the day.

We headed past a courtyard, water fountains, and concrete sitting areas made for a great place to have lunch on a sunny patio. Today was not that day, and I hugged myself trying to stay warm. We drove past an immense gymnasium with dark walls. Leslie stopped and pressed a button on her arm console. The glass walls slowly lightened as the tint dissipated, until they were clear and we could see inside the gym.

"That's a nice feature," Karo said.

Inside, a few robots were laying floor down. We kept moving until we found the destruction. The sidewalks were torn, rubble everywhere, and I noticed pieces of a space ship were littered among the debris. The building was cleanly torn apart at a corridor from off the gymnasium, and I guessed they'd destroyed at least thirty thousand square feet of construction.

"It's going to delay the building by a good six months, maybe a year," Leslie said.

"Better to do it right and be safe." We stopped, and I stepped out, walking over to a crater in the ground. It was at least forty feet deep, and I shook my head in awe. I couldn't believe some unknown entity had come to Haven attempting to destroy our school.

"That's it. We wanted you to see it. If you need to go, we won't keep you any longer. Set up the portal, and we'll keep in contact with each other. We need you on board with what we're doing here, Dean. Maybe you can come stay on Haven full time?" Leslie asked, her voice hopeful.

Mary and I had been talking about moving from our place on New Spero, but I couldn't commit to anything quite yet. "We'll see. All I know is we're going to miss Karo, but part of me is okay with hanging up my portal-hopping boots. I've seen more than enough excitement for ten lifetimes," I said with a smile.

"We can make a real pencil-pusher of you here, Dean," Terrance said, grinning widely.

"Ah, the good old days," I said.

"Let's take you to the lander," Leslie said. "Karo, we're

going to miss you too." He'd spent a good chunk of time living with Leslie and Terrance after we'd first found him alone on his home world, and they'd grown close. Karo had that effect on anyone he was around. He was so affable, and he made a mean dinner too.

"You have been gracious hosts, and what you're doing here on Haven is not only admirable, it's inspiring." Karo hugged them each, and we settled into the cart.

Seconds after we started driving to the front of the school, alarms blared out around us, and I caught Terrance looking up to the sky. "You have to be kidding me," he said.

"What is it?" Karo asked.

"They're back. And they brought friends."

TWENTY-THREE

"What's happening? How many?" I asked, wishing I had more information.

Leslie tapped her earpiece, nodding her head to words I couldn't hear. "Twenty enemy vessels have approached Haven. Our defenses are ready, the orbital team is in place. We're under attack," she relayed to us. She pushed the cart to the limit as we raced toward the parked ships.

"You guys can take the lander and leave. Go do what you need to do, and Karo, be safe. Take care of Ableen, and yourself for that matter!" Terrance shouted over the sirens and gusting wind. Small flakes of snow began to fall around us.

Karo and I exchanged a look at the same time, and he spoke for us. "I think not. We're taking the Kraski ship and joining the fight."

Leslie slammed on the brakes, and we skidded to a halt beside our lander. "Are you sure?" she asked.

"We're sure." I hopped off and opened the Kraski ship from the outside, running up the lowering ramp. The four of us entered the ship, and I was glad for the reprieve from

The Gatekeepers

the looming winter storm. I had the feeling we were about to enter a different kind of storm, one far more deadly than falling flakes.

I ran to the bridge and was startled to see a familiar face.

"Hello, Captain. Are we joining the defense?" Dubs asked from the pilot's seat.

"Hey, W. Great to see you," I told him. "Take us up!"

We gathered on the bridge, and Terrance took over the weapon helm position. The gray sky raced toward us, and seconds later, we burst through Haven's atmosphere. I checked the radar to get the lay of the land. Twenty red triangle icons were heading for the world, and we only had five green squares in line to defend against their arrival.

"Can we stop them?" I asked, not knowing what kind of weapons systems the enemy held.

"Captain, I'm intercepting a transmission," Dubs said, and I cringed at his casual use of the title *Captain* for me.

"Play it," I told him.

"*Haven, this is Admiral Yope of* Starbound. *We are on the way but won't arrive until twenty minutes after the attackers do. Stand firm and we'll cover you,*" Yope said, and I had to smile. I hadn't seen the man in a long time. I recalled the way he looked at me the first time we'd met. He sure hadn't liked me for some reason.

Now he might be our saving grace. "We only have to deflect them for twenty minutes. How hard can that be?" I asked.

"They'll try to spread out, enter the atmosphere. They won't know about our suborbital defense systems, so we should be able to blast them out of the sky upon entry if they make it that far," Leslie said. Her eyes half-closed, as if she was calculating a complex math problem and on the verge of a breakthrough.

"Captain, I've set the countdown timer according to the message," Dubs said, and I observed the top right corner of the viewscreen. The digital numbers ticked silently. It showed eighteen minutes and thirty-seven seconds now.

"How long before they're within firing range?" Karo asked.

Terrance ran the numbers. "Three minutes."

I had an idea. I wasn't sure we could fend off this many vessels with only five of our own, and even if the suborbital weapons worked, they might not be able to counter all of the enemies in time. We couldn't afford for the school to be destroyed, or even worse; an attack on our cities would be devastating. No other races would set foot on Haven again if that occurred. We had to take a risk.

"Dubs, fly us out. Move to the side of them… here." I pointed at the radar, and he nodded.

"Dean, are you sure? Maybe we should stand firm," Leslie said.

"Trust me. We'll be able to divert a few of them." I almost laughed, thinking about Slate's erratic flying while being chased around New Spero when we'd first arrived. "And worst case, they don't veer off, but we have a clear line at their cluster from behind."

"It'll work," Terrance agreed, and Dubs started forward. The red icons were blinking nearer, especially as we raced away from orbit.

The Gatekeepers

Terrance opened the line to the other allies and advised them of what we were doing. The Padlog ship took our lead and accelerated away from the rest of the defenders, moving to flank the enemy from the opposite side.

The clock continued its descent. It was at sixteen minutes and counting. "Almost in range," Terrance said, and he fired toward the enemy with a pulse cannon as soon as his screen flashed green. He let loose another five volleys, and as luck would have it, one of the red icons vanished from the radar. "I was trying to surprise them. But I'll take it," he said.

"I think that made them angry." I pointed at the viewscreen, where Dubs had zoomed the thousand kilometers to see the vessels. Five of them veered off toward us. Another five were moving toward the Padlog ship a thousand klicks the other way, leaving nine moving toward Haven.

"It's working," Leslie said. She grinned until the realization hit her. "They're coming for us. We can't fight five of them."

"You're forgetting something," I told her.

"What?"

"Dubs, engage the cloaking shield," I told the robot in the pilot's chair.

"Engaged, Captain." Our image blinked out on the radar, and the five vessels kept moving toward our previous location.

"Let's position ourselves behind them," I ordered, and Dubs swung our vessel around, letting the enemy ships pass through before following the vessels. "We only have one shot at this. Once we fire, they'll know where we are."

I took a look at the ships through the viewscreen. They were triangles, almost like the stealth bombers I had models of in my room as a child. My dad and I had bought the kits, and after hours of gluing and painting, we'd each sported a bomber. He'd let me keep both of them.

These enemy ships were black as midnight, sleek and pointed. They moved quickly, efficiently, and I wondered what kind of creature lay behind the controls.

"I have a lock on two of them," Terrance said.

I glanced at the radar and noticed one of the red icons was gone from near the Padlog, but the insectoid ship was in full fleeing mode, four enemy ships right on its tail. I silently wished our allies luck.

The timer was down to nine minutes. Terrance's nostrils flared as he waited for the go-ahead.

"Fire!" I shouted, and he tapped the console.

As soon as the cannons were off, Dubs arced the ship away, leaving the remaining three vessels scattering.

"They've arrived. We're going to hold them off…" The message from the Bhlat ship cut off as the nine enemies neared Haven. Two of them snuck past our defenses, moving toward the atmosphere.

Leslie was on her earpiece. "Take them down! Take them down!"

Dubs had another enemy in sight, and Terrance fired, hitting the glowing shield once before penetrating the defenses and blasting it to nothing. Then there were two.

"Captain, the Padlog vessel has been destroyed," Dubs said solemnly, and I saw the remaining four enemy ships change trajectory as they moved to join their initial cluster around Haven.

"Damn it!" I yelled. "We have to join them. Take us there."

Dubs shot us around, and raced toward Haven with the cloak activated. The two remaining vessels wandered around aimlessly, expecting to be attacked by a ghost.

By the time we were within firing range, the clock was at three minutes, and there were twelve ships left.

"The ground defenses are working. Another is trying to break through," Leslie said.

I spotted the Bhlat ship in the viewer now, and it bombarded the incoming fleet with everything it had, but there were too many of the enemies. Terrance shot at them, destroying one, then two more of the black triangle ships, but it wasn't enough to save the Bhlat. Their vessel exploded, a small piece at first, which escalated into a million fragments.

We were left beside an Inlorian warship and a Keppe vessel, neither of which had enough firepower to stop the coming vessels. Terrance continued firing, but our friend's shields were being decimated.

"Captain, they're here." Dubs veered us away, and I smiled grimly as *Starbound* arrived. The larger than life exploratory vessel fired ten beams at once, each striking its target with ease. Blue spheres shot out from the ship's underbelly, and seconds later, there were no more enemy ships around.

The Keppe ship and the Inlorian vessel were intact.

"Dubs, connect to the *Starbound*." I stood at the viewer, and Yope appeared on the screen.

"I don't know if I should be surprised to find you here, Dean Parker," Yope said with a smile.

"You saved our bacon today, Admiral. Thank you," I told him.

"Lucky timing. We were returning from our mission, and I decided to stop by this Haven I keep hearing everyone talk about." A Keppe woman marched over to Yope and whispered in his ear. "It looks like the Inlor need some help. Their life support and thrusters are inactive. We'll send help. See you on the surface?" Yope was being far more friendly than usual. Maybe the time exploring the universe again had given him a new outlook on life.

"See you there," I told him, and Dubs cut the line.

One of the black vessels was intact, and it sat there lifelessly in space. "Let's beam and board. We need to know who we're up against," I said, and Dubs flipped the cloak off and activated the tractor beam.

"Commencing lock," Dubs said, and we all collectively breathed a sigh of relief. No one had been harmed on the surface, and we'd suffered some casualties. Between the Padlog and Bhlat ships, I guessed that thirty or so of our finest had perished today, and those numbers were unforgivable. Any life taken was unforgivable in my books.

Snow fell in droves now, covering our lander as we emerged from the ship. The enemy ship had sat there idly for two hours while ground teams cleared it. They claimed nothing was alive on board, but we weren't taking any chances. I was in an armored EVA, and so was Karo.

"One last day of adventures for us, right, Dean?" Karo took long strides as he advanced toward the ship we were about to enter.

"For old time's sake," I told him. I'd called Mary to let her know what happened, and she understood the delay. She agreed we needed to see the inside with our own eyes, so we stuck around. On the plus side, I was able to spend a few more hours with Karo before the inevitable happened.

Terrance met us at the entrance to the ship. It was smaller than I'd initially thought. Seeing things zoomed in on the viewscreen in space as you're racing the opposite direction often gives the wrong impression.

Still, it stood about twenty meters from top to bottom, and at least a hundred meters from nose to thrusters. The entrance was at the side, near the belly, and a half-dozen armed Bhlat stood at the doorway, waving us inside.

"They're not messing around," Karo said as we stepped past them.

"Nope." I set foot into the ship, and felt like I'd been transported to a distant world. Everything was matte black inside: the walls, the floors, the ceiling. My boots clanked over the dark metal grates that made up the corridor, and Karo was granted enough head room inside here to not have to duck like he was used to.

"Where are they?" I asked a Bhlat inside. He pointed to the hall and tilted his finger to the left. "Thanks."

I took the lead, Karo close behind, and Terrance was

after him, taking his time as he examined his surroundings. We stopped at a computer integrated into the wall, but the ship's power was off.

"I can't wait until we can dissect this and find out where they come from," he said. "We're bringing in a secondary power source today to see if we can't breathe some life into the ship."

I would be long gone by the time that arrived. I took the first left doorway and saw the aliens. Two of them lay on the ground, dead. "What killed them? I don't think the life support could have failed that quickly."

They were wearing all black; thick padding covered their bodies. Their heads... that was where it became troublesome. I staggered back as white dots speckled my vision.

"Dean, what is it?" Karo asked, stabilizing me.

"Look." I pointed at one of the aliens, and Karo's eyes jumped open.

"They're..."

"They look human," I said. I knelt between the bodies. One was a woman, her black hair shorn short. She had a tattoo under her eye: three dark lines curving like a saber. The man had the same tattoo. He was scruffier, his hair shaggy, his face unshaven.

"Dean, remember, we look human too, but the hybrids aren't, fully," Terrance said from the doorway. He was right, but it bothered me that the attackers seemed so much like us.

"We'll find out soon enough. I take it there's a DNA sample being analyzed?" I asked.

Terrance nodded. "Already on it."

The Gatekeepers

We toured the dark ship, our suits giving us the light we needed to see. We found twenty more dead bodies, none showing signs of trauma, leaving me to think their deaths were by choice. "I think an autopsy will find they took their own lives with some sort of pill."

Karo nodded. "Likely."

After seeing all of these tattooed-faced human lookalikes, I needed to get off the ship and out of the EVA. My breaths were coming quick and shallow.

I left the other two behind, moving past the Bhlat guards and outside into the night. Snow fell harder now, and I recognized a man waiting in a lander nearby. Admiral Yope waved me over.

I entered the small ship and he shut the door. "Cold as ice." He outstretched his hand, and I shook it after popping my helmet off and setting it on a bench. "Dean Parker. I'd say it's good to see you, but under the circumstances…"

"Same here. You were gone a while," I told him.

"Yes. We saw some wonderful things, but I think it's time I retire from the stars. There are more pressing matters at home," he said wistfully.

I met his gaze. "Like Kimtra?" I asked, mentioning the smart woman he used to be involved with.

He nodded. "Like Kimtra. Very astute of you."

"Before I go, I wanted to throw something at you, Admiral," I said.

"Please."

I told him about the exploration ship we wanted to build, and advised him that Magnus would be taking the helm. I wasn't sure if Magnus had actually believed me, but I was going to make it a reality.

"We can help expedite that project for you. Do you want to build it here?" he asked.

"Haven would be best."

"The Keppe will happily trade the supplies needed, as well as leave you our blueprints. From the sounds of it, you have a few ideas of your own. Our base models are quite adaptable," he said.

Even after the crazy day of loss and victory, I was excited by this prospect. I sat down, and Yope joined me.

"Dean, you look tired," he said.

"I've been through a lot recently."

"I heard about you finding Magnus and *Fortune* out there. Thank you for bringing our people home," he said.

"It's more than that." I told him about the Gatekeepers, and the portals failing. Yope was surprised to hear it, and he almost stood up when I described the altercation at the prison world, then the shapeshifting animal that had taken Magnus' daughter.

"You *have* been through a lot. I think time on an exploratory ship is exactly what you and your family need," he said.

We chatted for a few more minutes, but eventually, I had to see Karo off. After a quick goodbye to Yope, I found Karo waiting for me in our lander.

I greeted him, and he forced a smile. "Ready to go?" he asked.

I wasn't, but I pushed the worry about the future aside for the moment. I shoved away the fear of seeing human

The Gatekeepers

faces on the strange new enemy's ship, and focused on the task at hand.

"I'm ready. What a day. We weren't expecting this." I laughed, and he joined me, the sort of hysterical sound you could only emit after too many hours awake.

By the time we arrived at the portals, we sat silent. They'd programmed the lock remotely to my DNA so I could gain access, and the door opened to my touch. I headed for the portal room, Karo beside me, and I paused in the doorway, placing my pen-sized device from Fontem's collection on the ground. The light emerged from it, sealing against the walls and ceiling before vanishing from sight.

"All set," I told him, and we were soon basking in the light of the portals. My very last trip through one, and his second to last.

TWENTY-FOUR

"*P*apa!" Jules ran toward me, hugging my legs as we emerged from the corridor.

Mary's eyes expressed her worry, and I squinted a smile at her, letting her know we were okay.

"Ableen, are you ready?" Karo asked, and the Theos woman nodded.

"I am, Karo. Let's go home," she said, and we followed them through the corridors. "Thank you for everything, Dean and Mary."

"You're welcome, Ableen," Mary said.

Ableen hugged me at the edge of the portal room. "Without your help, I'd still be on the Collector's ship."

"Take care of him for us, would you?" I whispered into her ear.

"I will," she promised.

Karo and Ableen stood past the doorway, and Jules was at my leg, looking up at me.

"Where Karo go, Papa?" she asked.

I knelt to her level. "Karo and Ableen are going home."

"No," she said defiantly. Her lower lip stuck out.

"Yes, honey. They have to heal the crystals," I told her, knowing she wouldn't understand.

"We can help," she said, holding her hand out.

"What's that about?" Mary asked.

"I don't know. She's said it a few times lately. I think she wants to be helpful. She must have learned it from a game," I suggested.

We'd all said our goodbyes, so we remained at a distance as the two tall Theos walked to the portal table. I couldn't believe this was it. They were departing to their home world, and we'd never see them again. The portals would be disabled after they released the Theos inside the complex system's main crystal, the resulting effect freeing every Theos from their captivity inside the Shandra. I hadn't thought of that name for a long time.

I recalled absorbing the Theos with Karo, placing his father inside the stone to activate it. Standing there, I could sense the ghosts of the Theos I'd merged with, the ones who'd helped me fight Mary's Iskios.

Karo gave me one last nod as he placed the Modifier on the table, his green eyes reminding me of Jules'. I tried to picture the Theos world's Shandra symbol, but couldn't. It was some magic protecting them, and even after using it, the memory was wiped from my mind.

"He'll be okay," Mary said. Her arm pulled me closer, and she kissed me on the cheek, leaning her head onto my shoulder as we watched them prepare to leave.

They both waved from the table, and Karo went to press the icon.

"Papa!" I heard Jules' voice before I saw her. She was

inside the portal room, running for Karo.

She was too close. She'd get beamed away with them! I ran for her. The second I scooped her up into my arms, Karo pressed the icon, and everything became white once again.

I was once again floating. Alone.

"Jules!" I shouted, but she was nowhere in sight. I wasn't sure how this worked, but I guessed she was already safely with Karo and Ableen. The others didn't seem to be pulled to this state of transition like I was.

"Jules is safe," the voice said. I recognized it. I'd once spoken using the same voice.

"Tagu. You're Karo's father," I told him.

The figure appeared. Tall, lanky, gray-skinned, with bright colorful eyes. He was an older version of my friend. "I am."

"Why did you bring me here?" I asked. I peered down, and I was wearing the same clothing I'd had on when I first met Karo.

"We have a bond. You've absorbed my energy, even for a moment, and that connects us. The Shandra will be unlinked, then?" he asked.

"That's the plan. We weren't supposed to go with Karo and Ableen," I told him.

His eyes displayed his surprise. "Ableen? Who is this Ableen?"

I told him the quick version, and Tagu acted very pleased with the news. "This is good. This is very good."

"What else do you need? We need to make it to New Spero before this all happens," I said.

The Gatekeepers

Tagu shook his head slowly. "I'm sorry, Dean. We can no longer allow travel through the Map."

Even here, my heart rate sped up. "What are you talking about?"

"We've been holding on by a thread. We cannot function any longer. This is the last trip through the Shandra. Our job is complete. The Balance is returned. Thanks to you," he added.

I ran a hand through my hair. "You have to let us go home. I have a daughter. She can't stay here."

"I'm sorry. Tell Karo I love him. Tell him to be happy," Tagu said, and began floating away.

I tried to swim in the white light, but my arms moved helplessly. "Tagu! Don't do this to me! One last trip, that's it, I promise!" I shouted at the top of my lungs as the figure grew farther and farther away until he was nothing more than a speck… then nothing. I was alone in the light.

"*P*apa!" Tiny hands held my face as I blinked my eyes open. I sat up in a hurry, grabbing my daughter.

"Jules, what have you done?" I asked her. She was clear-eyed, even smiling.

"Dean, I didn't see you. I'm sorry," Karo said. "What happened? Did you see your future self again?"

I jumped up, looking around the familiar room I'd only been in once, filling up with the energy of the Theos a few years ago, before Jules was even born. "No. I saw your father."

"My father?"

"Yes. Remember, we left him in here." I pointed at the table, which was no longer glowing.

"I remember well," he said.

"This was it. I can't feel him any longer. The screaming is done," Ableen said.

Karo turned to her. "What do you mean? We have to help Dean home," he told her.

"We cannot," Ableen advised.

I stumbled away until my back hit the wall of the crystal-covered room. Jules stood there like this was no big deal, and I wanted so much to be angry with her for running toward Karo, but I couldn't bring myself to feel mad. She was a little girl, an inquisitive kid who ran head-first into dangerous situations with her heart instead of her head. She was just like me.

"What do we do?" I asked softly.

Karo tried to activate the portal table again, but it failed. Nothing worked. The Crystal Map was here, but it showed none of the glowing portal worlds any longer. The table may as well have been meant for dining on. Jules walked over to it and I crossed the room, picking her up before she could touch it. Her eyes were brighter than ever as we locked gazes, and I almost dropped her.

"We can help," she told me plainly.

"Okay. Let's help by going to Karo's house and figuring this out," I said.

"Good idea." Karo grabbed the few packs they had, his stuffed with mementos of his time among us.

The Gatekeepers

We exited the portal room, and I was humbled by the beauty of the Theos world. I hadn't seen much last time, but now Karo was more open to sharing their secret planet with us. His home was nearby, and we emerged from the crystal caves into a village. The streets were lined with dark stone roads, and tall crystal buildings stood pristine as ever all around us.

Ableen took it all in with awe. "It's… different than I remember," she said.

"A lot has changed since you were taken," Karo admitted.

The sun was low in the horizon, and even from here, I could see the immense crystal mountain in the distance. The sun lowered a little more, and a thousand prisms scattered across the sky. If I hadn't been terrified at being stranded here for the rest of my life, I would have appreciated the sight even more.

"It's beautiful," Ableen said.

"Karo, is that…?" I started to ask.

"That's where we have to access the portals from, yes. It's the core that powers the entire thing," he said.

"Why didn't you tell me about it the first time I was here? I could have used them to defeat the Iskios," I said, a little confused.

"Dean, you were resourceful in coming here, but I couldn't risk giving you all of the information. You could have taken their power and become something… something terrible," Karo said.

"Or wonderful," I added, not liking the term he used.

"Perhaps, but I didn't know that. If you had, the

portals would have failed regardless," he told me, and it made sense.

"You do have space ships here, though, right?" I asked.

"Yes."

"It's going to be a long trip home, isn't it?" I asked.

He only nodded. Jules smiled up at me, and she grabbed my hand as we traveled toward Karo's home. I couldn't think of that journey yet. It might be years before we found home again, and I had no idea how we'd do it.

Karo took us into a building, this one squat and sturdy. "Is this the same place we were before?" I asked, not recognizing anything.

"No. That was more for show. We didn't want anyone to see our real world." Karo opened a door, and it slid to the side smoothly. The inside of the building was amazing. Wooden furniture over hard crystal floors. Lights came on as he stepped into it, and Ableen smiled as she took it in.

"This is nice. Nicer than the hut we had back home," she said with a laugh. I couldn't join her. My stomach was aching, and I found a seat on a soft-cushioned couch, obviously built for someone much taller.

"Dean?" Karo sat beside me.

"This is too much. We saved the stranded Keepers, we stopped the monster from killing, and now, I'm here with Jules while Mary's on New Spero. Is the universe really trying that hard to keep us apart?" I asked.

Jules was wandering around, touching everything.

"We'll figure it out, Dean. We always do," he said.

He wasn't wrong, but at that moment, it was hard to believe. "You know, it was only yesterday that we were fending invaders off outside Haven," I told him.

"I know. How about something to eat?" Karo asked.

"Let me guess, pizza?" Ableen beat me to it, and I finally broke a smile.

"Is this a house?" I asked Karo.

"It is. My house, I guess. It has three stories and six bedrooms. The layout is different than you're used to, I suppose." Karo was already moving toward the strange kind of device he'd concocted pizza from the first time we'd met. Moments later, fresh food came out of it.

"Now you know you need to share that technology with me, right?" I asked. For a second, I forgot I wasn't going to be able to bring it home through the portals.

"We'll share whatever you like, Dean," Karo said.

"Does this mean you finally trust me?" I asked, giving him a sideways grin.

Karo shook his head. "Not even close. I trust Mary, though, so I'll give you anything you need."

"You know, when we met, you weren't much of a joker. Do you think us humans rubbed off on you?" I asked.

"More than I'd like to admit. I'll surely miss everyone, including you and Miss Jules here. Will you help us tomorrow before you leave?" Karo asked.

"We will. I wouldn't have it any other way. You know, since I'm stuck here anyway. I did tell Ableen I'd help shut them off, didn't I?" I rose from the couch.

"You did, Dean. Perhaps this was a self-fulfilling prophecy?" she asked.

"I hadn't thought of that, but I wouldn't be surprised.

The universe seems to have a few tricks up her sleeve," I said, trying to relax. I couldn't change our situation, but I could accept it and work with it the best I could.

"Jules, time to eat," I said, and she tottered over to the table. "Do you have a sink to wash?"

Karo pointed to a spot in the kitchen that had two holes. He stuck his hands in the openings, and a red light shone out. He pulled them out when the light went off, and he grinned. "Saves the hassle of towels," he said.

I tried it first, feeling an energy vibrate through me rather than soap and water. It was some kind of disinfecting station.

"Okay, Jules. Your turn," I said, and she stuck her tiny hands inside, fully trusting it was safe.

She beamed as the light turned off, and she pulled them out, staring at them up close.

We ate in relative silence, not wanting to discuss the next steps. I stopped after one piece; the food sat heavily in my stomach. Jules sat playfully, like she didn't have a care in the world, and I suppose she really didn't. Her mother would be so worried about us, and I wished I had the communicator with me. We hadn't brought anything, because we were expecting to leave Terran Five and head home in our lander for a quiet night, just the three of us and Maggie cozied up in our house.

"We *will* figure it out, Dean," Karo promised.

"I know," I licd.

"Tomorrow," Karo said.

"Tomorrow."

Karo took us all on a tour of his home, and I watched

as Ableen searched through her new abode. It was endearing. Jules seemed to like it here, and I had a hard time wrangling her up when we were done.

"These are the bedrooms. I trust you'll find it to your liking," Karo said. He was different here, not so subdued. I could tell he was upset that we were stuck here, and he likely blamed himself for our situation, even though it wasn't his fault.

The room was spacious, with its own bathroom, one not too far off from a human's needs. The bed was soft, and Karo returned a few minutes later with fresh linens.

"Even your bedding doesn't grow stale," I said, taking the sheets.

"You don't become an ancient race by having poor sleeps," he said as a joke, but his face sobered as he probably recalled that all his people were gone, and he and Ableen were the last.

Ableen entered with Jules in tow. "I take it you'd like her back?"

I patted the freshly-made bed, and Jules ran over, letting me pick her up and place her beside me. She kicked out her legs and laughed as she fell on the bed. She was in a little romper again, and I couldn't believe how much trouble this tiny child had brought me. Still, I was glad to be with her.

"Goodnight," I told the two Theos, watching us like proud grandparents from the doorway. I saw the way Ableen looked at Karo, and I could almost read her mind. She wanted a child.

"Goodnight, Dean. Goodnight, Miss Jules," Karo said,

and the door shut, sealing us in.

"You are a piece of work, Jules," I said.

"Papa. Where's Mommy?" she asked.

"Home with Maggie," I told her.

"Can we see?"

"Not yet. We have something to do first," I said.

She nodded, as if that made sense to her young form of logic.

We fell asleep on the bed shortly after, me dreaming of finding a way to New Spero, one that didn't take years of space travel to happen.

TWENTY-FIVE

"This is the ship?" I asked, running a hand along the side of the vessel. It was sleek, almost like the perfect skipping stone: round and flat.

"This is it," Karo said. "It was my father's, and his father's before him. I guess that makes it mine," he added.

"Are you sure you want to part with it?" I asked. There were other similar vessels nearby, each glittering in the sunlight. It was a gorgeous day on their planet, and I suspected most days were this nice here. It was bright, but not too hot; there was a breeze, but not too gusty. Out here, on the outskirts of town, we were closer to the mountain range, and Ableen stood at the precipice of the hillside, staring out toward it, as if she was being called toward the remaining trapped Theos inside.

"I'll gladly give you this small gift. I've never used one of these ships, but I hear they're impressive. You won't go hungry on board, that much is clear," he said, implying it had food modifiers like his home.

I nodded toward the mountains and asked, "Do we fly there?"

Karo smiled. "No. I have something to show you. If I knew how to pass these on to you, I'd do so. It would help transport around the planet. They're not long-range, but you'd be able to travel from one Terran site to the next with ease."

He led us across the white stone ground, toward an outbuilding beside the parked vessels. I counted now, and there were five ships here, each about fifty meters long. It would be ample room for Jules and me to share. I pushed aside any worry for what Mary was feeling, because I couldn't control that. I had to focus on what was in front of me.

"Come on, Jules," I said. She was beside Ableen, holding the woman's hand.

Karo went first into the building, which I found sparsely furnished. There were seats outside and right in the doorways, and I imagined cloaked Theos guards posted there, allowing access only to those with permits. A doorway stood at the far end of the dim room, its green light flickering on at Karo's presence. The light glowed around the doorframe, urging us toward it with calming illumination.

"This will take us to our destination," he said.

"How is it powered? Surely not by the Theos' living energy?" I asked him.

"It harnesses solar energy, nothing more," he said, as if that explanation should make sense.

Jules walked up to it, and I held her away. "Sweetie, we'll let Uncle Karo go first," I said, grinning at Karo.

"It's safe. Come," he said, and waved us forward.

Ableen appeared to have used the doorways before, and she stepped through right after Karo.

"Ready, Jules?" I asked.

"Yes, Papa," she said, and stepped forward on balanced legs. I was right behind her, my hand on her back.

One step, I was at the building beside the idle Theos fleet; the next, we were at the bottom of the crystal mountain, looking up at the majestic sight. The doorway was out in the open here, and the green glowing energy surrounding it misted away as we moved beyond its sensors.

"Impressive," I said, and Jules started ahead, walking toward the mountain. "Someone's interested in the crystals." Jules was off-kilter today. She was quieter, more subdued, yet she was joyful; happy to be alive even here, so far from her home and mother. It was almost like she knew something the rest of us didn't, and it was off-putting.

"I suppose we should follow her." Karo smiled. I knew today was going to be difficult for him. His father's essence was in the main portal, and thousands, maybe even hundreds of thousands of them were inside the crystals around us. The air felt energized here, and I lifted my arm, finding the hairs on it standing straight up. A few of Jules' dark, erratic curls lifted as we went, but she didn't seem to notice.

"Do you guys feel that?" I asked, and Ableen nodded.

"It feels wrong," she said.

The sun was bright behind us, reflecting its voluminous glow across the smooth-surfaced peaks. There were too many similarities here to the Iskios world where we'd lost Mary. Only here, the stones were filled with Theos instead of Iskios, their rivals.

I was mentally prepared for a betrayal, for something bad to happen; only I wasn't armed, and I cursed under my breath at my stupidity. Karo moved with determination, as if there was nothing strange going on, and he was probably right. I couldn't deal with another Iskios scenario. Jules stumbled ahead, her tiny legs moving faster as we went. I should have left her at Karo's house. Maybe I should have stayed there, too.

"Come, Dean," Karo said, waving me forward. Lost in my thoughts, I was a hundred yards behind the other three. I jogged to catch up and arrived at my daughter's side. She smiled over at me, her green eyes brighter than ever before.

I'd been so lost in my own thoughts, I hadn't noticed how close we were to the vast peaks. Our path led us down now. Tall walls of clear crystal rose on either side of us, and as we walked, the stone lit up from a meter or so inside the surface.

"Have you been here before, Karo?" I asked, and his eyes said he had. They were glimmering with tears.

"I have. I was here when they entered. I saw them melt into the essence of this peak, fueling the portals. One last sacrifice for the good of the universe. For the Balance." His steps slowed, and Ableen was at his side in a second, her slender arm threading through his.

"It's okay, Karo. We have to do this. This is what they want," she told him.

"I know. I can feel it too. It's just… once they're gone, it truly will be only you and I left of our race." Karo stopped and laid a hand on the crystal wall, the light growing brighter at his touch.

"We'll make the Theos proud, Karo. Husband." Ableen reached for his hand, and he took it in his.

"Very well, wife," he said, and I didn't know if that made them a couple, but I supposed it did to them, and that was all that mattered.

"Papa!" Jules called from far ahead. She was at the end of the walled pathway, and she disappeared around the bend. I really needed to watch her better. I was so distracted, and she was like a slippery eel at this age, sticking her nose into everything.

"Jules, stay where you are!" I shouted, my voice echoing down the corridor. The angle of the pathway evened out, and now I could see we were entering the center of the mountain itself. It grew dimmer; even the sunlight was unable to refract through so many layers of clear crystal this deep inside.

I found her at a large arc-shaped doorway, and she peered toward me, her eyes burning green. She pointed into the room beyond, and I came to meet her.

"This is it. The Shandra Source." Karo stepped past us, and his long white mane rose in the air, the room thick with charged energy.

Ableen's did the same, and she tentatively stood beside her new husband, placing her hands over her ears as if blocking a sound I couldn't hear.

The moment I stepped foot into the chamber, I understood. Thousands of voices whispered at once; each of the Theos trapped within the pillars of crystal in the center of the space were vying for our attention, begging to be released. No wonder Ableen had been so upset about it, demanding we help them. They were in pain, tormented by the crystals. Ever since I'd banished the Iskios through the Shifter I'd bartered from Garo Alnod, the Balance had been off.

We had to right this. I attempted to block their voices from my mind, but it was impossible.

"Papa." Jules' voice was tiny, and I took her hand as she began to cry. I knelt down and wiped her tears away, pulling her into me.

"It's time," Karo told Ableen, and they moved toward the middle of the chamber. There were thirteen pillars forming a circle about twenty meters in diameter. At the center was a series of clear double-ended tourmaline crystals. As the flesh and blood Theos arrived, the crystals shone brightly, until I had to look away, blocking Jules from harming her eyes too. She tried to wiggle away, but I held tight.

"Thank you for your sacrifice Great Ones. You have done our people an honor beyond comprehension. We will continue our race. We will make you proud, as you have made us proud!" Karo was shouting, and I felt myself go weightless. My vision lowered to see my feet lifted off the ground.

The light had dimmed, and Jules poked her head from my chest, curiously watching Karo and Ableen touching the crystals in between the pulsing pillars.

"You are free!" Ableen shouted, and we stared at them from our floating position as thousands of lights emerged from the stones, slowly at first, then in a rush. We kept rising off the floor, and Karo and Ableen were doing the same now. They waved their hands upwards, thrusting their ancestors' energy from their trapped position, freeing them into… I wasn't sure. The universe, perhaps their afterlife. The whispers turned from fearful and anguished to happiness, relief, joy, and Jules and I smiled and wept as they lifted away from the surface, beyond the peaks of the crystal mountain and into space.

I felt them leaving, and I knew Jules did too. She waved at them, smiling widely and giggling. It seemed to go on forever, but when it was over, we lowered to the surface, and Ableen and Karo lay between the pillars in a heap.

Jules ran to them.

"Karo, Ableen, are you okay?" I asked, and Karo sat up.

"It is done," he said, smiling.

"It is done." Ableen was up now. Jules hugged her.

"Thank you for being a part of this, Dean Parker. You are the best friend one could ask for," Karo said.

"We wouldn't have missed it for the world, right, Jules?" I wondered if we were meant to come here. Jules running into the portal room at just the wrong time might have really been the right time.

"I'm sorry you have such a long trip home." Karo was on his feet, and he gripped my shoulder lightly.

"So am I. We still have one more thing to do first, right?" I asked.

Karo grinned. "We do."

The crystal mountain was dark, no longer glowing or luminous as the sun set. It felt like the end of an era I'd only begun to understand. The portals were dead. Without the Theos inside fueling the Shandra Source in the crystal mountain, we were stuck here. Karo had packed up the ship he was giving us, and Jules and I were ready to leave at first light.

We had one last task to be part of. Karo's father, Tagu, the same one who talked to me on our way to their home world, remained inside this portal.

"Why didn't he leave with the rest?" I asked Karo.

"When we took the others from this stone to help you fight the Iskios, we locked him inside as a precaution at the same time," Karo explained.

"Let's go say goodbye to your dad," I told him.

We entered the Theos portal room, a clean-lined space, made from nothing but the same rock as the rest of the world. The clear crystal walls no longer glowed; the table didn't activate. The symbols weren't there. It was no longer functional.

Jules was walking toward the table, and I snatched her up. "Let's give Uncle Karo some time alone."

Ableen stayed with us, letting Karo have the last few moments with his dad, even if they couldn't speak to one another.

Karo laid his hands on the stone beneath the table, and I heard whispered words, unable to understand them. One solitary light emerged from the table, a pure white glow that lifted, circled around Karo, and hovered into the ceiling and beyond. Karo stood, staring at the table that would no longer work.

"He's gone," he told us.

Ableen crossed the space over to his side. "They're all gone. It's what they wanted. I can no longer hear their cries for help," she said.

Jules demanded I set her down. She frowned at me, as if I'd been holding her captive. She pursed her lips and moved toward Karo and Ableen.

"What are you doing, honey?" I asked. She wasn't facing me, and Karo's eyes went wide in surprise as she neared the table.

She glanced towards me, her eyes glowing brightly. Their color reflected around the crystal room, and she lifted a hand. Green energy coursed from her fingertips now, and she smiled like she was playing a game. "We can help," she said again, and I finally understood what she'd been going on about for the last few days.

Karo and Ableen were standing in silence, frozen in awe, as I rushed to my daughter's side.

"What is it, Jules? How can we help?" I asked her.

Her hand was no longer visible as the cackling energy enveloped it. "Shandra poor tails." She said *portals* wrong, and it was the sweetest thing I'd ever seen.

"You can help the portals?" I asked from my crouched position.

She nodded. "I can help. See?"

Jules breezed past me to the portal stone and set her hand on it. The crystal exploded in light, and the force knocked me over two feet. I landed on my side, and Karo and Ableen were on the ground as well. Only Jules stood, her hand eagerly pressed to the portal stone, green energy beating from her body. The table glowed now; the symbols on the crystal walls burned hotly.

As quickly as it happened, everything ended, and Jules let go of the stone, her hand no longer a tool. She skipped to my side, and I pulled her in. "What did you do?" I asked. Her eyes were no longer glowing, only deep green, and she kissed my cheek.

"I helped," she said, as if that was all I needed to know.

Karo was at the portal table, and his voice boomed through the room. "Dean, it works!"

I leaped over to him. "What do you mean? How could she have possibly done this?" I asked.

"I don't know, but look." He turned the Crystal Map on, and every last pinprick of light around the universe where there was a stone was activated once again. From the looks of it, there were even more now, perhaps destinations that had once had portals, but where the Theos had failed long ago.

"It's... amazing," I said. I picked up Jules and squeezed her. "You did it, honey. I don't know how, but you did it." I was elated, but at the same time, terrified that my daughter held power like this. It was clear she'd gained the power from growing inside Mary's womb while Mary was possessed by the Iskios, and I was scared of what that meant for my little girl. She was so special, but this only meant she would become a target, a unique being that attracted too much attention.

"Dean, it looks like you can go home after all," Ableen

said softly, and I mouthed the word.

Home.

I returned to my house on New Spero, but Mary wasn't there. Instead of waiting it out, Jules and I went to the lander and headed for Magnus' place. There were other vehicles there: a couple of SUVs, a police transport, and a lander like the one I was inside.

People emerged from the house, and Jules pointed through the viewer. "Mommy!" She was right. Mary was standing in the front yard. I landed in a hurry, so anxious to see her, for her to know we were okay. When the door opened, revealing who was inside, Mary ran for us.

"Dean! Jules!" Her brown hair fluttered around in the air like a cape, and I met her halfway, enveloping her in a hug, spinning her around.

"We're home, babe," I told her, and Mary grabbed Jules, hugging her close.

"What happened?" she asked in my ear.

Magnus and Nat were there, and I noticed Reed beside Loweck, and another figure stood in the shade of the front porch beside the two kids. Maggie, Charlie, and Carey all ran for us, barking their joy at our arrival, and it was all too much.

Slate raised an arm from his seat near the house. "Jules did it. Jules fixed the portals," I spoke softly as I moved as fast as I could to the house.

"What do you mean, Jules fixed them?" Mary asked quietly, sensing my caution.

Jules was in her mother's arms, and she proudly said, "I helped. I told Papa I could help. Silly Papa."

I smirked at Mary as we walked, and shrugged. "It's true. She did tell me that."

Magnus and Natalia greeted us along with the others, but they stepped aside so I could see Slate. It felt like it took forever to cross the yard, but there we were, face to face again. His skin was sallow, his eyes sunken, but he was here. He was alive and well.

"Slate. You're here," I said, stating the obvious.

"So are you." He laughed, sticking out his fist. I bumped it and laughed along with him.

"How are you feeling?" I asked.

"Better than the other guy, from what I hear," Slate said.

"You going to be okay?" I asked quietly.

"Doctors say I'll be right as rain in a few weeks," he told me.

"Good." Everyone here was on the front porch, and they were all looking at me, as if waiting for some intense explanation of how we'd made it here.

"Well? Dean, you have to tell us," Magnus said.

I didn't know Loweck or Reed all that well, and couldn't have Jules's secret become known to anyone but those closest to my family. Only the few trusted members of our gang would ever know the truth.

"It was the craziest thing," I said. "The Theos were freed by Ableen and Karo, and..." I lied the rest of the story, and they nodded along, accepting my words as truth. I'd tell Slate, Magnus, and Nat later, but for now, the story I told them on the front deck was going to be the one the Gatekeepers learned, along with the Alliance of Worlds members. No one was going to see my daughter as a tool. Nobody would ever find out she held within her the power of an entire ancient race of beings.

EPILOGUE

"Welcome to the meeting, Dean Parker of the New Spero Gatekeepers. You all know him, and this weekend's conference is a good time for you each to pick his brain, to meet the man we've all heard so much about," Sarlun told the intimate gathered group. He spoke in his native Shimmali language, and the words translated into each Gatekeeper's personal earpiece in their own tongue.

We were inside the Gatekeepers' Academy on Haven, in the newly finished auditorium, and I stepped up to center stage, taking in the three hundred members of the Gatekeepers. They applauded loudly, coming to their feet. There were so many different races here, representatives from every corner of space. We'd been cataloging the new Crystal Map and were confident there were even more worlds to explore, more races to bring into the fold, and far more trade potential.

"Today, we are here because of this man." I pointed to Sarlun, who stepped away as the crowd continued to cheer. I raised a hand eventually, hoping to continue speaking. "We are Gatekeepers, and we will always persevere. The portals, the Shandra, were a basis for what we've been known for: traveling through them between worlds. We're explorers, peacekeepers, and warriors.

"Recently, the portals were failing, and we all now know the reason for that. Let's give thanks to the Theos, whose efforts allowed us to ever have our group, for without them, the portals would never have existed. Now, we not only have access to our old portal symbols, but countless more.

"You will each be able to expand your reach, and Sarlun has already begun a schedule for each team, which you'll receive over the next two days." I paused while they chattered to each other. They'd been grounded for so long, they were anxious to be stationed out there. I understood only too well.

Mary waved at me from the side of the auditorium, and Jules stood beside her, watching with interest. It had been six months since we'd left the Theos world, and so much had changed. Mary and I felt it was all for the best, but we no longer lived at our house on New Spero. We'd given it to Leonard, who had grown close with Reed. We'd planned to visit and see how the house looked now, but Mary and I were having a hard time with going there.

I realized the crowd was waiting for me to keep talking, so I moved on. "You also all know about the two separate attacks on Haven. The target has been our Academy, but we won't let anyone destroy what is ours. This school will train the next generation of children from all Alliance of Worlds planets, and we will only strengthen our alliance's foothold as well as the Gatekeepers' value to the universe."

An Inlorian stood, speaking loudly in his native tongue. My earpiece translated for me. "Have we determined the invaders' origin?" he asked.

I glanced over at Sarlun, who shook his head ever-so-slightly from the edge of the stage. "Not yet," I answered. We did know, but it was yet another secret I couldn't divulge to the public.

"Will we seek them out when we do?" the Inlorian asked again.

"That is yet to be determined," I told the crowd.

Others began asking questions, but I stopped them. "We can discuss some of these points later, perhaps in a better setting. This is the introduction to the conference, so please, have a seat, everyone," I said, and they listened. "As you know, our Alliance of Worlds seeks to barter before attack, but we aren't fools. We will defend ourselves when needed. That's all I'll say on the subject."

This appeared to appease them, and I kept talking, giving them an agenda for the next couple of days. When it was over, they all applauded again, and I made my way to the edge of the room, where Mary and Jules waited for me.

"If it isn't my favorite ladies in all of the worlds," I told them.

Jules took my hand. She was growing so fast. Another six months had passed, and she was over three now. Soon enough, she'd be heading to the Gatekeepers' Academy, making friends, becoming a teenager… fending off boys' advances. I admired my little girl, and was glad I still had time before all of that happened.

"They're all waiting. Are you coming?" Mary asked,

The Gatekeepers

and I nodded, waving Sarlun to the doors.

Sarlun was on stage, letting everyone know that the dinner started in two hours, and that they could use the next while to settle into their assigned dorm rooms.

We pushed through the doors and headed outside into the courtyard. The sun was bright, and the fountains were on, flowing water making calming sounds as we strolled over the cobblestone walkways toward the landers at the far edge of the school.

"What do you have up your sleeve today, boss?" Slate asked as we approached. Loweck was beside him, wearing casual clothes. Everyone here was in shorts or jeans, t-shirts and polos. I peeled off my Gatekeepers uniform, revealing the shorts and tank top underneath. It was nice to be out of uniform and among friends.

"Well, gang, we have something very important to show you all." I pointed at the landers. Magnus and Natalia entered first, with little Dean and Patty in tow.

"Papa, can I go?" Jules asked, wanting to take the lander with Patty inside. They were thick as thieves these days.

"Sure, honey. We'll see you in a few minutes," I told her, and Mary and I followed Loweck and Slate into the next lander. Sarlun ran up and jumped inside, still in uniform.

"The others meeting us there?" he asked, and I nodded while Mary took the pilot's seat.

Slate was suspicious. "What's this about? I'm your best friend, Dean. Can't you give me a hint?" he asked.

"You'll see in a few."

Mary lifted us off and followed behind Natalia's vessel until we crossed the low peaks, then settled back to the ground. The whole trip only took ten minutes, and I stayed behind in my seat as the doors opened, letting Loweck and Slate go first.

"This is impressive," she said, smiling at us from outside.

"Boss, you have to be kidding me," Slate said.

"What do you think?" Mary asked as we emerged from the lander. Magnus and Nat were coming over, staring at the huge object half a kilometer away.

"How did you do this so fast?" Magnus asked, unable to hide his excitement.

Another lander was already here, and Suma and Rivo came from inside, joining us. Terrance and Leslie arrived a minute later, and when I was sure everyone was here, I finally spoke.

"This is *Horizon*. Admiral Yope was gracious enough to donate a Keppe exploratory vessel to our cause, and we've already begun the modifications. It'll be ready in a year," I told them all.

"Ready for what?" Magnus asked.

"For Captain Magnus to take her out. And for anyone interested in joining to come along for the ride," I told him.

"Cool," Magnus' son, Dean said, making us all laugh along.

"Cool is right," Slate said. "What do you say, Loweck? Want to come along?"

She set her hand on Slate's forearm and nodded. "I'm in."

The Gatekeepers

Suma's snout twitched. "I'm guessing the *Horizon* is going to need some teachers. What do you say, Dean?"

I smiled. "It's not my call. I'm a passenger," I said.

Slate raised his eyebrows. "Does that mean…?"

Mary took this one. "We're coming too."

Nat beamed at this.

"I'm in too." This from Rivo, the small blue Molariun girl.

"You guys are going to have a great time, I know it," Leslie said. "Terrance and I will be staying here."

"And I'll remain on Haven at the Academy, helping it succeed," Sarlun said. "Take care of my daughter, will you, Dean?"

"Of course," I said. "Who wants a tour?"

Everyone raised their hands, and we headed toward the giant exploration vessel we'd call home in a short year's time.

The End

ABOUT THE AUTHOR

Nathan Hystad is an author from Sherwood Park, Alberta, Canada. When he isn't writing novels, he's running a small publishing company, Woodbridge Press.

Keep up to date with his new releases by signing up for his newsletter at www.nathanhystad.com

Sign up at www.shelfspacescifi.com as well for amazing deals and new releases from today's best indie science fiction authors.

Printed in Great Britain
by Amazon